NEVER

FOREVER

L. R. Johnson

L. R. Johnson

Printed in the United States of America

ISBN:0692565537
ISBN-13:978-0692565537

HAWAII Way Publishing

DEDICATION

This book is dedicated to my husband, Greg,
and my wonderful kids, Evan and Ashlyn,
who told me to never give up.

ACKNOWLEDGMENTS

I want to express my heartfelt gratitude to my
Associates in Writers Crime, Season Burch and
Pattie Sadler, whose inspiration, talent, and
support encourage me and lovingly criticize me
to become better. Thank you to my
loving parents who gave me the courage to never
give up on my dreams. Thank you to Shawndra Johnson,
your detailed eye is amazing. Thank you to all those
who gave me
feedback, and helped me correct my spelling
mistakes,
you all know who you are – my guiding angels.
Thank you to Season Atwater, who helped me
design my cover,
you have my eternal gratitude.

A New Beginning

Going to school in England has always been
my dream…always. To finally be able to put an
ocean between me and the poisonous influence in
my life has been what I've desired, but in my dream
I wasn't alone – like this.

Now I stand by myself in the middle of what I
hope will be my escape. The large elaborate
buildings of Cambridge University mark where I
will be starting anew. Several months ago my life
took a sharp left hook in a direction I could have
never dreamed of – even in my nightmares. Now I
gaze at all the eager, bright-eyed students dotting

the area with their lives just starting out, while I stand here with more experience in my eighteen years than I could have ever imagined.

The chill from eyes watching me dances on the back of my neck. Shifting my gaze, I notice several of the male students staring at me as if I am fresh meat thrown into a lion's den. One guy in particular is examining me with a sensual, penetrating gaze. His eyes narrow slightly as he gives me a quick, flirtatious wink. An embarrassing edge tickles my gut, spreading up across my shoulders and neck, triggering a shiver to rush through me. Quickly I look down at my over-sized sweater, pulling and tugging on all the edges to make sure every part of my torso is completely covered. Though his gaze is flattering, it is the very last thing I am or will be interested in. It's too soon. And who knows if I will ever be able to open my heart again.

Grabbing hold of my internal nerve I take in a deep breath. *Breathe, Breanna. Just breathe.* Exhaling a quivering breath I push back a loose strand of hair, clearing my vision as I slowly walk away from the flirtatious guy.

Moving through the maze of departments which are scattered throughout the college town, I try to find the English building. The archaic grandeur of the large structures makes me feel as if I stepped back in time instead of living in the twenty-first century.

Jumping out at me like a black sheep in a field of white stands the mid-century English building. This building has plain, clean lines with very simple yet elegant architecture. The building reminds me of being home in America, where nothing is as old as some of the structures here.

A cold sweat forms on my neck and my hands as I begin trembling, comprehending what I'm about to do. Here I am in a foreign country, all alone, about to embark on a new experience I'm not sure I'm ready for. A queasy sensation rises to the base of my throat with a heavy acidic tinge to it. I swallow forcefully, pushing the thick bile back down. This is not the time or the place to get sick right now. Pretending a deep hiccup, I try to hide the nausea flowing through me.

As I stare down the long hallway leading to all the classrooms, I notice many students moving through the hall like a fine dance choreographed by their professors. Their excited chatter fills the corridor and rolls over me like a tidal wave. It takes everything I have to walk against the sea of fear and disconnection. Because of my age this is a world I'm supposed to try to belong to. Theoretically this should be an exciting time of my life. But no matter what I do I will never fit in, nor am I really sure I want to belong.

Clutching hold of the doorknob, I fling the door open and walk into my new adventure. All of the students in my class turn and watch me. I begin aggressively wringing my hands as I turn my eyes to the floor and move to find an empty seat. Grabbing my pen and notebook from my book bag I start doodling vigorously, attempting not to look up.

I hear the classroom door open again. From the quiet murmurs, several girls call out, "Callum! I'm so glad you're in our class." Some of the girls even give a coy giggle after their statement.

The whole class starts making a fuss over him, with their overwhelming gratitude that he is in the same class as them. This is definitely someone I need to see. Perhaps I am in the presence of English Royalty or something along those lines. Shielding my eyes from my classmates I slyly look up, attempting to see this mysterious person. When, to my chagrin, I notice it is the same guy from earlier who was flirting with me. He's just an ordinary yet very good-looking guy.

He's perfectly put together with nicely shaped blue jeans accentuating the curves of his lower body. He's got on a soft blue button up shirt with a coordinating form-fitting cardigan. His clean cut light brown hair emphasizes his strong, chiseled features. Though his appearance is respectable, there is a rebellious glimmer in his eyes which I have seen in people multiple times in my life. I'm almost positive he is not a member of the royal family, so why is everyone making such a fuss over him? Pure curiosity pours over me, and I visually capture several mental images of his undeniably good looks.

Turning towards me his eyes look right into mine, narrowing with a surveying expression moving across his face. For just a brief moment my eyes lock onto his liquid caramel gaze, sending chills of energy shuddering throughout my body. The corner of his mouth turns up, revealing a slight smirk. A mischievous twinkle glistens just under the surface of his caramel ocean, as if he recalls his earlier attempt at flirting with me.

Abruptly the class door swings open, breaking my spell. In walks – I can only assume by the way everyone is rushing to their seats – our Professor. He briskly makes his way to the front of the class and takes us all in as if to ascertain what type of term this is going to be. Instantly his eyes stop on the same guy everyone was making a big deal over.

"Mr. Hughes, I see once again you have graced me with your presence. Do you think perhaps this term you might put some effort into your school work?" he utters, with a sincere tone in his voice.

A roar of snickers and giggles moves through the class. "Yes, Mr. Bramble," Callum answers in a low, masculine voice. His soft, buttery tone accentuates his English accent. Though I have a hard time understanding everyone here, I can understand him clearly. Perhaps his smooth tone makes it easier for me to comprehend him.

"Good, because I would hate to tell your father. He wouldn't like to hear that you are gliding through class again. Taking advantage of the faculty building which is named after your father," our professor responds in a firm tone.

Callum's jaw quivers slightly as his eyes narrow in anger. He faintly tilts his head in my direction, gazing out the corner of his eyes.

"No, Mr. Bramble, I wouldn't want that. Nor would my father like to hear about the happenings of his grown son," a sharp edge flutters off of each word as the atmosphere in the room takes on a new, thick reaction. The silence shrieks loudly within the room, filling every corner and crevice around us. No one has moved, let alone shown any signs of breathing. I can tell by Callum's stiff posture this is a subject he does not want to discuss, let alone mention.

"Good. As long as we are clear, Mr. Hughes," Mr. Bramble adds flatly.

"Crystal," Callum snaps back.

Our professor bounces back quickly, instantly bringing our class's attention to him. He reveals what he expects from us this Easter term. The air within the room softens, gently heaving away any anger and doubt once residing within its grasp. Now all I have to do is successfully figure out how to keep all attention off of me.

I am effectively able to sink into the background for the rest of the class time by staying quiet and avoiding any eye contact, only listening to what our term schedule is going to be. As soon as the class ends I hastily grab my things and bolt out of the room, trying to avoid a possible conversation with Callum.

Standing out front of the Hughes English building, I realize there is no possible way I am going to be able to locate my next class without asking for help. Streams of students hastily swim past me with very little attention directed towards my confused state. I know if I'm going to make it to my next class on time I have to take the initiative and ask someone for help. Looking around, I notice a petite blond girl gazing questionably down at her class schedule. Her sharp features blend into each other, as if a sculptor has chiseled every detail flawlessly. Her blonde pixie haircut frames her face perfectly. A twisted smile creeps into the outer edges of her thin mouth. She looks about as confused as I am.

"Excuse me. I don't mean to bother you, but you look like you're lost. Maybe we can help each other?" I inquire timidly.

"Am I that bleeding obvious?" she asks. The words seem to spin around deep in the back of her throat, occasionally she snaps out the last letter of each word. Her thick English accent makes it hard for me to understand what she is saying. Trying to process what she just said, I mumble out, "Well…" my mind searches for the right words to say without offending her.

"Oh buggers. Don't worry about answering the question. I already know the answer." A swift smile forms as a sweet, high-pitched laugh gracefully escapes her mouth. "My name is Olivia," she says as she lifts her hand towards mine.

Grasping hold of her delicate hand I shake it fervently, "Nice to meet you Olivia. My name is Breanna." She lets go of my hand, rubbing hers gently. "Oh, I'm sorry. I hope I didn't hurt you." I softly bite the corner of my mouth as the furrow between my eyes deepens in embarrassment. Heat presses up into my face, tainting the color of my cheeks.

"Let me guess. You're American?" she asks sarcastically as a wide smile spreads across her face.

"Does my accent give it away?"

She exhales a slight laugh, "Sure, but I was more thinking of your grip. What is it with Americans and your bloody firm handshakes? Do you all practice on bricks or something?"

With a quick wit I add, "No. We start with wood then we graduate to bricks." A burst of laughter rushes through both of us.

Though Olivia's petite frame gives the appearance of an insignificant or meek girl, her strong, sarcastic personality commands your attention. This is a girl who can definitely hold her own against anyone. I highly doubt she has ever let anyone pull the wool over her eyes. Her self-assurance is not in any way rude or uncouth. On the contrary, it is very captivating. There is something about Olivia's boldness that makes me not only trust her, but feel the need to have her fully in my corner here. I admire her brass way of stating what is on her mind. This is a character flaw I have, I keep everything inside of me and allow it to tear me apart like a ragdoll in the clutches of a bear's mouth.

"Well, Breanna, should we find our class?" a slight giggle still resonates within her words.

"Yes, please. I'm supposed to go to my history class, but the buildings are all spread out here."

"Don't worry about it. I'm from England and I still get confused. My arse of a brother was supposed to meet me here, but as usual he's a no show." Her eyes narrow, causing a dark veil of anger to briefly wash over her. Then as quickly as it appeared, the shroud of irritation is gone. "Well, that's a story for another occasion. I don't think we're too far off, though. The faculty of history is just on the corner of Queen's Road and West. It's just a bit of a stroll."

"Thank you so much," a sigh of relief escapes my lips as I gaze around. "I feel like I have been walking forever today. I never thought Cambridge University was made up of so many schools."

"If you want we can share a cab? That way you don't have to walk anymore," Olivia adds, as she sweeps a stray strand of blonde hair behind her ear.

"No, I don't mind walking. Now hopefully I can help you find where you're going."

"Well, actually I'm heading there myself. Maybe between the two of us we will be able to find our bloody course."

Nodding gently, I join her and we head down the street towards where the history building is located. This is not how I envisioned my new start, but at least I have grabbed hold of the reins to my run-away life.

Though Olivia never stops talking the whole time, I can't recall one thing she is saying. Her accent is too thick to follow along, besides my mind is completely captivated by my new surroundings. The grand arches and sheer magnitude of all the buildings is absolutely amazing.

Looking around, I take in everything. How the River Cam gently cuts through the breathtaking backdrop to all the well-manicured grounds. The crisp, clean air is such a sharp contrast to the dirty, smoke-filled environment I am used to. Raising my head I lift my eyes towards heaven, taking in a deep, cleansing breath, smelling the fresh rain tainted with moist dust and the sweet smell of the white willow trees. The cool, fresh air washes through my body, filling my soul with a sense of renewed possibility and hope.

"This is our building," Olivia's high pitched voice dances on the edge of excitement. "It's about bloody time! If this wasn't the building then I was going to scream," she adds flatly.

"Thank you, Olivia. I couldn't have done this without your help."

"No problem," she declares emphatically, as a glimmer of excitement shimmers in her eyes.

"It was nice meeting you, Breanna. Hopefully we'll meet again."

"Absolutely, now I can at least say I know one person in England," I state matter-of-factly, as I try to hide the loneliness within me.

"Blimey, you don't know anyone here?" Olivia's voice deepens as a hint of surprise whirls off each word.

"No," uneasiness coats my shaky voice as I try to hide my insecurities.

"You are braver than me. Why did you decide to come to school here in England?"

My heart immediately speeds up, sending a wave of unresolved pain and fear throughout my body. I'm not prepared to answer anyone's questions yet. This is my hell to live and no one else's.

Fighting back my tears, I utter softly, "I got accepted to the University." A simple answer is better than nothing.

Her eyes soften as she stares deep into mine. She nods in a hesitant, yet compassionate way. "Alright then, you have your reasons and they are yours alone. But if you ever feel lonely you know you can find me here."

"Thanks," I express genuinely.

We go our separate ways, and though desolation is left swirling around me after she leaves, I have a suspicion our paths will cross again, soon.

Tragedy

With each day that passes by I manage to slip into my classes completely unnoticed. I am able to successfully melt into the walls and the surroundings next to me. From this vantage point I can survey the class and the intricate workings of the ever present air of privilege surrounding me. The snobbish and snide remarks oozing out of the girls' mouths are immature and disgraceful. They speak so humanly to each other's faces, but no sooner than their backs are turned the berating comments begin, like heat-seeking missiles out for blood.

I'm effectively able to go about my routine of school, then home to my flat and well needed rest. The marathon my body is going through takes everything out of me. But this is my perfect situation, where I need to be right now. No pain, no memories, just living in the middle of life, where nothing on the outside can reach me. I have found my safe spot – until today.

Walking into my English class a word is written up on the board in large letters, TRAGEDY. A swarm of stinging bees vibrates within my stomach. A tingling sensation races through my hands and feet like fire ants consuming them. What in the hell can we be doing already? We have been studying English writers from the Romanticism period. I know the way they wrote placed a heavy influence on their imagination and emotions. But, I am not ready for this subject just yet. If only I was still feeling sick to my stomach, I could leave, but I haven't felt sick in days and I lack the nerve to try and sneak out. A boisterous discussion reverberates all around me as to what our lecture is going to entail today.

A deep boom echoes from the front of the room, "That's enough! Everyone, take a seat," our professor yells as he slams one of the books down on his desk.

I have discovered over the past few weeks our professor is very matter of fact in the way he addresses his lectures. The technique he has mastered matches his appearance. His starched, pressed shirt is tucked into his crisp, clean khakis, while his trim, dark hair is slicked back impeccably. Everything is planned, even down to his flawlessly polished shoes. His middle-aged appearance marries beautifully with his speech. He enunciates every syllable with a posh, crisp British accent. Each lecture he has given has been void of emotions. Perhaps whatever he has planned will not be too bad, considering his flat approach to everything.

Slouching comfortably into my seat, I gaze around at the classmates rushing feverishly to prepare for the impending discussion. Everyone but Callum Hughes opens their bags for some sort of writing instrument and paper. Callum simply pulls out a pen and folded piece of paper from his blazer pocket. He nonchalantly places them in front of him. There is a lackadaisical attitude in his efforts towards any note-taking in class, yet he has one of the highest grades in our class, so far. It's not fair how his grades seem to come easy to him while I have to work hard in my classes just to stay afloat. I have been observing his natural charismatic skills on everyone, charming them – including Mr. Bramble. His friends naturally gravitate to him like he's a superstar. His appearance screams natural good looks, with his thick brown hair and tall, athletic body. Even this building is named after his father. Not to be rude, but what can Callum possibly know of tragedy?

Professor Bramble pulls a stack of old novels from his briefcase and lays them on the table. These tattered leather books have definitely come from a different era in time. The bindings have seen better days, with deep cracks revealing the mesh beneath the leather. I'm surprised the pages are still hanging in there.

"Now that I have your attention, can someone explain to me why I have brought these books to my lecture today?" Professor Bramble asks, while stroking the top of the stack of antique books.

Silence falls over the classroom, and I can almost hear the wheels in everyone's head spinning. Someone finally raises their hand, "Is it because we are studying writings from that era?"

"No, but that was an adequate attempt Ms. Locke. Would anyone else like to try at a more developed answer?"

A pulsating sour taste rises up from my nauseous stomach. My heart pounds against my chest like a sledge-hammer trying to break through. Slowly I raise my hand, not quite sure why I am doing this. I had successfully made myself inconspicuous, but what I am about to do will destroy all of that. I can't sit here any longer while the answer is completely obvious to me. The compulsion to answer his question is far too strong for me to fight.

Mr. Bramble's eyes widen as he notices my hand going up. He gives a slight nod in my direction. "The fact that you have the word tragedy on the board, along with these books, makes me think of two different reasons. One is most of the stories in that time period have some type of tragedy the protagonist has gone or will go through. But my second reason is to never judge a book by its cover. No matter how much the world has destroyed it, there is still a beautiful, worthwhile story within its pages."

The entire class instantly turns and looks at me, as if they have just realized I am in their class. Their expressions range from utter shock to complete amazement. Some of the girls exhale forcefully through their noses, giving off a sound of disgust. Their eyes begin searching over every detail of me. An unnerving wave of embarrassment sweeps over me, causing my cheeks to blush.

"Thank you Miss…" He looks down at the list of students in his class. "…Miss Hayes. That is a fairly decent answer." A feeling of satisfaction prickles through me. Though I am happy about my answer I am also frustrated with myself. I can no longer hide. I am a visible participant now. I know it and now everyone else knows it, too.

Mr. Bramble grabs his lecture notes and tucks them neatly into his briefcase. Turning towards us he adds, "We're going to do something a little different today. We're going to take the first reason Ms. Hayes gave us and run with it. I'm going to break you all up into small groups of two or three. I then want each of you to share a tragic experience from your life." A mixture of gasps and shrills of excitement reverberate through the class. "We're all the protagonists in our lives. If you have not yet experienced the effects of tragedy, I assure you, you soon will."

A numbing sensation spreads fervently throughout my quivering body. This is not possible. I can't be here. I can't do this. There's no way in hell I am going to share with any of these people my tragedy. My only hope is that no one will want to have me as their partner.

Mr. Bramble interrupts my optimistic thought by adding, "So we get some truthful experiences I am going to segregate you into my own groups." As he begins dividing the groups up my panic increases, causing sweat beads to form on my upper brow. My shallow breathing escalates into a state of distress. Why did I have to speak up? Now even my professor knows I exist.

"Ms. Hayes, will you please join Mr. Hughes at the back table."

Oh shit. Why did I have to come today? Closing my eyes tightly I audibly exhale discontentedly as I head to the back table where Callum now sits patiently waiting. His immaculately polished appearance is such a sharp contrast to his relaxed and nonchalant posture. Hastily grabbing my chair I sit down, adjusting my bulky sweater. Cautiously I look up into his liquid caramel color eyes. His posture does not adjust a bit. Callum stays in his slight languid position, examining me with his intensely scrutinizing eyes. My trembling hands grab onto my sweater, adjusting and covering every part of my torso. His penetrating gaze almost seems to peer right through me. My eyes narrow, deepening the furrow between my brows as a conundrum of thoughts rally around in my head. I'm not sure if he's disgusted he is stuck with me, or if he's truly trying to figure me out.

Attempting to get this over with quickly, I demand, "You go first."

A brief smile tickles the corners of his mouth, "Bloody hell, you just want to bang to it, huh. Don't want to get to know each other first?" he asks without adjusting his reclined posture the whole time.

Disgusted by his sly and sexual reference, I answer flatly, "No. I prefer not getting to know you. Nothing personal, I just want to get this over…"

He immediately sits up, causing the once relaxed aura about him to evaporate. His eyes widen as his jaw quivers slightly, "Wait a minute. You're telling me to not take it personal. You don't want to get to know me before we share some deeply tragic experiences in our lives. Well, I hate to tell you, I do take it personally."

Using my trembling nerves as fuel I add, "Like you have ever experienced something deeply tragic before."

"A lot more than you," he scans over me, visually taking in my appearance. "You're a spoiled American who knows nothing about tragedy, let alone experienced any. You're just like most of the young American girls I have met, bored with their environment so you decided to run to England in hopes of having a fairytale experience."

My gripping fists tighten, causing my nails to cut into the palms of my hands. Heat races up my stiff spine, "You know nothing about me or why I'm here. Trust me, the reality of a fairytale for me is over," I shout, louder than I intended to. "My reasons for coming here are mine alone. I don't need some egotistical boy assuming something about me." Grabbing my things I rush out the door, trying to fight back my tears.

Hastily I head down the long hallway as my tears now spill down my overheated cheeks. The months of pent up sadness mingled with anger explode forcefully from my body. This is not possible. I came here to escape my pain so I can deal with the aftermath on my own. Why am I allowing this arrogant jerk to drag this kind of pain out of me? Blindly I stare down at the floor as I run at full speed, instantly slamming into someone.

"Bloody hell, watch where you are going!"

I look up to apologize, when I catch sight of a feisty pixie face staring up at me, "Olivia."

Olivia's face beams with surprise as soon as she realizes it is me. Slowly her expression takes on a downward spin as she observes my plight, "Breanna, are you alright?"

"No. Can we go somewhere and talk?"

Her eyes narrow as a soft, deflated expression washes over her. A slow exhale rolls over her lips, "Absolutely. Where would you like to go?"

"I don't care. You decide."

We sit on a bench at the edge of the River Cam. I watch the shimmering ripples dance on top of the water, completely unaware of the dangerous undertow lying beneath the glow. I may put on an aura that everything is okay, but I'm completely aware of my troubles lying beneath my surface. I carry the reality of what I have gone through and will still be going through on a daily basis. Quietly I watch all the punts on the river full of people enjoying their journey. A sense of resentment consumes me, causing my tears to well up in my eyes again. Warm drops fall gently from my eyes and land with forceful stings, seeping through my pants, causing the skin on my thighs to heat up.

Olivia rises up, turns towards me and asks in a soft, smooth voice void of her usual sarcasm, "Breanna, do you want to talk about it now?" Olivia's voice is coated with concern.

"I can't. This is my burden to bear. Besides, I don't want to put a heavy load on you. I think I'm just feeling very lonely. And I allowed some jerk in my class to get under my skin, that's all." I can't look up at Olivia for fear she'll be able to see right through me. The core to my sadness is not something I'm sure how to explain, nor am I sure I want to reveal it, either.

A soft exhale rolls from her mouth as she gives my shoulder a gentle squeeze, "Fine, I told you once before that your reasons are yours alone, but I can do something about your loneliness."

Tilting my head questioningly I look up at Olivia. She is now wearing a mischievous smile prickling the corners of her mouth, causing my heart to drop into the sour bile within me. "What do you mean?"

Her posture changes as she stands at attention with a wave of excitement rushing through her. Her hazel eyes, which are already large, swell with the possible thrill of what she is about to propose. "You obviously have had a bleeding day. There's no better cure for it than to go and get pissed."

"Excuse me?" I ask, slightly caught off guard.

"Oh, I forgot, you're American. I mean go and get drunk. There're some great pubs around here and I'm supposed to meet some friends at one soon. Why don't you come?"

"Thank you Olivia, but I can't." A heavy weight of desolation pushes down on my shoulders, deflating my posture.

"Why not? It's just going to be my brother and a few of our friends. They will love you. Besides, this will be a great way to forget about your problems."

If she only knew how it would just make my problems so much worse, "Thank you, but I don't think it will be the best place for me right now. Besides, I don't drink."

Her eyes widen as her bottom jaw drops, revealing her gaping mouth, "Wow. You don't drink. Drinking tea and meeting at the pubs for a pint is a big thing here in England." A sarcastic laugh pushes out of her, "What, are you pregnant?"

Though Olivia is just kidding, a searing surge shoots through my core causing an internal pain to envelop me. The once hard and protective shell shielding my core rips wide open. Tears fall heavily down my cheeks. I foolishly believed I was going to be able to hide my pregnancy from everyone. This is something I thought I didn't want to talk about, but her guess leaves me with a sense of relief encapsulating me. I have been going through all the pain and uncomfortable struggles by myself. As my tears resume I gaze up straight into her eyes whispering, "Yes."

Olivia's face drops, the once gaping mouth reappears, only wider, "Bloody hell. You're what?"

"I'm pregnant," though my voice is soft it is laced with frank honesty.

I watch as the disbelief flows down her body like air pressing out of a deflating balloon. She drops down right next to me, forcing me to scoot over onto the edge of the bench. Her wide eyed expression stares straight ahead, not even acknowledging what she is staring at. This is the first time I actually have seen Olivia speechless. Regret slowly consumes me with the fact that I perhaps should not have revealed my predicament to her. I don't know her well enough to know how she is going to handle this kind of information. Though this is just the tip of my iceberg, this is my hell, not hers, and I should have kept it that way.

"I have to see this for myself," she declares, in complete frankness.

Turning towards me she lifts up my sweater and places her hand on my stomach. My frozen body shatters, causing me to jump back slightly with the intrusive touch of her hand. The invasion of privacy vibrates into my core as I sit motionless watching this molesting of my stomach take place. I always knew this type of invasion is a very common occurrence for pregnant women. Once someone's baby bump is showing their stomach becomes public property for anyone to touch. But because I have been successfully able to hide mine with large sweaters or jackets, I have not experienced it before – until now.

"Blow me. You're very pregnant."

My rigid body remains motionless as I gaze down at her hand still firmly placed on my now exposed stomach, "Yes. I'm almost nine months."

"How old are you?" she innocently inquires.

"I am eighteen."

"You're the same age as me."

"I know," stating frankly, considering I have been assuming she is my age the whole time.

"How?" Her hand grips my stomach like a basketball.

I gaze up at her with a wide eyed expression. My face must be revealing the question running through my mind, because she immediately gives a rebuttal to her previous statement.

Her cheeks flush a soft pink color, quickly adding, "I know you need to have sex in order to get pregnant. I just mean, how were you able to hide this, thus far?"

Slowly I reach down, grabbing her hand, gently removing it from my exposed mid-section. Pulling my sweater back down over my pronounced stomach, I anxiously adjust it, making sure every part of my torso is protectively covered. A ringing stings my ears as a tingling sensation pricks my mind with a fear of swarming questions to come. I can't tell her any more, but I can't chance losing my only possible friend either. My hands begin aggressively twisting and turning around each other as I brutally take out my nervousness on them.

"I am actually not that big for how far along I am. But I was successfully – until now – able to hide it with my loose fitting clothes. I would really prefer to keep it that way, too."

Olivia's furrow between her eyes deepens as she stares at me with a questionable gaze, "You know you won't be able to hide it for very much longer."

"Yes, I know. But I am at least hoping to make it to the mid-term break."

A laugh suddenly escapes out of her, "That's a bleeding good plan. But I will be surprised if that happens. You may not be showing very much, but since you are almost nine months along then you are knocking on that delivery door."

The reality of what she says pulsates through me. I knew I would be taking a chance of going into labor while in the middle of this term, but I had to come here. I couldn't stay where I was any longer. I had to leave before I was destroyed. Though I am far from the surroundings I am used to, this is exactly what I need right now.

The cool, damp air washes over me, leaving shimmering droplets of water all over my clothes and hair. The thick mist slowly pours down over everything. The once sunny and bright day is beginning to be overtaken by the invading clouds rolling in. The light is extinguished by the haze, leaving only gloom and darkness. Everything around me and within me reflects my feelings, like the consuming darkness has won.

As I sit here in silence contemplating my situation, I watch the swarms of people running around in the mist having a carefree time. The sounds of their happiness are muffled by the intense veil of haze now enveloping all of us. Heavy droplets of water fall from my now curly brown hair.

Olivia's voice cuts through the thick haze I am in, "I don't know about you, but I can't sit here in this anymore. I am getting soaked."

"If you want to go, you can. It is okay with me," my voice is gruff under the circumstances.

"What do you think I am, some sort of wanker? I am not leaving you here. You are coming with me whether you want to or not." Standing up she grabs tightly onto my hand.

"No, I can't go and you now know why," I utter forcefully, trying to fight the tight grasp she has on me. Though Olivia's frame is petite she is extremely strong for her size. She tightens her grip around my arms while she continues pulling me up from the bench.

"Just because you are in this state doesn't mean you can't have fun. You are coming with me even if I have to bloody drag you the whole way. You are still young and deserve to let loose and have some fun. So let's go."

Cat's Out of the Bag

Olivia has to practically drag me the entire way. I try to come up with a million and one reasons as to why I can't go with her to the pub, but she isn't listening to me. She drags me down a narrow street lined by quaint four-story row houses, where the bottom floors are filled with commercial institutes. Each row building is unique in its style, giving the street a mystical illusion, as if everything has stepped back in time. The charming street gently curves, allowing me to see the details of the intricate buildings. Hanging on the outside of all the businesses are traditional oval signs, enhancing the archaic yet picturesque feeling to the street. No cars are allowed on this street, making me feel as if I too have stepped back in time. As the night approaches it brings with it swarms of people heading to the multiple pubs and restaurants lining this trendy lane.

My nerves abruptly explode as we stop in front of an enchanting pub called The Black Cat. The front has two very large paned windows situated on the bottom floor of a Tudor style building. I grab Olivia's hand tightly in nervous reaction, and she gives my hand a gentle and reassuring squeeze back. As Olivia swings the door open a bell hanging on the inside rings loudly, causing everyone nearby to turn in our direction. Loud cheers from the back of the small and modest pub echo towards us.

"Olivia, we are back here!" someone shouts.

Olivia starts to head back when I abruptly stop, causing her arm to be yanked hard, "Buggers, Breanna. That hurt."

"Sorry, but can I at least go to the bathroom, the loo, first and make myself somewhat presentable before I meet your brother and friends?" She stands here quietly observing me like a bounty hunter scrutinizing her skipper that is ready to escape at any moment.

"Aye, but if you don't come back I will come after you," she states with a half-smile slightly curling up the edges of her mouth. I am not sure if it is a joke or if she is serious, either way I am not about to test her. She is stubborn enough and strong enough to take me down.

"I promise I will meet you back there," pointing to the back of the pub where everyone is waiting for her.

Apprehensively I walk out of the bathroom, knowing I did the best I could to freshen myself up by calming down my soaked, curly hair and putting on some lip gloss. As I approach the back I can hear all the loud laughter coming from their group. Abruptly I stop when I recognize a low, yet smooth voice speaking up.

"Aye, today was a mess during our lecture. I was about ready to bloody throttle my partner. Thank God she decided to storm out of the classroom instead."

A high-pitched female voice chimes in, "What was Professor Bramble thinking when he bloody put you two together?"

"It had to be because of our last names," he utters, with a twinge of an unexplained emotion looming within the statement.

Silently I watch from the background as this berating dance takes place. Complete irritation and disbelief collides within me. Out of everyone in the school Olivia's friends have to be the jerks from my class. Instantly the urge to run consumes me, no matter the possible repercussions from Olivia when she confronts me later.

Quickly I turn to leave, when I hear Olivia's voice cut through all the rumbling echoes within the pub.

"Back here!" she shouts sharply with a commanding tone in her voice, as if she is aware of what I am about to do.

Slowly I turn around, noticing Callum's wide eyes and frozen expression as he picks up his bottom jaw off of the floor. Mustering up every little bit of confidence I have within me, I stand erect, walking with an air of self-assurance towards the now stunned group.

Olivia stands up to greet me, turning to her friends she utters, "This is my friend from America, Bre…"

"Breanna," Callum interrupts.

"Yes. How did you know, Callum?"

I stand with my chin erect, staring deep into his eyes, as if daring him to continue with the criticizing conversation he has been entertaining. Olivia begins alternating her gaze between Callum and me, taking in our visual battle. Her eyes narrow with a sudden realization of something, "Let me guess, Breanna, the arse in your lecture today is my one and only sod of a brother."

Callum turns hastily, gazing angrily up at Olivia, "Who in the bloody hell are you calling an arse? This girl," he nods his head aggressively, gesturing towards me, "was being just as much of an arse as I was."

"Excuse me, but I am standing right here, and I am going to defend myself. You were passing judgments on me in class that you had no right to do," I snap, while my body stiffens in reaction towards my accuser.

"Judgments, you say? I think you were doing fairly well at passing your own judgments," Callum remains comfortably reclined in his chair as he surveys me with scrutinizing eyes. His lackadaisical attitude towards me and my feelings infuriates me. My eyes bore deep into his caramel eyes as the rage swirls within me.

"Callum, don't get your knickers in a twist. She is just Miss Emotional."

"Sod off Emily, you wanker! You don't know anything," Olivia breaks in.

"On the contrary, Olivia, I was there. I know a lot more than you do," Emily snaps back. Emily's sharp, clean voice balances nicely against her thick British accent. Her long, dark hair blends perfectly with her smooth olive complexion. Every detail of her has been flawlessly put together. Not a single strand of hair is even out of place. It appears to be that way with everyone here, but me and Olivia. Olivia's natural beauty, however, supersedes all of the girls' plastic made up enhancements. Though Olivia and I are products of the recent weather condition, Olivia still looks as if she belongs on the pages of a magazine. When an English woman's features are exquisitely put together by her maker, her beauty is unmatched. This is definitely the case with Olivia. She is absolutely stunning on the outside and on the inside.

I watch as Olivia and the others begin arguing back and forth. They are speaking so fast and with such thick accents, I can only understand a few words here and there. Several swear words are thrown into the mix of British derogatory statements. I feel like I am in another country that does not speak English. There is no way for me to even defend myself, because I can't even understand enough to join in. As I turn towards Callum I notice he is just staring at me in an amused sort of fashion. His eyes glisten with sheer enjoyment as he watches me fidget in my uncomfortable situation. A coy smile creeps into the outer edges of his full lips. Staring at me with an air of arrogance, he reaches over, patting the seat of the empty chair next to him.

My eyes narrow with mere curiosity, stating flatly, "Why?"

"Why not? I won't bite," a slight smile appears as the words roll off his tongue, "This time."

Gazing back at him I decide to challenge his game of poker. Sucking in my internal strength I proceed to walk over to the illustrious awaiting chair. Turning the chair in his direction I sit directly across from him, trying to match his nonchalant attitude as I meet his gaze head on. His face reveals a slight amusement towards my parallel response and my ultimate wager I am placing on this obvious game he is playing. Throwing my bet into the pot, I utter in a smooth voice, "I am not afraid of getting bit."

His eyes widen as a sly smile lifts the corners of his mouth, "Really, then what are you afraid of? I know you are not here for the bloody weather." His smooth voice gets deeper, causing the inflections within his brogue to increase. I am not sure if this is a reaction caused from nerves or by his sheer delight over the fact that he has just raised the bet. His gaze never leaves mine, locking me into his penetrating eyes. I try to match his as I fight back the anxiety rolling within me. An uneasy twinge in the pit of my stomach turns, causing the baby to kick me violently. For just a brief moment I had forgotten that I am pregnant, but this sudden movement instantly brings me back to reality. Callum has raised the bet, but I am not about to play my hand. No matter how much I try to bluff, this is a game I will ultimately lose.

Trying to fold my hand in this game, I state flatly, "I am here to go to school, that is all. Why is it such a mystery that an American wants to come to a University in England?"

He suddenly leans forward, placing his elbows on his knees while resting his chin on his knuckles. His strong, masculine features cause my heart to race as his stimulating eyes bore deep into mine. His face is now just within a foot or two from mine, causing me to nervously push myself further back in my chair. "That's bollocks. There is more to you than meets the eye."

His statement sends a competitive wave throughout me. Though his features are perfectly put together, like his sister's, his is heaving with intense masculinity and sexual confidence. His immediate proximity to me causes an unexplained uneasiness to quiver within the pit of my stomach, slowly consuming me. Trying to retain my poker face, I breathe in as I call his bluff, leaning forward to meet his gaze. Our faces are now just within inches of each other. Embracing my competitive edge I look deep into his caramel eyes with my hazel green eyes, stating flatly, "And don't you wish you knew?" A slight satisfied smile spreads across my face.

"Yes, I do," he adds resolutely. Instantly he grabs hold of the back of my head, pressing his lips firmly against mine, tightly holding me against him. Mere shock vibrates through me as his warm lips move passionately over mine. His kiss has an unfamiliar edge to it, as his lips move with tender speed, like this is his only way to discover my secrets. At first, the touch of someone's kiss on my lips sends a wave of pleasure through me, but the moment does not last long. Rage begins pulsating within my core, superseding the sensation of pleasure. How dare he throw himself on me like this! Instantly I push him away, slapping his face with great force. The palm of my hand tingles with a numbing pain where it connected with Callum's skin. Turning towards the group, I notice everyone staring at us in complete shock.

Fervently I push my chair away from him, "Don't you ever do that again!"

"Callum, you bloody wanker!" Olivia snaps. "What in the hell were you thinking, kissing her like that?"

Gently massaging the side of his face he glances over at Olivia, "I wasn't thinking, obviously, or I wouldn't have gotten bloody slapped across the face."

"I wouldn't have just slapped you, you sod." Olivia turns towards me, "Are you alright Breanna? I am so sorry about my brother. He's not usually like this. He must be completely pissed."

A feeling of nausea washes over me as a swarm of mixed emotions overpowers me. One part of me is flattered by the attention and the feeling of someone desiring me again. I have missed that intimacy towards me. At the same time a feeling of betrayal rips through me, tainting everything within me with a vile taste. I need to get out of here, "Don't worry about it Olivia. I think I am going to head back to my flat though."

"Okay. I will go with you."

"No, I will just catch a taxi."

"No, really, I am going with you and you are not stopping me," she firmly adds.

As we start to leave Callum yells out, "I am sorry Breanna. I didn't realize."

Turning towards him, I utter questioningly, "You didn't realize what?"

The side of his face still burns a flaming red color from the slap I inflicted upon him, "I didn't realize that you are queer."

Shock instantly washes over me. I have had enough of his arrogant attitude for one night. I don't care if it is because he is, as they say, pissed.

"You think I am gay just because I didn't respond to your forceful kiss?"

Olivia, who has been standing next to me in utter astonishment towards her brother, couldn't hold in her anger any longer, "Sod off you bloody bastard! You have no idea what you are talking about. I love you Callum, but right now I don't like you very much."

"Stay out of this Sis. You know nothing about her. As far as you know she may have a thing for you," Callum chimes in.

"She doesn't have anything for me other than as a friend. She is here all by herself. And besides, you bloody idiot, she can't be queer. You have to like having sex with men in order to get pregnant."

A still silence takes over the room as everyone's mouths fall wide open. Instantly my heart drops as I look down at Callum's face. His eyes widen to the size of silver dollars as he stares at me in total disbelief. An uncomfortable wave rushes over me and I feel as if I am standing in front of everyone completely naked. Their eyes bore right through my clothes, trying to see this mystical baby bump which has eluded them. Instinctively, I wrap my arms protectively around myself, trying to hide my virtual nakedness. Callum's eyes drop down to the floor as if it is made of glass, allowing him to see to the center of the earth. His eyes will no longer meet my gaze, as if embarrassment has consumed him. He just silently sits staring at the floor as everyone else visually rips my clothes off, causing me to feel sick.

"Shit, I am a bloody idiot. I am so sorry, Breanna," Olivia's voice is a soft whisper, full of regret.

"It's alright. Like you said earlier I won't be able to hide it much longer, at least the cat's out of the bag now." As I turn to walk out I notice Olivia is still attempting to follow me, "Please don't come with me. I need to be alone." She starts to resist, when I gaze into her eyes, uttering softly, "Please." Reluctantly she nods, agreeing to my request.

As I walk away I can hear one of the guys say, "Well, Callum now we know she's a slapper, not gay." A thunderous rumbling noise ensues behind me, followed by a loud shout from the same obnoxious guy, "Bloody hell, Callum! What did you hit me for?"

As I open the pub door and walk out into the damp fresh air, I instantly am aware of how alone I really am. Now that everyone knows I am pregnant, how are they going to treat me in class? Will I be alienated even more?

Don't Let Go

Winter slowly loses its grasp on the cooler weather. Warm air now begins to invade the outer edges of the breeze, leaving everyone to slowly start shedding the bulky layers once covering their bodies. I am no longer able to hide my fully formed baby bump. Everywhere I go I receive stares from all directions. Since everyone in my class already knows my predicament, either from that embarrassing night or the rumors flying around about me, I now care less about what I wear to my lectures. The stares and low vibrating whisperings have become an everyday occurrence. The onslaught of daily attacks is something I have now learned to embrace with a sense of familiarity. This is the only stability I have here. Everything else around me feels like a constant changing roller coaster. Olivia has tried talking to me, but I can't let her in any more. This is something I have to endure alone, that way I am less likely to get hurt again. By keeping my shell thick and not allowing anyone to penetrate it, I am able to not fall apart. There is only so much I can handle before I become a useless mother for my future child. I have already had to endure more than any other eighteen year old, and I still have more I have to suffer through.

Unlike all the mud-slingers in my class, Callum has been eerily quiet. His eyes never turn in my direction. It is as if I have never existed to him. I don't know whether he is embarrassed about kissing a pregnant woman, or just the plain fact that I am without a doubt having a child and there is no way he can get involved with someone like me. Getting involved with anyone is the furthest thing from my mind. I wish I can at least talk to him, explain that I will not ever be interested in him or anyone else. And whatever guilt, regret, or even disgust he has over the situation, he shouldn't worry about it, I am a big girl. My biggest concern, though, is that he needs to patch up whatever ravine has been formed between Olivia and him. Olivia is a great person and doesn't need to feel the burden from my situation. Having a family who cares about you, even if they piss you off, is something that should never be taken for granted. Every time I have tried to talk to him he has scurried out of the room like a rat running from a pouncing cat.

As I walk into my lecture today, the roaring sounds of everyone talking instantly comes to a halt. I go about my routine, heading back to the corner seat I have inhabited the past two months. Everyone's eyes follow me as if I am a bride walking down the aisle. The sudden outbursts of derogatory comments such as, "*slut*" and "*slapper*" rip through the silence, slashing right to my core. I have asked myself so many times lately, why did I decide to come here? But as soon as my mind utters the question, I instantly recall my promise and the hell I would have to confront if I were home. I am not ready to face that reality yet. I'd much rather deal with this situation than have to face my world back home, yet.

Quietly I stare straight ahead trying to ignore all the berating comments, when suddenly I catch sight of Callum. His head snaps straight up, glaring out at everyone with fiery darts of chastisement. The class instantly silences, other than a few snide remarks directed towards Callum. His eyes briefly lock onto mine as he gives me a half smile. Returning his sentiment I nod my head in a grateful gesture. Then I resume my traditional position, gazing straight ahead, waiting for Professor Bramble.

A sharp pain tears through me again as I grip the edges of my binder and try to ignore the Braxton-Hicks contractions I have been having all day. The stress I have been going through lately has not helped in this situation. They seem to be coming with more intensity and frequency. The muscles around my stomach harden, causing intense pain to hastily roll up in intensity. Slowly my stomach relaxes slightly as the pain begins to decrease back to a normal level. Trying to hide what is going on, I breathe out slowly, gazing right through the table until it all washes away.

Thankfully, Professor Bramble walks in. He is carrying a large stack of papers. Placing them on his desk he turns and faces us, "We have gone through a variety of subjects and now it is time to pull it all together. I want each of you to write a thesis about your favorite fictional protagonist." The moaning and deflated sighs vibrate throughout the room. "I am so pleased that you are all excited," he adds sarcastically. "But that is not all. I want you to take your character and do a comparison to the tragedies of your partner's."

Instant shock rolls through me as I close my eyes tightly in reaction to the horrific news. A sharp tingling sensation forms in my chest then drops, like a heavy rock into a still pond, causing a brutal contraction to develop within me. Doubling over in agony I grip my fists tightly under the table, as I hold my breath and wait for the intense pain to pass. Gratefully no one notices me, they are too busy whining and moaning over the apparent thesis we all have to do. Slowly the tight contracting of my stomach eases up, allowing me to open my eyes just in time. Mr. Bramble turns his attention toward me, "Miss Hayes and Mr. Hughes, I need the both of you to stay after."

Callum remains facing forward. From the look of his frozen and erect posture he is in as much shock as I am. The grumbling voices slowly subside, transforming into an air of mocking and bantering back and forth. Most give comments on how they feel bad for him, while others state how he may just get something out of this situation. One chimes in stating, "You may be able to get your willy off mate, if you don't hurl first." Laughter begins to fill the room, while Callum's body remains motionless.

"Mr. Beddows, you twit. I have had just about enough from you. Please exit my class." Mr. Bramble's tone, which is usually flat and reserved, is now firm with a cutting edge to it.

"What?" the rude guy I have come to know as Gavin Beddows, one of Callum's friends, utters in surprise.

"I am hoping you are smart enough to understand what I mean. I don't want to have to ask you again."

Gavin grabs all his things and starts walking out. As he walks past me he looks in my direction and purses his lips together, simulating an insulting kiss. Meeting his gaze head on I raise my hand lightly off the table, giving him the universal crest with my finger. A low, rumbling laugh comes from the front of the room, as if whoever this person is approves of my gesture towards Gavin. Angrily he pushes the door open and stomps out of the room.

"Is there anyone else who would like to join him?" Mr. Bramble asks as he gazes scornfully around the room.

For the rest of the lecture the class is uncomfortably quiet as he explains what he is expecting from our thesis. Occasionally I gaze around at all the immovable statues staring up at our Professor. Callum remains facing forward, but a sense of ease now envelops him instead of his once rigid frame. As soon as the lecture is over everyone bolts from their desks as if they are fleeing from the scene of a crime. Slowly I grab my things, trying to avoid eye contact with my Professor, hoping after our eventful class he has forgotten about meeting with Callum and I. Nonchalantly I stand up and try to exit.

"Miss Hayes, where do you think you are going?" Mr. Bramble asks softly.

As I turn around I notice that Callum is waiting at Mr. Bramble's desk with a mischievous smile streaming across his face, "Oh, sorry, I forgot."

"That makes two of us. If it wasn't for Callum coming up here and reminding me, I would have let you both leave without talking to you."

Instantly, I shoot Callum a lethal glare. Why is he so interested in working together again? The last time was a nightmare. Grabbing whatever strength I have left I head over to the desk. Another contraction suddenly bursts through me, causing me to quiver with pain as I hold onto my stomach.

"Are you alright Miss Hayes?" My Professor asks.

"Yes," I utter softly, trying to hide the agony in my voice.

"Good. I want to talk to you both about what happened during your tragedy discussion a while back. Everyone else did it, but you two. Why?"

Callum immediately chimes in, "I have no idea. I was a willing participant until she stormed out. So you might want to bloody ask her." Callum looks over at me with a luring expression, baiting me to answer the question.

As I look at his arrogant face a surge of anger rushes through me. How can he question my reason for leaving now that he knows I am pregnant? "You absolute jerk. You now know why I left!"

"I know one of the reasons, but I don't know it all, like if you are married," he barks back in response to my accusations. A lingering ripple of fear resonates within him.

"And you will never know the rest. It is none of your business," my trembling anger vibrates throughout my body now.

"I think it is my bloody business, since I kissed you and I'm pretty positive you kissed me back, too," he snaps back with an edge of disappointment and disgust vibrating through him.

"How can you believe I kissed you back? I think I gave you a very strong response to your kiss."

"Oh, you bloody well did," he states firmly, as he gently rubs the side of his face, remembering the pain, "I felt the sting of your response the rest of the night."

"Well then, what gave you any idea I wanted the kiss, least of all that I kissed you back?" This discussion is causing a rising wave of nausea to form in the pit of my stomach. Just the mere situation of having to talk about that night causes my stress and anger to escalate to an unsafe level.

The corners of Callum's mouth pull up in pure satisfaction over a lucid discovery he is apparently about to share with me. His caramel eyes twinkle with mischief as a wide smile spreads across his face, revealing deep dimples sinking into the sides of his cheeks, "You accepted my kiss at first, lingering there before you decided to slap me."

Just as I am about to share with him the logic behind my lingering lips, destroying his theory, Mr. Bramble butts in, "Wait a minute, is there something sexual going on with the two of you?"

Caught off guard we both shout simultaneously, "NO!"

Without warning a sharp pain explodes right through me, causing me to grab onto Callum's arm for support. The throbbing agony is centered directly in my abdomen, but the pain vibrates throughout my back and down into my vaginal area. Grabbing onto his arm I begin squeezing it firmly, trying to fight the torture ripping through me.

"Ouch! Bloody hell, Breanna! What are you doing?" Callum's obvious pain I am putting him through vibrates within his voice, causing his voice to lower and tremble.

The intense agony I am going through isn't allowing me to talk. All I can do is hold onto Callum's arm for some kind of stability. Severe pressure pushes down on me, as if something is ripping me open from the inside. I begin focusing all my attention on my breathing, trying to survive this penetrating attack. Slowly the contraction eases up, and for a brief moment my breathing seems as if it is going to stabilize, but no sooner than the sensation of respite tickles my body, another intense contraction immediately seizes down on me. This time the cramping within my abdomen reaches an excruciating level. The only thing I am able to utter is, "Help!"

Mr. Bramble jumps to his feet and hastily announces, "She is in labor!"

"What?" anxiety slashes through Callum's question.

"She is going to have her baby any moment," his voice is firm and full of authority. "Mr. Hughes, I need you to take her to the hospital, now."

"Why me? Shouldn't you take her? You're the bloody professor," honest terror of what to do vibrates within his voice and oozes off of his petrified body.

"I cannot, I have another lecture. Besides…"

"I don't give a shit who takes me! Someone just help me!" I shout.

All of a sudden the realization of how serious of a situation this is for me rings heavily within Callum's action. Reaching down, he immediately swings me up into his awaiting arms and begins rushing me out of the building. Wrapping my arms tightly around his neck, I bury my head into his chest as I fight the intense cramping pushing down on me. Tears roll down from my eyes as the fear of what is about to take place consumes me. I am fully aware of how my child is going to enter the world, but I am not ready yet. I always had dreams of when my child would come into this world to the awaiting arms of its parents. Dreams of both a mother and father there, gushing over the miracle being placed in their grasp. While they stare down at their child, realizing they are now a family. But instead of that fantasy, I am now being rushed to the hospital in the arms of an almost stranger, to greet my child all alone, robbed of the wondrous family event.

Reacting to my apprehension I mumble softly into Callum's chest, "I'm scared."

Pressing me tightly against his firm, muscular chest, he utters softly onto the top of my head, "It will be okay. I promise."

He continues rushing through the campus, ignoring all the shouts and curious eyes gazing in our direction. He tightens his grip on me as he pulls out his phone, calling for an ambulance. The trembling distress and exhaustion shows in his voice as he tells the mysterious person where to meet us. Callum pushes his way past several crowds with expertise. Making our way through the masses of people swarming all around us takes some skill. And by the ease of his movements I can tell he has had some experience pushing his way through crowds.

Everything around me seems to be moving in slow motion as Callum rushes to the rendezvous spot he has arranged. Every detail and every sound washes heavily over me as we move across the campus. The warm sun rolls over my body, heating me all the way throughout my core. The sighs, gasps, and occasional birds singing merge delicately with the heavy panting coming from Callum's mouth. His breathing, while heavy, rolls out an unchanging rhythm. Focusing in on his steady, fervent breathing, I am able to remain in some kind of control. Laying my head against his chest I begin counting each one of his breaths, as I focus intently on the embroidery of his thin sweater. I notice every cross stitch and detail of the thread used in forming it. Each movement his chest makes lulls me deeper into a state of hypnosis. The intense pain is still pushing down on me, but following his breathing is allowing me to endure each wave of contractions.

I try to put the fear of the situation out of my mind as he hastily cuts his way amongst the main section of the campus. Suddenly I hear him yell towards someone, "Here we are. She's in a lot of pain. You're going to need to rush her there."

Another set of hands grab onto me, attempting to take me from Callum. Wrapping my arms even tighter around Callum's neck I hold on for dear life, refusing to let go, "No! Don't touch me."

"Breanna, it's okay. These are the paramedics. They are going to take you to the hospital," he breathlessly adds, as he tries removing my hands from around his neck.

My fear completely takes over me. The only thing that has helped me remain in some sort of control has been focusing on Callum's steady breathing, and now he wants to take it away. I wrap my hands even tighter around his neck as I bury my head into his firm chest. I can't do this. I can't do this all alone. Waves of intense cramping intermingled with a deep surging anguish, flood my body. The echo of my life I once had calls to me from the corners of my mind, leaving me to only feel the want that will never come. As I grip even tighter onto Callum a wave of comfort radiates from his enveloping arms. This familiar sensation triggers in me some kind of feeling of security amidst the abandonment I am succumbing to.

"I can't do this alone. I can't!" I forcefully mumble, as my tears freely fall. Everything I have been holding in now explodes, allowing the deep anger and pain to release from me like giant flood waters overpowering a dam. My tears saturate his sweater as I begin sobbing uncontrollably. My breathless and shaking voice vibrates against his chest while I keep repeating over and over, "Don't let go of me. Please don't let go of me."

Callum places his hand firmly against the back of my head, holding onto me tightly. Bending down he whispers softly into my ear, "I promise I won't let go of you." Turning towards the E.M.T. he utters fervently, "I am bloody going with her."

The paramedic gazes towards us with a firm, annoyed expression, "I can't mate, not unless you are a family member or the baby's father."

Callum's muscles tighten around me as I bellow in agony with another onslaught of contractions forming within me. "Look 'mate,' she is not about to let go of me and I am most definitely not about to let go of her. So, either you let us both in this bloody ambulance or I am going to run her there myself," his livid voice resonates throughout the whole vicinity, causing a large herd of students now forming around us to jump back in shock.

The emergency worker looks all around at the crowd, taking in every reaction that is now being verbalized. Turning his head sharply towards Callum he states flatly, "Fine, but when we get to the hospital you can be the one to tell them who you are. As far as I am concerned, for the sake of this girl, you are family."

They open the back of the ambulance, allowing Callum to gingerly maneuver his way in while still carrying me in his arms. Lying within the small but safe boundaries of the ambulance is a narrow gurney off to one side. A thin white sheet lay over the top of it. At three different locations there are thick black straps to hold a patient firmly against the stretcher. On the opposite side of the gurney are two single seats, mainly for the paramedics, but in this case one will now be occupied by Callum.

Callum proceeds towards the awaiting gurney, "I promise I won't leave, but I need to put you here."

As he bends over the gurney I reluctantly let go, landing on the hard cold surface. All the emergency workers instantly swarm around me, forcing Callum out of the way. Panic envelops me as they begin pushing and probing all over. My breathing increases as waves of anxiety pulsate throughout my overstimulated mind. One of the paramedics says something about having to remove my pants and undergarments, but his words sound as if he is speaking down a long tunnel. Everything dances around me like a kaleidoscope of smeared colors and muffled noises. Out of the corner of my eye I notice something pushing its way through the wall of paramedics. Then suddenly something warm grabs hold of my hand, squeezing it softly. A warm wave of comfort rolls through me, relaxing my rigid muscles. Any sense of modesty is thrown out the window in this situation, and honestly it is the furthest idea from my mind. At this point I don't care if I am flashing the entire city.

A whirl of emotions spins rapidly throughout my mind. Though Callum irritates me on multiple levels, I am so grateful for his presence right now. Grabbing onto his hand I close my eyes, allowing my tears to freely flow again. One of the paramedics' voices cuts through the mumbling commotion, uttering, "We may have to deliver the baby in the ambulance if we don't get her there soon."

Turning towards me the paramedic adds instantly, "I need you to breathe through your contractions. If you feel the need to push, I need you to blow hard, trying not to push if you can."

"I can't do this," I stammer out. My voice trembles violently under the pressure from all of my nerves.

"Yes, you can," Callum replies.

"No, I can't. You don't understand. My body is bearing down whether I want it to or not. I can't stop it," I state, with a thick layer of apprehension vibrating within my voice. The heavy pressure pushing down on me is unbearable. All I want to do is push, but I can't. My abdomen tightens up like a hard rock with every rolling contraction and does not seem to be easing up at all.

Callum's grip tightens on mine as he gently adds, "Just do what they are telling you to do…breathe." I can hear his slow breathing take on a rhythmic tone. He slowly breathes in for a steady count and then gently blows out, as if he is just causing the flame on a candle to flicker slightly. I gaze at him through the tiny sliver between all the paramedics standing around me. Watching his mouth and chest move at a steady, rhythmic pattern, I begin mimicking his breathing, trying to slow mine to match his. Control gradually washes over me as I gaze down at our fingers intertwined. Suddenly I notice his thumb gently forming circles on the top of my hand. This simple action instantly brings to my mind a vision from my recent past. This mere tender display of sympathy gives me the strength I have been searching for. Gripping onto his hand I fight the urge to want to push.

Gratefully the ambulance comes to a stop and the back door flies open. A sea of nurses and paramedics rush around the back of the ambulance, hastily carrying the gurney out. Callum's grip tightens up, never letting go of my hand, forcing him to have to nearly jump out of the ambulance.

As we rush through the double doors, one of the nurses turns towards Callum. Placing her hand firmly against his chest, she utters authoritatively, "Excuse me, but you can't come in here unless you are the baby's father."

"What?"

"I am sorry sir, but only the husband or father of the baby is allowed in the delivery room. Those are the rules. You can wait in the waiting room, where someone will come and get you…"

"No! I need him to be with me. You don't understand," I immediately intervene, as another wave of sharp cramping washes through me, causing my heart rate to increase.

The nurse turns towards me. Seeing the sheer distress and agony within my face she looks down and notices my hand gripping fiercely onto Callum's. Bending down she whispers into my ear, "I need you to nod yes at the next question I am going to ask. Do you understand?" I shake my head in affirmation as she stands up, gazing directly into my eyes. "Is this man the father of your child?" she asks, pointing towards Callum.

Shifting my eyes back and forth between Callum and the nurse, trepidation pushes down on me. If I tell her the truth then I will have to go through this all alone, but if I answer yes then I am betraying my heart and everything that is real. A hot surge forming in my heart seeps out with poisonous shocks of sorrow. I am alone. No matter how much I wish my life would have turned out different, this is my world now. My mind knows it and my heart accepts it, but right now I can't be alone, I need someone. I cannot go through this experience by myself. Though this is not the person I want by my side, fate put him here and I will not let him go.

Taking in a deep breath I slowly gaze up into the nurse's eyes, "Yes. He is the father of my child."

Callum instantly turns towards me. His eyes narrow, forcing the furrow between them to deepen in hesitation. Gazing back at him I plead with my eyes for him to participate in this charade. I know this is not how he is hoping to spend his day, but something threw us together and there is no way he is going to leave now. His eyes suddenly soften, revealing a hint of a smile creeping into the corners of his mouth. Compassionately he squeezes my hand, reassuring me, once again, that he isn't going to leave. I renew my tight grip on his hand and the nursing staff begins to hastily push us through the large double doors into the awaiting delivery room. As the doors close, so too does my past and a new world now lies ahead of me.

Welcome to the Real World

My eyes remain affixed to the large light hanging right over my head as waves of muffled uproar envelop around me. A strong beam from the overhead light pushes down on me, warming my body to the very core. A sense of calm comes over my heightened body as I hear a low, soothing voice cutting through the chaos.

"You are doing great, Breanna. It is almost over. Push! Push!"

"Aaahhh!" As I bear down an abrupt sensation of feeling like I am being ripped in half sears through me. Then all of a sudden all the pain and agony I have been going through dissipates like a destructive tsunami finally receding back into the ocean. Cutting through the air, like a glorious call to me, is a high-pitched cry. The sound pierces me to my very core, causing a deep sensation of unimaginable love to fill the loneliness which has been consuming me.

"You have a beautiful baby boy," the doctor announces as he holds him up.

Without warning he places my baby on top of my stomach. Tears of joy begin to freely flow as I gaze down at this tiny and magnificent child. His dark hair frames his miniature features, as he looks up at me with an almost celestial understanding. As our eyes meet for the first time, an exchange of complete understanding of whom he is and who he is a part of, passes between us. The room that once held a sea of commotion is now so quiet even the doctor is beginning to whisper out of respect.

"Dad, would you like to cut the cord?" the doctor whispers, handing surgical scissors over to Callum.

Instantly I snap out of the trance I have been in. Reality suddenly comes to the forefront of my mind. Turning quickly towards Callum, I notice he is staring down at me and my miraculous newborn baby boy lying tenderly against my chest. A slight tear is forming in the corner of his eye, while he witnesses the newly formed bond between a mother and child. Wrapping my arms around my baby, I gaze up at Callum with a sense of possession.

Noticing my sudden reaction, his shoulders slump slightly and he utters softly, "If you don't want me to cut the cord then I won't, but if you don't mind I would love to share in this experience."

Allowing him to do this act that is usually reserved for the father is both an honor and a heartbreak. Knowing this irritating and obnoxious boy will be the one cutting the cord causes a conundrum of emotions to roll through me, shredding me up inside. Though he irritates me, I cannot deny the bond now formed between us. Looking into Callum's strong, yet gentle face, his caramel eyes gaze down upon me, reminding me how he willingly stepped into the role of knight in shining armor. Looking up at him I realize everything he has been put through today. I now see him with very different eyes. His well-built physique and good looks is usually thrown off by his lackadaisical and arrogant shroud, but his protective covering has melted away. A sensitive and kind core now pours out of him, causing him to appear even more charismatic to me.

Looking into his liquid caramel eyes, I respond to his statement, "I would be honored if you would cut the cord."

"Thank you!" A beam of joy spreads across his face, lighting up his seductive eyes.

Reacting on his impulse he bends down, placing a soft, passion-filled kiss on my mouth. His soft, moist lips gently move against my mouth, causing a wave of passion to vibrate within the pit of my stomach. The intense situation we have gone through together is liberated as our lips vigorously connect. Freely I respond to his now fervent kiss with equal zeal. Our mouths move aggressively against each other, as we surrender the overpowering need pulsating within us, causing my heart to hammer aggressively against my chest.

While we are lost in the hypnotic state of our passionate and overzealous kiss, a sudden low coughing sound of someone clearing their throat snaps us out of our state, "I don't mean to bother the both of you, but you are going to have to remove your lips from hers if you are going to cut the baby's cord. It is very blatant how happy the both of you are, but this little boy can't wait any longer."

Callum slowly pulls his head away from mine, staring deep into my hazel green eyes. The countenance within his eyes immediately transforms from a soft passion-filled appearance to a completely terrified expression. The furrow between his eyes narrows, causing a cold business-like façade to wash over him, guarding his emotions.

"Thank you Breanna, for letting me cut the cord, even though we both know I am not the baby's father," he whispers, in a flat icy tone.

His words pierce right through me as I watch him walk over and cut the tie that binds my baby and me. A surge of revulsion and anger forms in the pit of my stomach then vibrates through me, causing my hands to tremble against my innocent child. What was I thinking? This is not supposed to be an emotion for me. I can't have any feelings for someone, least of all this arrogant ass. I am now a single eighteen year old mother. I cannot act like I am still a teenager anymore. I can't and won't be Callum's play-thing.

Gazing down at my miracle, I stare into his eyes, uttering softly, "Looks like it is just me and you… Noah. I want you to always know you were conceived in love and will grow in love. I promise."

The nurse walks over to me, gently removing Noah from my protective grasp. She carries him over to the examining table to weigh, measure, and clean him up. My eyes anxiously follow them when suddenly Callum utters, "You did great, but now that you don't need me here anymore, I think I am going to leave. I am abso-bloody-lutely exhausted."

Shutting my emotions off I respond to him in an impersonal tone, trying to mirror his sudden distance, "You fulfilled your duty completely. I appreciate it, but you are right, I don't need you anymore."

He stares at me with a cold yet quizzical expression on his face. The brick wall which had crumbled during our episode together now re-appears. It seems Callum is rebuilding the wall, brick by brick, uttering flatly, "Well, I always know how you feel about things. You either state the obvious or you have no problem showing me." Callum begins rubbing the side of his face, recalling the sting I left on his cheek after I slapped him.

"I guess that is something we both have in common then," glaring deeply into his eyes I add, "Your stings hurt just as bad. They just don't leave a physical mark."

"I have no idea what you are talking about," he utters emotionlessly, with an air of conceit.

Shaking my head back and forth in disbelief at the sudden transformation he has undergone, I utter with a thick note of disdain, "Oh, I am sorry. That's right, I am the idiot here. Why should I be upset at the fact that you kissed me again?" Looking into his eyes with regret, I add, "This time though, I did kiss you back, only to feel like a foolish girl afterwards, falling for your meaningless kiss. As soon as you realized your mistake you became as cold as ice, trying to get out of here as soon as possible." The recent experience I am still enveloped in causes my emotions to ride on the knife's edge of self-control and a hormone imbalance. I immediately fall off of the edge, succumbing to an uncontrollable crying fit.

"Breanna, it wasn't meaningless, I…" he gazes back at me with the same fearful expression now streaming through his face, again. Immediately he stops what he was going to say, uttering firmly, "You don't bloody understand."

"You are right, I don't understand, but you don't understand my situation either."

His normal relaxed posture tightens up as if his spine instantly turns to stone, "No one knows your mysterious *situation*. Breanna, where is your baby's father? Why are you here in England all alone and not in America with your family? Why…"

"Stop!" I yell as I continue my crying fit, falling deeper into the emotional pit of despair, causing a tremulous wave to roll over me.

The nurse instantly comes over to me, "Are you alright?"

"Yes. Mr. Hughes is just leaving, that is all." I look up at Callum with tears streaming down my face. Anger flows through me as I realize this beautiful experience has been poisoned by his pride and arrogance. Not wanting to look at him anymore, I stare down at my slightly exposed breasts. Grabbing the blanket I pull it up over me, protecting my body from any more unneeded exposure.

"You want to leave, now?" A bewildered expression flashes across the nurse's face as she adds, "Don't you want to hold the baby?"

Though my eyes remain affixed to the blanket over me, I can feel his gaze cutting into me like lasers zeroing in on my thoughts, "No, I think it is best if I go and get some rest. Thank you and take good care of…" He looks down at me then over to Noah, who is now being swaddled in a hospital blanket, "…Noah."

The hospital door instantly closes, causing a bolt of sorrow to pierce through me with the reverberating sound it makes. The loneliness I have grown accustomed to once again wraps around me like an old wool blanket. The warmth and familiarity I can appreciate, but the uncomfortable itch it leaves on my skin is unbearable. I may put on a tough shroud, but the painful circumstances I have had to endure are taking a toll on me. My tears flow down my cheeks like giant waterfalls. Suddenly the edge of my bed pushes down from the weight of someone sitting on it.

"Would you like to hold your little boy?" a nurse asks. I look up only to discover this is the same nurse who wasn't going to let Callum in unless I said he was the baby's father. She is the only one here who knows that Callum is not Noah's father.

"Yes, please," I grab hold of Noah, firmly holding him against my chest. Looking down I examine his every detail. His soft olive skin, thick brown hair with golden highlights painted delicately across the tips, and almond shaped eyes balancing perfectly on either side of his adorable pudgy nose. His features bring to my mind a mixture of joy intermingling with painful memories. The similarities are absolutely uncanny. His sweet hand opens up, revealing his long, delicate fingers. Placing my finger into the palm of his hand, he instinctively wraps his fingers tightly around mine.

"I am a single mother also. You will be fine," the nurse utters softly.

"I hope. He came into this world under unfair circumstances. I pray that an angelic soul will be sent to help us."

"Do you have any other family here besides the man who left?"

A slight snort pushes through my nose, "He's not family. He's not even a friend. I barely know him. He is just an arrogant jerk that is in one of my classes. I have no one. I am a stranger in a foreign land." Looking up into her eyes I add, "I am completely alone."

"Wow. Why did you come here then, especially being pregnant? Shouldn't you be with the baby's father or at least your family?"

"I should, but that scenario is only in my dreams. The real world has a much harsher plan for me. I am only here to keep a promise."

Enveloping Noah in my secure arms, I press him tightly against me, noticing that he is beginning to fall asleep.

"Remember, dreams are the kindling to hope. And with hope and faith anything is possible," she adds, stroking Noah's hair delicately.

"I guess," I skeptically sigh.

"And what about the arrogant jerk? There is definitely something resonating between you both, it is blatant. The way you wouldn't let go of him, nor was he about to leave you, either. And, well, let's just point out the obvious kiss between you both. He appears to be more than just someone you barely know."

"There is nothing between us. It was just a heat of the moment kiss," I state flatly, trying to hide the fact that I actually enjoyed it. During the moments of my labor and frantic delivery, his chivalry and kindness formed a bond linking us together, like oil and water emulsifying, creating an inseparable union. But that too is just a dream. Besides, I would be cheating on my heart and that I can never do.

"Not blooming likely, but you can just go on fooling yourself," she states blatantly. "I better let you rest while you have a chance to, because once he is awake you will be entering the world of

Zombieland." A sarcastic laugh escapes her, "Would you like me to take your baby to the nursery so you can sleep?"

"No! I don't want him leaving my side!" Realizing the intensity in my voice I instantly tone it down, "Thank you, though."

"If you need anything just give me a buzz," she states, pointing to the call button on the side of the bed.

Extreme exhaustion flows over me as I listen to the slow, soft breaths Noah is making. My breathing begins to mirror his as I gaze out the window. I watch how the rippling rivulets of raindrops hit different areas of the glass, yet roll towards each other like magnets, combining their forces as they stream down the glass. As I examine this paradox, a hypnotic state slowly consumes me, sending my languid body deeper and deeper into a state of relaxation.

A quiet sense of peace floats throughout the room as my mind dances around the reality of being a mother. As I silently soak in all the details of Noah's face I can hear boisterous cries of joy from the people in the room next to me. The myriad of elated comments piercing through the wall sends a sensation of tremendous loneliness to conquer my mind. All the comments seem to be coming from family members who are completely overjoyed for the blest couple.

This is a joyous day for me also, but there is no one here to share it with. Out of my peripheral vision I notice the phone sitting ominously on the night-stand. Trying to fight the urge to call, I begin debating with myself as to how ridiculous I am being.

Instantly I hear a low voice coming from the room next door stating enthusiastically, "I am the luckiest bloke right now. I have a beautiful wife who just blessed me with a handsome baby boy." Their room erupts with roaring cheers, causing my internal debate to end.

Grabbing hold of the phone I begin mindlessly dialing. The chance of her even answering the phone is slim to none, but I need to at least try. The anxiety pulsing throughout me increases as the phone feels like it is ringing for eternity. Just as I am about to hang up, the ringing stops and a gruff woman's voice states firmly, "What kind of idiot calls me this early in the morning? Someone better be dead!"

Immediately I remember the time difference, realizing it is about 5:00 o'clock in the morning. Trying to buffer the shock, I quietly respond, "Hi, mom."

"Who is this?" her voice has a hint of irritation to it as she slurs out the words.

"It's me, Breanna."

"What the hell? Why are you calling me? Please don't tell me you are in jail," her jumbled speech compliments her foul mouth perfectly.

"No mom, that is your area of expertise," I state coldly, remembering all the times I got a call from her in the middle of the night stating she was in jail, and could I come bail her out.

"Did you just call to remind me of how much of a lousy mother I am? If so, then at least give me the decency of allowing me to pour myself a stiff drink first."

Alcohol has always been my mom's first and only love in her life. Every memory I have of my mother always involved her being drunk or getting drunk. The inconsistency of where we lived or what job she had, was the only consistency in my life. The small glimpses of sobriety were either court-ordered or child protective service-induced. When she is sober she is a completely different person. There were a few times she really tried to be the kind of mother she knew she should be, working two jobs to pay the bills and give me everything she thought I needed. But all I wanted was a stable mother, something she couldn't give me longer than a few months here and there. When she would go through one of her binges I would usually leave, running to the only person I could trust. I could go for months without even talking to her and she wouldn't even realize I was gone. I haven't seen or talked to my mother for a year now and she has no idea. It is as if her brain has been pickled by the alcohol, affecting the way her mind now works. She has no concept of time or reality.

Wanting to get off the subject of alcohol and her parenting skills, or lack thereof, I utter, "I am sorry for the rude statement. I just called to tell you that you are a grandmother."

"You had a baby?"

"Yes. I just gave birth to a beautiful little boy, today."

"Who is the little bastard's father?" she blatantly states.

I can almost smell the alcohol through the phone. What am I thinking, calling her? I am an idiot. I just wanted to have what the family next to me is experiencing, someone excited about Noah's birth. My anger and disappointment towards my mother pushes out. "He is not a bastard child! You know nothing about me or my life anymore. All you care about is where your bottles of vodka and gin are. I just wanted to talk to my mom and attempt to share in this celebration. But I can see I am asking way too much from you. I am sorry for disturbing your hangover respite, but look at it this way, you can now continue drinking. Good-bye."

My loud and disdainful conversation causes Noah to wake up, immediately realizing he is starving to death. Freeing his source of food from my hospital gown, I begin feeding him. Looking down into his sweet face I utter softly, "I am at least excited you are here."

My breathing is beginning to return to its normal rhythm. That is a conversation I don't ever want to have again. I cannot let her in anymore. I have to come to grips with the fact that the mother within my dreams never existed. My mother is a constant disappointment, hurting me too severely for someone my age to handle. I have already experienced way too much for an eighteen year old, I don't need my mother's problems also. It looks like it is just me and Noah, and I am okay with that.

Suddenly there is a soft tap on my hospital room door. Trying not to disturb Noah I whisper, "Come in."

"Well, now I know what kind of a bloody friend you are. I may have been the first person here in England you told about being pregnant, but I had to find out about your delivery from my brother," Olivia sarcastically states, as she comes walking in carrying a small bouquet of blue flowers.

I have never been so excited to see someone as I am to see her. Her beaming take-no-prisoner attitude is such a sharp contrast to her beauty and petite features. But even more shocking is how her tough attitude is such a sharp contrast from her loving and compassionate nature.

An immediate elated sensation washes over me, "Olivia, I am so glad you are here. I'm not alone now."

A large smile spreads across her face, "Of course you are not alone. You have me, remember?"

The Space Between Us

We sit in the cab outside of my flat, preparing to enter my new world, "Olivia, it is nice enough that you brought Noah and me home from the hospital. But you didn't need to buy me a car seat also. I could have bought one myself."

Her eyes narrow as she tilts her head slightly, adding, "Not blooming likely. When would you have had the chance to get one? Were you just planning on leaving Noah in the hospital while you run out and purchase a car seat? They would have never let you leave without one."

She definitely has a way of pointing out the obvious. A huge smile spreads across my face as I stare at her in complete appreciation, "I could have never made it through this without you."

A quizzical smile dances in the corners of her mouth as she searches my eyes for a deeper answer, "And who else?"

I know what she wants me to say, but the anger I feel for him and the embarrassment I feel towards myself is still fresh in my mind. He literally carried me through my labor and delivery, but what happened afterwards left me feeling confused and disappointed with the both of us. It is the first time I have felt something in a long time. I couldn't have asked for anyone better to help me through it, but how he just shut me off after we kissed left me feeling like a piece of useless trash. The look in his eyes held an enormous amount of regret, causing me to feel like I had just committed adultery. The resonating sickness and humiliation is still spinning within me.

Looking away from Olivia I refuse to answer her. I highly doubt Callum told her anything about our kiss. I am sure he is disgusted with it and would prefer to keep the surreptitious kiss private. I am not even sure how I feel about it. Conundrums of emotions roll around within me. I teeter-totter between feeling ashamed and feeling an undeniable gravitational pull towards him. It is like a schoolgirl crush on steroids. The angrier I get at myself the more my mind replays the entire event. I can still feel his firm, protective arms around me as he rushes to meet the ambulance. I can hear his gentle, warm commands encouraging me through the whole process. He never left my side. I saw such a compassionate part of him, which left me with a resonating feeling of coming home again. But after we kissed I was only left to feel like a used rag, dirty. Looking up at her I utter, "What are you talking about?"

"Bloody Hell! What happened? Both you and Callum are tight lipped about the details."

Immediately I look up at her, "What did he tell you?"

"Just that you went into labor right after your lecture and he went with you to the hospital. He told me he was able to witness the most miraculous event. I have never seen Callum look so happy and exhausted at the same time. And that is saying a lot."

"Well, if that is all he told you, then he divulged everything." Opening the cab door I grab the handle of the car seat, awkwardly getting out of the cab. Turning to say goodbye to Olivia I notice she is now standing next to me, paying the cabbie for his service. "What are you doing? You don't need to walk me into my flat too."

Completely ignoring me she grabs some of my things, proceeding to walk into the building as if she knows exactly where she is going. I watch her quizzically as she walks towards the correct flat. A strange sense of fear rushes through me. She has never been to my flat before. How does she know where I live? "Olivia, how did you know which flat is mine?"

A huge smile spreads across her face as she beckons me with a quick sideways nod to come and follow her. Hesitation rolls up my back, causing the hair on my arms to stand straight up. A hint of something mischievous lingers in the corners of her smile. My feet are like lead anchoring me to this very spot. I am not about to move until I know how she found out where I live.

Olivia notices my trepidation and calls out, "Breanna, stop being ridiculous, I am your friend, not a bloody stalker. I will tell you how I know which flat is yours, but first you need to come in.

Resolving to trust her I walk over to my door and open it up. Disbelief washes over me as I stand in the doorway in complete shock. Immense heat forming in my chest explodes out, causing tears to freely flow. I have never seen anything so beautiful. There in one corner of my tiny flat is a spectacular oak crib fully decorated in a soft blue palette. Every piece of furniture has been arranged to flawlessly fit within my tiny space. On one side of the crib is a matching dark oak dresser. Flanking the opposite side is a beautiful light blue club chair. The quality of the furniture is something I could never have afforded but have dreamed about.

This act of incredible kindness I have never experienced before. My heart swells with emotion as I take in this act of love. Closing my eyes tightly I try to fight back the flowing tears, but it is to no avail. I have always had to struggle for just the basic necessities in life, never thinking I would ever be able to have something so beautiful for my son. To save on money, I was just planning on purchasing a portable crib.

Grabbing the handle to the infant car seat I carry sleeping Noah into the flat. As I approach the miraculous gift I notice all the intricately carved details to the crib and dresser. These pieces look as if they stepped right out of history. The antique quality to each piece shows they have come from nobility. The elaborate carvings on each piece of furniture show that a skillful woodworker took his time in cutting each piece. On the inside of the headboard is carved a family crest bearing a capital H in the middle of it. My fingertips gently stroke the top rail, tracing every shape and detail etched into the wood.

The soft blue and white toile bedding fits the vintage feel flawlessly. Plush bumper pads encircle the inner edges of the crib, ending perfectly on top of the layers of toile pattern and checkered bed skirt. Thrown over the side rail is a plush blanket awaiting the use of its future inhabitant.

As I look at this unfathomable gift I mumble in a soft, tearful voice, "Thank you, Olivia. Thank you."

Olivia's hand gently wraps around mine, "Don't thank me. This was all Callum's idea."

Instant shock pierces my mind, causing chills to race throughout my body. Confusion flusters me, making it nearly impossible to talk. "What? I don't understand. This was Callum's idea? Why?" I stammer out.

"Callum told me that before he left the hospital he got your address off of the hospital records and then drove to your flat. He had someone let him into…"

"Who?" I interrupt, "And how?"

"God knows. That boy is so smooth he can probably talk the queen into giving him her crown." A large, proud smile spreads across her face, "He is a perfect combination of power and persuasion. Once he finally knows what he wants, neither Heaven nor Hell will be able to stop him from getting it."

A soft laugh exhales through my nose as I recall his forceful conversation with the paramedics. He was going to get in the ambulance with me and there was nothing they could do to stop it. There is a definite persuasive air to him.

"So you are going to have to ask him the details about how he actually got in. But once he was in he noticed you had nothing prepared for when you brought your baby home." Walking over to the top portion of the crib she gently traces the crest engraved into the ornate oak crib. "You know, your baby must have made quite an impression on him."

I watch as she strokes the crib. Her voice had lowered to a contemplative tone, one that I had not yet heard in her before.

"What do you mean?" I ask, completely confused by her statement. The only impression I thought I left him with was one of shame and embarrassment.

Turning towards me she states, "This isn't just any crib set, this was Callum's. It has been in our family for generations."

Disbelief and shock floods my body as I try to understand why he would let Noah use his crib set. "Why would he do this?" I utter softly under my breath. Everything about him confuses me on a profound level. I can't figure him out. One minute he is arguing with me and then the next he kisses me, followed by ignoring me, then becoming my hero, kissing me again, running away, and now this. I was beginning to get comfortable with hating him, but now all the emotions I had for him in the hospital return. A warm sensation invades my entire body, causing a tingling feeling to rush through me.

"He had it brought over to your flat. Then he asked me to help him pick out a baby set for the crib." She turns towards me, revealing a softer side. Usually her breathtaking looks are encased within a shell of sarcasm and spitfire. But this time her true beauty shines forth, unprotected and vulnerable, "I hope you like it."

Uncontrolled tears stream down my face. "Like it. I absolutely love it." My gruff voice muffles as a multitude of emotions flood my body.

Olivia tenderly wraps her arm around me. Pulling me closer to her she utters softly, "Then why are you crying?"

Using the back of my hand like a napkin I begin aggressively wiping the tears away. "There are so many reasons. Most of them you wouldn't understand, but there is one I am completely confused about."

"What do you mean?"

Trepidation rolls deep within my gut. I have no idea how to tell her and when I do, what is she going to think? If I don't even comprehend what is going on, how can I expect her to know? My mind and heart seem to be battling over what they feel is right. My heart is telling me no, to hold onto what is true and right, but my mind is telling me that it is okay to feel again. But I am no longer a single person anymore who can make mistakes and have them only affect me. I now bring a child along on this rollercoaster of life. I have no idea if Callum is just looking for fun, but my only way of finding out is to tell Olivia. Turning towards Olivia I look into her eyes and just spit it out, "Callum and I kissed."

"I know, but when you slapped him I think he got the picture," she states, with an air of confusion dancing on the tips of each word.

"No, we kissed again in the hospital. But this time I kissed him back. I don't know why. Maybe it was just the intense situation we both were in, but there was something to the kiss. But…" Hesitation swirls within my mouth as I notice Olivia's shocked expression. Her eyes are about as wide as her mouth, causing a sick, shameful sensation to curdle my stomach.

"Bloody Hell!" is the first thing out of her mouth, then after a long pause she asks questionably, "We are talking about my arse of a brother, right?"

"Yes." I state, in a slow, reassuring way.

"Well, that explains all of this," she affirms, as she points towards the beautiful gift he left for me to discover. Turning back towards me, she looks deep in my eyes. "But I thought you hated him."

"I do…I did…I don't know. I thought I did, but when we were in the hospital together he revealed a part of himself that reminds me of someone I miss."

Turning my back to Olivia I continue, "I needed him at that time and he was not about to leave me. There was a bond formed between us…so I thought."

"What do you mean, so you thought?"

Turning back towards Olivia I notice she is now sitting in the club chair leaning forward, listening to me intently. Her eyes are no longer as wide as saucers, but instead they are now narrow with a deep furrow between them. A distorted twist to her face reveals a curious misunderstanding, as if she is cognizant of some sort of information I am missing.

"Well, after we kissed everything changed. He looked at me with an expression of regret and became very cold and distant. At a moment when I should have felt joy, he made me feel cheap. I should have trusted my first impression and avoided him like the plague."

My tears begin to flow freely, again. Sorrow rips through my heart, slashing at whatever pieces I have left. I can't take anymore loss. The weight of the past year pushes down on me, causing me to collapse under the enormous pressure. Damned up emotions explode within me like flood waters destroying everything within their grasp. I have been successfully able to run from my pain and tragedy until now. It is funny how something so immature and meaningless can break down the wall I have successfully built around my heart.

Burying my head in my hands I begin to release my internal pain and suffering. My breathing vibrates against my chest from the sobbing motion I am making. A soft, warm hand presses gently against my back. "If I could, I would kill my brother, but you need to understand something about him first."

Gaining enough control over my emotions I am able to talk slightly, "Olivia, you don't understand. I have repressed my emotions over the past year and whether good or bad, Callum has allowed me to let it go. I have not completely cried over my circumstance. No matter how hard it is for me to let go, I have to."

"I am confused. Please don't let go of Callum yet." Olivia's eyes are moist and filled with sincere sympathy.

"I am letting go of my husband."

Olivia's hand suddenly drops as she backs up, completely taken aback by what I have just divulged. "Your bloody what? Please don't tell me my brother has been pulled into an affair."

Wiping my tears away I utter softly, trying to not lose control again. "No. My late husband… who… died eight months ago." The deep furrow between her eyes returns. I can see the wheels in her mind turning, trying to figure everything out. "I married my best friend and true love as soon as I turned eighteen. He was my savior in more ways than one. I could have never imagined my world without him in it. He was my… everything. One month after we were married I got a call that he had been involved in a serious car crash and was being taken to the hospital."

Warm, salty tears pour down my face as I relive the worst night of my life. The vision of that night opens up, allowing me to recall every detail. The cold, sterile feel of the hospital matched my numb, empty feeling, as if I was walking in a dream. The rush of people swarming all around me mimicked my chaotic mind. Everything within me seemed to be moving in slow motion as I headed to a private section of the emergency room. "As I rushed into the emergency room, I was led back to the secluded room. As I walked into his room the man lying on the gurney did not look like my husband. This man's body was broken, bloody and bruised, making him unrecognizable. My mind kept telling me over and over that this could not be Andrew. No matter how much I tried to convince myself that it was a dream, the reality of what had happened screamed in my face. He couldn't die. That is a selfish thing to do and he is not a selfish man. The choice was in neither of our hands, though. I didn't want him to leave me, but no matter how much I didn't want it to happen, I knew deep down he wasn't going to survive this. His injuries were too extensive. I held his battered and bruised hand and," I close my eyes tightly trying to fight back the tears, "watched him leave this world. A huge part of my heart died that night with him."

I look up at Olivia's shocked and sorrowful face. "My nightmare was not over yet. The universe was about to throw one more challenge at me." As I close my eyes again I can see and smell every detail. The different types of sweet Jell-O salad, funeral casserole, and many different combinations of heavy amounts of cologne flood my senses. "The day of his funeral I had been extremely sick. I had to just power through that day with a detached sense of obligation. I thought it was just the stress and emotional heartache I was under until one of Andrew's friends jokingly asked if I was pregnant. It was no joke. I found out that night, the same day as his funeral, that I was in fact pregnant. So there I was, an eighteen year old pregnant widow."

As I open my eyes I notice that Olivia's face is completely soaked by the tears freely flowing down her. Her contorted face is now mirroring my broken down expression. We both sit here in complete silence as the thick, depressive atmosphere within the room envelops us in sorrow and pain. I never meant to share my burden with anyone, least of all my one and only friend here, but now that I have a heavy weight has been lifted. The affliction I have been carrying is now floating all around us and can finally dissipate. I have been bearing the weight of that for so long, though it is a heavy burden for Olivia, I now can breathe. At last I can hope to let go, whereas before, I had no hope.

Olivia's eyes are transfixed onto the floor, while she shakes her head back and forth. "Blimey. Knock me down with a feather."

Instantly I look up at her with a taken-back expression. "What in the hell does that mean?"

Olivia looks over at me, instantly remembering that I am not from here. A wide smile spreads across her face as she tries to muffle a snicker forming within her. An immediate transforming sensation comes over me. All the pain and sorrow bubbling within me burst into a hilarious rolling freight train. No matter how hard I try to contain it I can't stop the laughter from coming. A loud, rolling laugh explodes from my mouth, followed by an incredibly embarrassing snort.

Huge bursts of giggles roll out of Olivia's mouth, "What was that sound?" she states, referring to my lovely pig-like snort. I don't usually make that sound, but because of the heavy emotional shift happening within me the snort was coming out whether I like it or not.

We both just lose control and begin laughing hysterically. The swing of emotions causes my body to tremble. No matter how hard I try to stop laughing I can't. Everything within me embraces this change in my emotions. The giggles form in the pit of my stomach, where my intense pain once resided. This new sensation is a welcome change, but is also sending my body into a state of exhaustion.

Our hysteria slowly subsides, leaving us feeling confused and fatigued. I have no idea whether to laugh or cry again. A forceful sigh escapes my mouth as I stare at Olivia gratefully. "Please don't tell anyone my situation, especially Callum."

Her eyes widen as she slowly regains her control, "This time I will not let it slip, I promise." Her body relaxes slightly as she takes on a more serious tone, "But I wish that you would tell Callum." I immediately try to interrupt, but she lifts her hand, stopping me before I can utter a single word. "You have more in common than you realize. I promise I will not tell him, but you also need to drop your prejudices towards him. You are judging him by his cover and that is unfair. Not everything you think about him is true. There are things from his past constantly nipping at his heels. I know he can be an arse sometimes, but he is my arse and I would do anything for him. And I know he would do anything for the ones he cares about." Her eyes scan to the beautiful crib set he set up in my flat. "At least think about it."

I silently gaze at her as I take in all the emotions I have been through today. Miraculously Noah has been able to sleep through the whole thing. I stare at him, envious of his innocence and simple life. What I wouldn't give to have a simple, untainted life. My life has never had an innocent, blank slate. From my birth I have had colors scattered all over me. Some have formed beautiful pictures, while others just have been random streaks of mindless scribbles.

I can't see how Olivia thinks that Callum and I have a lot in common. He comes from a very different world than me. He comes from a home with a mother and father. He is somewhat close to his sister. They come from a long line of aristocracy and privilege. I, on the other hand, am an eighteen year old mother and widow who comes from an alcoholic mother and a mysterious one night stand father. The space between us is wider than she realizes.

Closing the door behind Olivia as she leaves, I turn around and there facing me is the crib set that was once Callum's and is now Noah's to use. This is my world now. While most eighteen year olds are just starting out in life, I feel like I am exhausted. I am tired of the pain, the struggles, and the heartbreak. Looking out across the room I notice that Noah is starting to wake up. Walking over to him I pick him up, holding onto him tightly.

Looking down at him I utter softly, "You fill the empty space perfectly." Walking over to his new crib I lay him down in it. As I watch him surrounded by the incredible gift Callum has allowed Noah to use, I am filled with an overwhelming sense of gratitude again. I have been judging him by his outer appearance. There is more to Callum rippling beneath his protective shield on a subterranean level. I was able to witness his core surging beneath his tough exterior. Maybe I should give Callum a chance, just maybe.

The Invitation

Walking onto the portion of the campus again after being gone for two weeks feels like my first day. Thanks to Olivia I will be able to continue going to school, completing the Easter term. She has been getting my assignments from her brother and from my professor in my one other class, bringing them to me. My attempts at doing my classwork while breastfeeding and getting very little sleep, have been nearly impossible. But because of her efforts, I have been able to keep up with all my coursework. She knows the only way I am going to be able to finish my courses is if I have someone to watch Noah while I am gone, so Olivia sent over the lady who used to be Callum and Olivia's nanny.

Leaving Noah this morning was the hardest thing for me to do. He is still so new and fragile that it felt like my heart was going to rip out of me. Though I will be only gone for a few hours I feel like I am having a panic attack. I know I can trust the nanny Olivia has sent over, but I still worry. The nanny's appearance exemplifies the perfect model of an upper class British caregiver with her thick pinned-back grey hair, prim and proper dress attire. Every part of her has been meticulously put together. As she speaks, her thick, precise British accent places several enunciations within just one word. Just being around her this morning caused me to consciously correct my posture and speech. I felt like I was in a finishing school and if I slouched or used incorrect grammar I was going to be firmly corrected. Though she seems rather stiff and prudish I have no doubt she knows what she is doing.

As I stand in front of the door to my classroom the nerves bubble up within my stomach. I haven't seen Callum since he left me in the hospital. We haven't talked about anything, least of all our kiss. Olivia has told me several times that she has caught him debating whether to come over or not, but she says there is something holding him back. She has never seen her brother like this before. Her words have given me hope that maybe our conversation will go over well. I have wanted to thank him for the amazing gift, but I have been meaning to do it face to face. There are so many things I want to talk to him about, but as I stand in front of the door I am not sure my nerves will be able to allow me to talk to him.

I close my eyes and take a deep breath as I grab hold of the knob, quickly opening the door. The multitude of boisterous conversations rapidly halt with my surprising entrance. All eyes span towards me, but the only eyes I care to notice are Callum's. Gazing around the room I notice Callum looking straight at me with a kind, reassuring grin on his face. Seeing his supportive smile I return the sentiment as I walk over to my usual seat.

Just as I am about to sit down Mr. Bramble utters, "Ms. Hayes, welcome back. I am glad you are able to join us again."

"Oi, what have you done with your little bastard child?" a low voice chortles from the front of the room.

"Belt up Gavin! You bloody arse! I won't let you talk about her son like that," Callum snaps.

"Mr. Hughes, I don't usually allow abusive talk like that towards another student, but in this case I am grateful for it." Turning towards Gavin Mr. Bramble firmly states, "Mr. Beddows, I think you owe Ms. Hayes an apology. That kind of disrespect is absolutely not allowed in my class."

Gavin turns slightly towards me, "I am sorry, Breanna."

His apology on the surface appears sincere, but the heart of it lacks any authenticity. I have no idea what I did to make Callum's friends hate me so much. There has to be something deeper than my pregnancy and now the reality of being a young mother. They have always held some kind of animosity towards me.

I pretend to accept his apology by giving Gavin a slight insincere smile. The class immediately turns their attention back to the front of the room. We are heading into the final preparations for our mid-exam before our week vacation. I try to stay focused on the discussion, but my mind is fully anticipating the conversation with Callum. The thick air within the room wraps around me with an unexplained excitement. I am counting down the minutes left in class.

Finally my professor finishes up, causing a herd of students to hastily flee from our lecture room. I notice Callum slowly gathering his things, as if he is stalling for some reason. Realizing that it is now or never, I head over to Callum.

"Hi, Callum," I state pragmatically, trying to hide my nerves.

A radiant smile spreads across his face as he stands up to greet me, "Well it is about bloody time. I wasn't sure how much longer I could stall waiting for you."

"Well, if you were waiting for me, then why didn't you come over to me?" I sarcastically snap back.

Rolling waves of nerves pulsate throughout my body. A new sensation tickles my nerve endings as I stare into Callum's stimulating caramel eyes. Callum has never made me nervous before, but now things feel different to me. After my breakdown with Olivia, the tough shell around my heart crumbled, allowing me to see for the first time how much I really missed Callum.

A soft laugh exhales through his nose, "I'll give you that one." We both laugh as if we are trying to stall the inevitable. Suddenly he asks, "How is Noah?"

"He is doing great. Better than me. I am exhausted from not sleeping at night. They need to tell future mothers to sleep all the time, so when your baby is born we will have some reserve to live off of," I state honestly. I am sure he notices the dark circles under my eyes.

A smile spreads across his face, as his eyes seem to long for something, "Can I come and see him?"

My heart fills to the brim as he asks to come and see Noah, "I would love you to. You are the one who cut the cord."

He laughs hesitantly, and then adds, seemingly to change the subject, "So, what do you think of Miss McNally, the nanny?"

A little snicker explodes from my mouth, "Well, I can tell that she is an experienced nanny and knows what she is doing. But she is also very…"

"Proper, and a bit scary," he interrupts.

We both start laughing together at poor Miss McNally's expense. Though I know she is a great nanny, her sterile and business-like nature is hard to get used to. I can only imagine the stories Olivia and Callum have about her. I never grew up with a nanny watching me. I was lucky if my mom was even sober enough to look after me. Some of my earliest memories are of me taking care of myself. I never had an additional someone to watch over me. Having a nanny is just part of their world.

"Yes. She is a bit scary. This morning I felt like if I didn't walk correctly or use proper British English, she was going to crack my knuckles," I laugh as I try to imitate her sharp crisp British accent.

His laughter increases to a full rumble, "I think you need to work on your accent. That was horrible."

Our laughter blends together forming one bond. I watch as his wall is completely tumbling down, exposing his vulnerable side. The shimmering lights of joy twinkle within his beautiful eyes. Though Brits are not known for their teeth, his are gleaming white and perfectly straight. His full, masculine mouth spreads across his face forming a perfect smile. I take in every detail of him now, with a very different emotion.

He continues laughing as he adds, "Remind me that I need to not only pay her for taking care of Noah, but she needs to work on your proper English."

Instantly my laughing stops, "What do you mean? Are you the one paying for her and not Olivia?"

His relaxed expression vanishes, along with his joyful laughing. He looks at me quizzically as he tries figuring out what to say. Resolving to fully embrace the question he answers, "Yes. I am the one who arranged for Miss McNally's services and payments."

A deep furrow forms between my eyes as I look at him with wonder, "Please don't take offence to this question, because I am extremely grateful for everything you have done for me and Noah, but why? I will never be able to repay the things that you have given us."

"I don't want you to repay me," he states firmly, interrupting me.

"I have never in my life received this kind of kindness. The crib set is beautiful and Olivia told me that it is a family heirloom. I promise I will return it as soon as I find a new one to replace it."

He walks within inches of me, placing a hand on my shoulder, "I want Noah to use it. I don't want you to find another one."

His caramel eyes bore deep into mine, sending a warm sensation to pierce my heart. His touch penetrates my skin, sinking into my very core, causing butterflies to soar within me. Warmth crawls up my spine and radiates throughout my head, causing tears to form within my eyes. "Callum, why? Please, tell me why?"

His hand starts trembling on my shoulder as he looks deep into my eyes. A tangible heat fills the space between us, causing our breathing to increase. His eyes hold a hunger and craving within them, sending chills throughout my body. An aching need pulsates between us. Reacting to the yearning, he slowly begins to lean in towards me, uttering in a smooth buttery tone, "Say my name again."

Suddenly out of the blue I hear, "Callum, there you are."

The fire burning between us instantly extinguishes as Callum's body immediately stiffens. Looking up I notice Emily, the dark haired petite girl from our class and also the night at the pub. Walking gracefully over to Callum, she interlaces her arm purposefully within his. Standing up on her tippy-toes she leans over and kisses him on the cheek, "I have been waiting for you, babe. What has been keeping you so long?" she glances over at me with a crooked smile.

Callum looks at me with a petrified expression on his face. His hand slowly drops from my shoulder as he takes a timid step away from me. A searing edge of disgust and disappointment roll through me. I keep trying to look Callum in the eye, but he refuses to meet my gaze. If he has been in a relationship with Emily the whole time, then he should have never kissed me…twice, wait… almost three times now. And if they just became an item, then that is even worse, because as soon as he made a mistake with me he decided to run to Emily. A shivering surge of anger rushes up my spine. Of all the people at the University, why her? She is such a pompous snob.

"I was just asking Breanna about her little baby," he states, with an irritated edge to his tone.

"Oh, that's right. I forgot you have a baby now. That is too bloody bad. You won't be able to go to Callum's family home for the holiday now. We were thinking about inviting you." Her condescending attitude vibrates within every word. A subtle smile spreads across her face as she looks right at me.

"Why can't she go? It is mine and Olivia's home. Both Breanna and her baby are welcome anytime," Callum snaps back.

Emily's jaw clinches down tightly, causing a subterranean quiver to vibrate in her jaw just under her skin as she stares at the ground. Callum looks up and meets my disappointed gaze. As he opens his mouth to say something I immediately interrupt him, "Wow, let me just start by saying, I am done. I am not about to play any games so I am just going to say, you both are perfect for each other." Grabbing my things I proceed to head out the door when I hear Callum call my name. Turning back towards him, I state coldly, "You are still welcome to come and see Noah, but that is it." Hastily I walk out of the room as the fire within me now transforms into a deep sadness. All I want to do is go back to my flat and hold onto Noah.

Walking down the stone street the cool air washes over me, shedding the frustration off of my body. Gingerly I walk through the crowds of people, stalling my return to my flat and Noah, as a heavy sigh rolls through me and I fight back my anger towards Callum. Finally getting control of my emotions I head back to my flat. As I open the door I am taken aback in shock. There, sitting in my club chair, is Callum holding Noah who is fast asleep.

"What the Hell are you doing in my flat? And where is Miss McNally?"

"I let her go home," he whispers softly as he looks up right into my eyes.

Glaring down at him I snap, "You have no right to come in, or even let Miss McNally go home."

Tilting his head slightly to one side he looks at me patronizingly, "I disagree. She is under my employment and what I say, she will do. Besides, you gave me permission to come by and see Noah."

"I didn't mean right now. What did you do, jump in your car and rush over here, dragging poor Emily along?" I begin looking all around my tiny flat for Emily. "Where is she, by the way? It's not like she has a lot of places to hide here."

A coy smile spreads across his face, "Why do you want to know?"

I look at him as my rigid shoulders drop in irritation. Rolling my eyes at him and his arrogant game he is playing, I utter coldly, "I am not going to partake in this game. Just answer my question."

"She's not here." Holding Noah firmly against his chest he carefully pulls himself up from the club chair and walks closer to me. "You are playing a bigger game than you realize." His eyes bore deep into mine, causing my heart to race fervently against my chest.

A surging wave of heat forming in my gut pushes its way up, causing all the hair on my arm to stand straight up. Forcefully my mind pushes the sensation he is causing me back down, as my anger now supersedes any other emotion residing within me.

"I have no idea what you are talking about. I am not the one who kisses you, then almost immediately turns my attention towards someone else." Deciding I am completely done with this conversation I grab hold of Noah and forcefully remove him from Callum's arms. "Get out."

He moves just inches away from my face. As he looks down at me, his caramel eyes ignite with a flame of passion, "No. I am not about to leave. If you want some answers as to why I kissed and ran then you need to answer some bloody questions of your own first."

His eyes bore deep into me, piercing my heart to the very center. Reacting to his piercing gaze I back away from him, trying to close the door to my heart. Immediately Noah belts out a loud scream, shattering the uncomfortable silence looming between us. Instantly I try bouncing him up and down, attempting to calm him down. Nothing I am doing is working, though.

"Here, let me try," Callum insists, reaching for Noah.

"No, I can do it," I snap, as I turn Noah away from Callum's reach.

"I never bloody said you couldn't do it. I am just saying that he was asleep with me and just maybe I can put him to sleep again," he says, reaching for Noah. He gently takes him from my reluctant, yet consenting arms.

He begins rocking him side to side as he walks around my tiny flat. I watch, completely enamored by his gentle and soothing touch. Noah's boisterous screams slowly subside to just a quiet, vibrating whimper. Callum gazes down at him with a completely smitten trance. Something definitely was formed between them in the delivery room, because Noah has never been like this with me. The anger flowing through me dissipates as I watch this gentle action. Conundrums of emotions roll violently within me. The pain of longing for Noah's father, Andrew, vibrates against the passionate feelings towards Callum, like bumper cars against my heart. My young heart can't handle this, especially if Callum is just playing games with me.

Turning towards me Callum utters in a buttery soft voice, "It looks like he just wanted me after all," he smiles, with an air of satisfaction.

My heart swells as I watch Callum's soothing nature towards Noah. Life sure knows how to play games on us. Here Noah has been robbed of the experience of knowing his biological father and what a wonderful man he was. Then to form a bond with a man that will never be part of his life. The pain that is constantly rippling within my heart slices through me as I watch this kind gesture. He slowly walks around the room humming a soft lullaby I have never heard before. Callum's eyes gaze down into Noah's, as his eyes slowly start to close. Tears begin to well up in my eyes as I realize the tender male influence Noah has been robbed of.

"What are you humming?" I ask, softly.

Not even skipping a beat, he tenderly turns towards me, "It is just a lullaby my mum used to sing to me."

"How did you know what to do?" I uttered, completely confused by his sudden and tender action.

"I care about Noah, and when you care about someone everything comes naturally." Placing Noah tenderly into his crib, he turns to me asking frankly, "Where is his father through all of this? If he truly cared about Noah, or even you, he would be the one bloody putting him to sleep, not me."

Completely taken aback by his sudden question I snap, "You have no idea how much I wish he was here rocking him to sleep." Tears start to freely flow down my cheeks now as I whisper, "But he can't."

"Do you still love him?" Callum's voice holds a husky tone to it, as if his vocal chords are tightening up as he speaks.

Gazing down at the floor I utter softly, "Yes, and I always will."

A heavy, deflated sigh rolls from his mouth, "Why would you do this to me? Have me in the hospital room with you, let me cut his cord and then kiss me, when you are bloody in-love with someone else the whole time?" His voice takes on a deep, dark tone, like a painful growl of a lion. "Don't talk to me about playing games. This is the cruelest one of them all." Walking over to me he places his body just inches from mine, his proximity close enough to be disquieting, "You are a daft girl for hanging onto someone who obviously doesn't care about you both."

Anger tears through me like a wild tornado, ripping through my core. My hand instantly reacts to the searing fury pulsating within me, causing me to attempt to slap him again. This time though, he catches my hand just before it hits his face.

Holding tightly onto my hand he states firmly, "Not bloody likely, this time."

Yanking my hand away from his, I shout, "Get out!"

"Gladly, but don't think that I am going to play this game anymore. I am also done."

Just as he opens the door to leave, Olivia walks up to my flat. Her face ripples with surprise as she stares at Callum. "What are you doing here?" she utters, questioningly.

"I am just leaving," he states in a sharp, crisp tone as he hastily walks past her.

"What the bloody hell is going on here?" she asks, in a sharp tone.

My tears spill down my cheeks as I begin to sob uncontrollably. His harsh words leave me feeling both angry and heartbroken at the same time. His statements about me playing a game with his emotions reverberate within my ears. I never put myself in his position, and to him I am messing with his heart. I did use him, when I went into labor to fill the void caused by Andrew's death. I did need Callum and at a point I wanted him also. I never told him the truth, because I didn't want to be judged or treated different, but in so doing I have led Callum on, hurting him in the process.

My tears slowly subside as I begin to be upset with myself. "I screwed up! I should have been honest with Callum, but I can barely be honest with myself. I just wanted to escape. The last thing I want to do is confront my reality, causing others to bear the brunt of it."

Olivia gazes at me in a reproving way as she walks over to me, "You didn't screw up, but you weren't smart either. You may think that you botched up everything with Callum, but I know my brother and it takes a lot for him to really give up on someone he cares about." A soft tone now rolls within her voice as she gazes at me solemnly, "And trust me, he cares a lot about you. Besides, he has not been honest with you either."

Tilting my head to one side I recoil in confusion, "What do you mean?"

Her eyes sear into mine, as she explains, "Callum is my half-brother. His father died when his mum was pregnant with him."

"What! Why didn't he tell me?" I utter in complete shock, as a tingling sensation ripples up from my feet, penetrating my legs with a numbing sensation. I am not sure how much longer my legs are going to be able to support me. Rushing over to my chair I quickly sit down before I fall down.

"Breanna, why didn't you tell him about you? Pride is a dangerous thing to dance with. It will always hurt you in the end," she sincerely, yet lovingly lectures. My eyes drop in shame as she continues, "His mum married my father soon after she gave birth to Callum. He has always loved Callum and has treated him like he is his own, but Callum has always felt like something was missing, until he came home the night of your delivery. The hollow spaces within him seemed to be full, leaving him complete for the first time. Do you see why it is not over for him yet?" Her eyes beam with a sudden proposal, "Come to our house for the Holiday week."

"What? Olivia, I don't know what I want. I am too messed up right now. I don't need to ruin someone else's life, too."

"Who said anything about ruining someone's bloody life? I am just saying to come and have fun." Noticing my sideways glance towards Noah she utters, "Both of you come. Noah needs to get out of this tiny flat anyway. Besides, what kind of friend would I be if I left you here for a week all by yourself?"

Closing my eyes tightly I take in a deep, cleansing breath and utter, "Fine, we will go."

Olivia's face brightens as a large smile spreads across her face. A secret plot shimmers within her expression. My heart races with fear tinged with excitement. I am thrilled to be able to get out and have fun. I haven't done anything since I have been here except school work. But I am also terrified at what could lay before me. I am straddling two different roads, and I cannot remain this way for much longer. I am going to have to choose one of the roads, leaving the other one behind me, soon.

He's Oh So...

Olivia picked me up early this morning; we loaded up her car with an excessive amount of baby things and my one small suitcase. Why is it the smaller they are, the bigger the items? What I am bringing is nothing compared to what I have to bring for Noah. After a few encouraging words from Olivia, we head out on our hour and a half drive to their home in West Wycombe.

Anxiety pulsates through my chest as we drive away from my tiny flat. Cambridge is the only area in England I have been. I have no idea what I am heading into this week. I will be surrounded by a strange environment, for the most part strange people, and an unknown situation with Callum. Olivia never told Callum I was planning on coming this week. She thought it would be fun to just surprise him by showing up with both myself and Noah in her car. I hope she is doing the right thing.

I had to spend this past week listening to everyone talk about the big holiday at Callum's house, and how they are going to have so much fun. Emily was very boisterous about her intentions towards Callum and her hopes in sharing a room with him. It took everything within me to keep my mouth shut. Callum never looked at me the whole week, as if I no longer existed to him. Except on one occasion when Emily was being particularly pompous, flaunting her sudden relationship with Callum by hanging all over him. Callum gave a quick glance in my direction, and then proceeded to push her off of him, glaring at her in a disapproving way. I hope my sudden appearance at his family's home will put a damper on his carnal plans with Emily.

As we drive, the scenery all around us transforms from large ancient buildings, to gently sloping hills dotted by sporadic clumps of small wooded areas. The green ancient hills appear to step right out of the past, like a picture book opening up its pages, revealing its ancient story. The grassy pasture areas are separated by crisscrossing rows of hedges, like a giant chess board. The historic

Georgian country houses dot the landscape, giving a perception of stepping back in time. The grandeur and beauty of the landscape marries perfectly with the historical buildings, washing over me with a sense of peace.

We follow a narrow, shrub-lined road that leads us through a small grove of trees. Suddenly the trees open up revealing a breathtaking sight. I always knew that Callum and Olivia came from a privileged and wealthy life, but this is ridiculous. There in front of me stands a breathtaking stone Georgian house. The large abbey-looking structure is surrounded by a park-like setting. The grove of trees seems to envelop the back of the house, causing the grey stone to appear to illuminate off of the green backdrop. A large historic garden is positioned perfectly within the front of the breathtaking structure. Off in the distance of the property stands a small lake surrounded by weeping willow and large trees with their branches dancing delicately over the rippling water.

A surge of tremendous inadequacy floods my mind as we drive down the private road. This is a world I don't belong in. I feel like a fish that has no business soaring in the sky with the eagles. The only type of environment I am used to is trailer parks and small residential neighborhoods.

Nervously wringing my hands I utter under my breath, "I don't belong here. What was I thinking?"

"Of course you bloody belong here. Just because this is my home doesn't make me a pretentious prat. Most of the people here have underlying insecurity and self-doubt, anyway. They tend to confuse money with the man, but my mother didn't raise us to be that way. Maybe it was because of her own tragic situation, which taught her the value of a person's true character versus their inheritance. Breanna, please don't feel like you are unwelcome here." She looks at me with a true expression of love. "This is both yours and Noah's home now. Please make yourself comfortable here."

Her words cause my anxiety to momentarily dissipate, until we pull up to the circular drive and I notice Callum walking out their front door. His huge smile is now surrounded by a slightly thick and scruffy five o'clock shadow, making him appear even more masculine. He looks to be enjoying the holiday in more ways than one, because his lackadaisical attire is mirroring his facial hair. His well-fit jeans and form-fitting t-shirt emphasize his lean, yet muscular build. I have always thought Callum was good looking, but this new look screams sexuality, causing my heart, and my jaw, to drop. He energetically walks towards Olivia's car, when suddenly his eyes catch sight of me. He stops dead in his tracks as he stares at me with incredulity.

I manage to give him a rather uncomfortable smile as I get out of the car. Nervously I utter, "Hi."

A slight pause vibrates between us as his mind appears to be grasping the reality of my presence. "What are you doing here?" he asks, in disbelief.

"She came with me," Olivia snaps as she gets out of the car. "If you have a bloody problem with it you can talk to me."

His features soften as he notices me taking Noah out of his car seat. "Do you need any help with…" He surveys the massive amount of baby items I have shoved into Olivia's small car, "…all your things?"

I watch Callum questionably as a slight smirk streams across his face. Though he is examining all the baby items his eyes lock onto Noah with an intense yearning. A warm sensation pierces my heart as I am reminded of the bond that he has with Noah, "I would love some help. Would you mind holding Noah, so I can get all my things?"

Olivia turns towards me, revealing a large smile, completely aware of the olive branch I am handing him. Callum walks closer to me as he looks into my eyes, "I would love to hold him, but how about I first bring all of your things into a room for you." Slinging the strap of my bag over his shoulder he starts stacking all of Noah's baby items into his arms. "Blimey Breanna, did you leave anything in your bedsit? We are only here for a week."

Olivia lets out a loud laugh, as she chimes in, "I think I put the kitchen sink in the boot."

"I know it looks like an insane amount of things, but the smaller they are the more things they require. I didn't even bring anything for Noah to sleep in, either. I would need a moving truck if I had to bring the crib you let him use."

"We are just winding you up." Callum muffles his low laugh as he adds, "Don't worry about not having a place for Noah to sleep. I can go and pick you up something if you'd like."

I gaze at Callum with new eyes. After my meltdown with Olivia I was able to remove the storm shutters from my vision, opening my eyes and heart to the world around me. I now notice every expression and gesture he makes, as if a spotlight is illuminating his every action.

"Thank you Callum, but I am here for only a week, so I think I will just have him sleep with me."

Olivia adds, "Breanna, I forgot to tell you that I have Miss McNally coming here. That way you can have some fun also." Turning toward Callum she states, "I know you weren't planning on Miss McNally's services this week, but under the circumstances I figured you would want her here." A mischievous smile streams across her face.

Complete shock hits me like a tsunami wave, enveloping my entire body. I thought Callum quit helping me after our fight and that Olivia had taken over paying for the nanny service. Callum's face drops in aggravation at what Olivia has just revealed. Olivia's face, though, lights up in sheer delight at her deliberate revelation.

"Callum, have you still been paying for Miss McNally's services?" I ask in a soft, grateful tone.

Callum turns away from me and begins to walk through the large front doors, "Come with me and I will show you to your room."

"Callum, answer the question."

He continues to walk through the front door, never turning to face me, "Yes. Now follow me."

We walk through a labyrinth of hallways until he reaches a large, ornate door. As he opens the door my eyes widen, trying to take in every detail to my room. A large four-poster bed sits against the middle of the south wall. The bed is layered with heavy amounts of matching comforters and vintage quilts. Coordinating curtains hang from the railing around the bed and also the large windows, which overlook the garden. An oversized fireplace is flanked directly across from the large bed, bringing a cozy feeling to the enormous room. Down-filled overstuffed chairs are positioned by the window and in front of the fireplace, seemingly beckoning me to sink into their comforting warmth. A large, fluffy blanket is thrown perfectly over the back of the chair in front of the fireplace, adding to the comfort of the room. Light floods through the windows giving the room a bright and cheerful feeling. The walls are decorated with oil paintings of renaissance men and women. I can only assume that these are paintings of his ancestors.

"This room is incredible. Are you sure this is for me?" I mumble in complete amazement.

"I am glad you like it. This room is for you and Noah." He places all my things on the large four-poster bed. As he drops them down, I notice all my things melting into the bed, slightly sinking beneath the surface.

"Is that a down mattress?" I ask, as I watch my things being enveloped by all the soft coverings.

"Yes. My mum likes anything down. If you don't like it I can have them taken off."

"Absolutely not! I have always wanted to sleep on a down bed," excitement reverberates within my voice.

A heart melting smile streams across his face as he tenderly walks over to me. With every step he takes my heart begins to pound even harder. The thunderous beats of my heart echo within my ears, causing my hearing to be muffled. He now stands just inches away from me. His soft brown hair falls perfectly around his face, causing his caramel eyes to sear right through me. His scruffy stubble forms perfectly around his luscious, soft, full lips. A nervous sensation forming in the depth of my stomach climbs up my spine and rolls down my arms, causing my hands to tremble.

"May I take Noah now?"

For a brief moment I had forgotten that Noah was in my arms. Shaking my head slightly, trying to bring my mind back to reality, I mindlessly answer, "Absolutely. He just ate about thirty minutes ago, so he should be good for a while."

"Great, then you wouldn't mind if I took him to my room." Noticing my sudden apprehension he adds, "This way you can explore the house and get acquainted with it. I wouldn't want you getting lost this week." A playful smile tears through his face, as if there is more to his statement than I am aware of.

A heavy sigh explodes through my mouth as my shoulders deflate in defeat, "Fine, but where is your room, so I can come and get him when I am done?"

Gently he takes Noah from my arms, swaddling him against his firm chest. Giving me a slight wink he replies, "How 'bout I just bring him back to you when he wakes up?"

"No, if you are going to take him to your room then I need to know where it is. Besides, you know where my room is," I state emphatically.

A mischievous smile lights up his face as a deep, quick laugh shoots out of his mouth. "That's right, I do know where your room is." He opens my door and proceeds to walk out into the hall.

"Callum, that's not fair!" I yell down the hall.

"See you soon," he responds, never turning back in my direction.

I watch as he turns down a hallway, causing me to lose sight of them both. A quiet lull and a sense of freedom prickle over me as I stare down the hallway. I fully decide that Callum was right, this is the best time for me to go exploring. Closing my door I begin to walk down the long, wide hallway. Though the house has got to be several hundred years old, it is surprisingly bright and cheery. His mom has done a great job of marrying the past with the present. Because they are both important, the modern details don't supersede the history of the home. A home cannot live without its past and cannot thrive without a future.

The hall leads to a large sitting room where enormous ceiling to floor windows line one of the walls. Out of the windows I can see the expansive green lawns and a historic stable in the distance. The room is massive in size yet the oversized down furnishings, placed in quaint little seating arrangements, allow the room to feel smaller than it actually is. Another large fireplace is the focal point to the room, giving the expansive room a feeling of warmth and coziness. Huge framed oil paintings depicting another era of time hang above the fireplace and line the walls with pride of where they came from.

Continuing down another long hall, it takes me to a room I have always dreamed of having. The warm tones to the room blend perfectly with all the books lining the entire length and width of the walls. The plush fabric and deep, rich colors of the furniture allow someone a perfect reading environment. A large fireplace is in this room also, but the mantle is done with a natural dark wood stain. Silver and china tea sets are placed perfectly on a soft, oversized ottoman, inviting the room's inhabitants to have a cup of tea while they read their favorite book.

I proceed to the large couch, sitting down and listening to the sounds around me. In the distance I can hear the laughing shrills of Callum and Olivia's friends. Their cheers of excitement echo down the hall and push through the library. As I sit here listening I am reminded just how different I am from them. The immature giggles and overacting is not part of my world anymore. Though I am the same age or even younger than some of them, my mind is now on a very different level. I am not looking for a one night stand, but someone who will stand with me. A sense of longing washes over me. Fighting my instinct to give in to the loneliness I get up and proceed down another, narrower hall.

This one takes me up a slight sweeping staircase. The intricately carved wood resembles the carvings on the crib Callum let Noah use. At the top of the stairs I take a right towards a large set of double doors. Turning the knob, the door instantly swings open, revealing an enormous and breathtaking bedroom. The dark, masculine colors bounce perfectly off of the light flooding into the room. Another large fireplace is in the room. Next to it, though, is a carved wood desk with books streaming all over it. Substantial area rugs line the wood floor, bringing some warmth to the room. I notice the oversized canopy bed and suddenly realize I must be in Callum's parents' room. Just as I go to leave I notice something slightly moving on the bed. Straining my eyes to see what it is, my heart instantly takes a leap, "Noah, there you are."

Walking over to him I notice that he is still sleeping, with a pillow positioned protectively behind him. Gently I pick him up trying not to wake him. This must be Callum's room, but where is Callum? Just as I start to quietly walk out of his room, Callum steps out of the bathroom completely wet, and… oh, so naked. Utter embarrassment shoots through my frozen form, as I stare at his well-defined and dripping wet body. It is not like I haven't seen a naked man before, but I haven't seen *Callum* naked. Our wide eyes suddenly meet as he catches sight of my wandering eyes. In just a split second I notice the droplets of water running down his cut and well defined physique. The droplets ripple down his washboard stomach, running into rivulets down to his perfectly formed V shape, which his lower oblique and abdominal muscles have molded nicely.

My eyes remain watching the streams continuing down his relaxed and immovable body, when suddenly I am brought back to reality. "Oh shit!" I shout, as I hastily turn around, trying to push the erotic image out of my mind. "I am so sorry. I was just leaving."

In trying to fumble my way out of his room, I trip over the corner of his settee at the end of his bed. The jerking motion jars Noah awake, causing him to belt out a scream. As if I am not already mortified, now I have to calm Noah down when I can barely calm myself.

"Breanna, cool down. I am decent now," Callum states, with an edge of amusement to his voice.

"I just need to go," I yell, as I try to talk over Noah's blistering cries.

Callum grabs my shoulder, spinning me around towards him. A large towel is now wrapped tightly around his waist covering all the necessary parts, but still revealing his perfectly sculpted physique.

"You don't need to leave. See, I am covered up now."

"I thought you were going to watch Noah, not take a shower," I stammer out.

A soft laugh pushes through his nose. He is having way too much fun reveling in this situation. "He was sound asleep, so I thought it was a perfect time for me to take a shower. Besides, I am supposed to bloody bring him back to you, not you come to me. You are the one who came into my room unannounced."

Trying to defend myself I add, "I didn't realize this was your room. I thought it was your parents' room. But when I saw Noah on the bed and you were nowhere to be found, I came in. I am so sorry." My obvious humiliation rolls within my quivering voice. Trying to let my nervous energy out I begin bouncing Noah rapidly, attempting to calm him down.

He looks deep into my eyes with a glint of satisfaction, "You didn't have to look as long as you did." A smile tickles the corners of his mouth.

Dropping my head in shame I try to explain, "I…well…"

"Don't worry about it. I would have done the same thing if I saw you buck-naked," A soft laugh flows out of his full, supple lips. Reaching for Noah, he gently demands, "Here, let me try. I am not as wonky as you."

Callum holds him against his now dry torso as he tenderly jostles Noah up and down. My quivering body evolves into a searing wave of passion, as I watch Callum hold Noah tenderly against his barren chest. Images of Callum's soaked, inviting and very naked body run through my mind, causing my skin to ignite like gasoline thrown on smoldering embers. My breathing increases, while Noah's resumes to a slow and steady rhythm.

Callum turns towards me and notices my heavy breathing matching his own. His flaming eyes pierce right through me as the room charges with a strong electrical current. We both stand motionless absorbing the electricity pulsating between us. The room fills with a tangible heat causing our bodies to explode with goose-bumps.

"What have you done to me?" he utters in a low, growling tone. His tight, quivering body maneuvers towards me like a cat getting ready to pounce on its prey. "I thought I had given up on wanting you, but then you had to come here. Why?" he asks in sharp rebuking tone, as he places Noah on his bed.

"You don't understand. I…"

He fiercely chimes in, "I don't want to understand. I am going to make you forget about that wanker!" He rushes towards me like an animal on attack, pinning me against the wall. His mouth presses firmly against mine as our lips move in simultaneous bliss. He compresses his firm body against mine, while his hands grab forcefully at the wall behind me. Wrapping my arms tightly around his waist I aggressively pull him against my trembling body. Months' worth of pent up passion lets loose on each other. His soft, tender lips transform into powerful vessels, taking me to a place I have never been. His sweet, hot breath fills my mouth as his tongue mixes up the concoction within me. My hands delicately trace up his spine sending chills throughout his body. His quivering exhale rolls across my lips as he takes in my tender touch. Everything I am pours into our kiss, like a rushing river out of control.

My heart bursts into flames as life pushes its way back into it, jump starting my soul. Intertwining my fingers into his wet hair I grab onto a large handful, as I mumble his name under my breath. A deep surging desire of want encapsulates the both of us. Soft growls escape his mouth as his teeth gently grab hold of my bottom lip. An explosion of exhilaration vibrates throughout my body, causing a vehement moan to roll from my mouth. Freely letting go of my inhibitions I begin to claim Callum, when suddenly a loud knock at the door vibrates through the both us.

"Callum, are you ready yet? Remember you promised to take me to the stables where we can be alone," Emily's shrill voice pierces through the door, instantly transforming the mood.

Callum exhales forcefully as he dejectedly slams his forehead against the wall, next to my ear. His chin rests tenderly on my shoulder as his heavy breathing rolls down my neck. Closing my eyes I instantly feel the regret and anger consume me. My body stiffens as I fight back the rage building within me.

"I am not ready yet, Emily. Go wait for me downstairs," his voice, though breathless, is firm in his direction towards her.

"What am I doing? You came here with Emily." Pushing him slightly off of me, I look at his face as my eyes burn into his. "What are you thinking, that you could have your way with me then move on to the next conquest? I will not have me or Noah dragged into something like this." Pushing my way out from beneath his grasp I head over to Noah. Gaining my breathless control I gently pick him up.

"I would never drag Noah through anything," he snaps, as he turns and faces me.

"But you would drag me. Thanks."

"Breanna, you love someone else. Don't you think that is dragging me through shit?"

Rage forming in my stomach pushes up as I yell, "And I will always love Noah's father, my *late* husband!" A deep furrow forms between Callum's questioning eyes. "Yes Callum, my husband died a few days before I discovered that I was pregnant. I

am an eighteen year old mother and widow."
Taking Noah I aggressively walk past Callum's
frozen body. "Andrew is not the wanker…you are!"
I shout, as I walk out of his room, fully deciding I
need to move on.

Dinner Party

I begin pacing back and forth in my room as I try to stifle the anger pulsating throughout my body. Gripping my hands into firm, tight fists, I struggle to fight the urge to hit something. The quiet lull flowing around me is such a sharp contrast to the storm raging within me. After leaving Callum's room I wanted to leave, but I am trapped because I came with Olivia. Fully resolving that I am forced to stay, I decide to hide out in my room. After feeding and changing Noah I put him back to sleep. That is a great thing about this age, all he does is eat and sleep. But now that Noah is asleep, I am left alone in this quiet room with nothing to do but replay every erotic detail of Callum's mouth on mine; while he is most certainly off with Emily doing who knows what with her.

As my mind wanders with the possibility of what Emily and Callum are doing, a disgusting sensation in the pit of my stomach, mixing with my anger, causes a toxic explosion within me. Throwing myself onto the plush chair I grab a blanket and fling it over me as I furiously scream out loud.

Immediately there is a knock at my door. My heart begins beating rapidly as to who it can possibly be.

"Who is it?" I desperately ask, with a hope swirling around me.

"Are you alright? I heard a scream," a huge disappointed sigh flows out of me as I hear Olivia's voice at the door and not Callum's.

Dejectedly I open the door, gazing straight into her eyes. "No, I am not alright," I utter as I head back to the comfort of my chair.

Closing the door behind her she walks over to the chair, squeezing in next to me, forcing me to scoot over. Grabbing hold of the blanket she places it over her, too. Looking straight at me she states, "Okay, talk."

I have never had a close girlfriend, or even just a friend for that matter. While most girls have mothers, sisters, or best friends to vent on, I have nothing. Andrew would always try to be there for me, but he was a guy, always trying to fix it instead of just listening. I think it is just men. They have to fix things, whereas women just want to talk, especially teenagers. My mom was never emotionally or mentally there for me. She was either too drunk or too sick from the withdrawals to ever listen to my problems. I just learned how to vent on the world by screaming at the trees, the sky, or even God, wherever he is.

My eyes begin to tear up as I realize for the first time in my life I can just talk and someone is willing to listen, "I am an idiot, that's all."

"If you are an idiot then I must be completely daft in my head."

Pressing the furrow between my eyes tightly together, I state, "You have no idea what I have done. And…"

"I think I know more than you realize. This has to do with my brother, doesn't it?" Her soft eyes melt into me as a wave of compassion and understanding flow from her.

"Yes. I…I…" I mumble, trying to figure out how exactly to say it without embarrassing myself.

"Did you do the Rumpy-Pumpy with him?" A slight snicker rolls out of her.

"What?" I ask, completely confused by her question.

"Did you have sex with him?" she asks, point blank.

"No!" She looks at me in disbelief. I meet her gaze with a sudden sense of comfort, realizing that I can tell her anything. "But if truth be told, it was likely heading in that direction."

A huge smile spreads across her face as a glimmering light flickers within her eyes, "It's about bloody time. I have never met two people with more chemistry than you two, and yet you are both so bloody stubborn you won't act on it."

"Well, I wish I hadn't," I added, flatly.

"Why? Was it that bad?"

"No. Not at all. I haven't felt like that in a long time, if ever. What Andrew and I had was a love built around friendship. This was a raging inferno burning between Callum and me," I look up into her completely enthralled eyes. "I felt like I was going to melt into a puddle on the floor."

A heavy, satisfied sigh rolls out of Olivia's mouth, "Wow. To have something that powerful is rare. What is the problem then?"

"Emily," I state coldly.

"Emily? What does she have to do with it?"

"She knocked on Callum's door. They were supposed to go to the stables together for some…" I look into her eyes with a disappointed rage, "…alone time. That is why I am an idiot. I am just one of his conquests. I know you want there to be more between us. Hell, I wanted there to be more, but we are both wrong."

Olivia's face drops in disbelief, "There has to be some misunderstanding."

"No, he is there with her right now," my stomach turns with disgust.

Olivia's body straightens up as a glimmer of excitement washes over her, "No he's bloody not. Emily has been in the study with Gavin this whole time. She hasn't gone anywhere with anyone, least of all with Callum."

"What? Is Callum still in his room then?" My body is now mirroring Olivia's erect position, as some kind of hope springs through me.

"No. He left a long time ago. I thought he went to get some things for dinner, but he hasn't come back yet."

Sinking back into my dejected position on the chair, I hold onto the corner of the blanket for security, "Do you think he is coming back or is he gone?"

"I am sure he is coming back. Callum has lined up the cooks for dinner tonight. We are planning a nice supper in the dining hall. Everyone will be dressing up for it. So if he doesn't show up I will bloody be brassed off."

"You didn't tell me about a nice dinner. I don't have anything nice to wear."

A wave of panic rolls over me, as I gaze down at my basic comfortable attire. All I have been wearing for months are loose fitting clothing. Though I am no longer pregnant, I haven't had any desire to go out and buy more form-fitting, flattering outfits.

A wide, mischievous smile spreads across her face, "Well, that is why I came down here in the bloody first place. I bought you something before we left." Maneuvering her way out of the chair she heads over to the door and retrieves a large, thin box. Walking back over to me, she states, "I hope you like it."

"Olivia, you didn't need to buy me anything! I can just miss dinner." Gratitude washes over me as I stroke the top of the box. No one has ever just surprised me with a gift. Andrew would have loved to buy me gifts, but we were so poor that those kinds of things were only for the future. A future we never got to have.

"Not bloody likely. I am not about to let you miss this dinner. And I know that I didn't need to get you a gift. I wanted to get you a gift. Can you just say thank you and open the bloody thing." Her excitement is contagious as she bounces on the arm of the chair.

Lifting the lid to the box I discover a delicate black tea dress, folded precisely within the box. Shaking it free from the tissue I notice the beautiful, yet deep plunging neckline which is accentuated by a thin strand of small diamonds following the trim of the neckline. The cut to the dress is form-fitting, revealing every curve of a woman's body. A thin layer of black chiffon covers the entire dress, giving it a soft, elegant sheen. Turning the dress around, I am taken aback at the even deeper plunge to the back of the dress. The same thin layer of diamonds continues down the cut of the back of the dress, but at the bottom of the V-line hangs a long cluster of diamonds. It gives the dress the appearance of wearing a plunging necklace that dangles in the back just above one's bum, once again calling attention to another part of the female asset. Placed also in the box is a pair of red stiletto strappy shoes, adding to the highly sexual appearance.

"Do you like it?" she shrills in an over-excited tone.

"It is absolutely beautiful. No one has ever given me anything this nice." My hand gently caresses the soft, silky fabric, tenderly stroking the diamonds that follow the deep neckline. "Um, my only thing is the neckline is awfully deep," I stammer out, not wanting to offend her.

A boisterous laugh rolls out of her, "Breanna, that's the point. I thought you might want to take advantage of the wonderful rack Noah has given you. You have a blinding body which you hide behind baggy clothes. It is time to show it off.

Besides, what better way to knock my brother off his trolley?" She continues laughing as she smacks me on the back and walks towards the door. "Miss McNally is here, so don't worry about Noah. She is planning on watching him tonight. Dinner's at seven. See you soon."

Holding the dress up to me I turn to face the full length mirror, realizing that I have been hiding behind things. It is time to step out from behind all my coverings and reveal myself.

Anxiously I begin wringing my hands as I close my eyes, preparing to enter the dining room. I can hear all the laughter echoing from the room when suddenly Gavin belts out, "Callum, it's about bloody time. Where have you been all day?"

Hearing Gavin's comment causes a deep peace to wash over my mind, like a warm blanket wrapping around my heart. He didn't leave for good. He came back. Realizing that Callum is now here I know I have to walk in before I chicken out. Taking in a deep, cleansing breath I proceed to walk into the dining room.

As soon as my shoes start clicking on the wood floor the whole room turns in my direction in complete shock. Every mouth in the room drops wide open as they observe a very different girl standing before them. My hair is pulled up into a messy bun, with just a few curly strands delicately hanging down, revealing every detail of the deep plunging neckline. The air within the room washes over me, causing my visible skin to explode with goose-bumps. The cool air swirls around my bare back, sending chills racing up and down my spine. I feel completely naked standing here in such a revealing dress. But I do have to agree with Olivia, since having Noah I now have a perfect hourglass figure.

Looking over the entire group I notice each of their faces tell a very different story. Olivia's face is beaming with pride, like a mother watching her daughter take her first steps. Gavin's wide eyes seem to be surveying every detail of my body with great pleasure. Quickly I scan the room until suddenly I see him. Callum's eyes are not wide with shock, like the others, but are piercing right through me, as if there is no one else in the room. The heat surging off of Callum fills the room, enveloping me with passion. My eyes lock onto his, causing everything but him to vanish. His dark black, slim-fitting suit is tailored perfectly to accentuate his well-built body flawlessly. The undone top two buttons of his white collar shirt reveals just enough skin to cause my heart to speed slightly. His messy hairstyle blends impeccably with his masculine and scruffy face. My breathing quickens as I look at his striking facial features marrying effortlessly with his perfectly positioned stubble.

Slowly I walk into the room when Olivia rushes up to me, "Bloody hell, you look stunning. I am abso-bloody-lutely jealous right now. If I had a body like yours I would never wear clothes."

Turning nervously towards her I whisper, "I feel like I'm not wearing any clothes the way everyone is looking at me. I feel like hiding right now."

"You are not about to go and hide. The girls are just jealous, including me, while the boys are…well, let's just say they're not having the most pure thoughts right now." A huge smile streams across her face as she revels in her obvious good choice in picking out this dress. She surveys all the onlookers then turns to me, "Oh, and by the way I think my brother has gone into shock." She giggles as she walks me over to the long dining table.

The table is decorated with crystal goblets and beautiful off-white china. A large vase in the center of the table has a myriad of white roses and white tulips mixed with baby's breath and green fern sprigs. The elegance to the table balances perfectly with everyone's formal attire.

Immediately Gavin rushes over to my chair and pulls it out for me. Completely taken aback by this uncharacteristic gentlemanly behavior, I stand here not sure what to do. Placing his hand on the middle of my bare back, he gently guides me to my seat as he pushes my chair in.

"Blimey, your skin looks and feels like cream," he utters in amazement, as his hand remains on my back.

Callum slams his fist on the table, causing everyone to jump, "Gavin take your hand off of her and have a seat." His voice is firm with a dark growl to it, "We need drinks. Where the bloody hell is Rosie?" he shouts at the top of his lungs for the waitress to bring in the alcohol.

I can see a tangible irritation vibrating throughout him as he refuses to meet my gaze. Insecurity runs through me, causing me to wrap my hand around my arms, trying to hide my exposed cleavage. Leaning over to Olivia I ask, "Is Callum upset because I am wearing this?"

Olivia smiles slightly, as she rolls her eyes in Callum's direction, "No, he is just jealous, so he is acting like a daft arse."

Rosie rushes into the dining room carrying a large decanter of an amber-colored alcohol. No sooner than she fills his glass, Callum has completely emptied it. He taps his glass and she proceeds to fill it again. I watch in disgust as Callum seems to be having an internal argument, causing him to drown himself in something I despise.

"Callum, have you been to the Hellfire Caves here?" Emily asks, trying to lighten his mood. "I hear that it is amazing and scary at the same time."

"Blimey, I have always wanted to check them out." Gavin turns towards Callum, "Was one of your relatives part of the Hellfire Club?"

Olivia jumps in while her brother drowns his confusion in his glass, "Our mum never let us go there. She said it is an evil place with an equally evil past. She won't tell us if any of our relatives were participants in the Hellfire Club or not."

"Which to me translates as, yes, they were part of the club," Callum smugly remarks, as he pours himself another drink.

"What are the Hellfire Caves and Club?" I ask, completely fascinated with the conversation.

"It is where in the eighteenth century wealthy men would go, get drunk, and then act out all of their sordid fantasies with a female of their desire," Callum chimes in as he glares deep into my eyes, causing my heart to race. Picking up his glass he slams down another drink.

"It looks like you're getting the drunken part down," I snap.

"If you have a problem with alcohol then you are in the wrong place, Breanna," he slams back.

"I have a problem with what it does to people. It is a vile drink that transforms a good person into a monster, like Dr. Jekyll into Mr. Hyde. It will ruin your life and the lives of those around you." The memory of what I had to grow up with as I watched alcohol destroy my mother, turning her into a delinquent monster while ruining my childhood, resonates within my voice.

Callum leans forward onto both elbows, placing the backs of his interlocking fingers under his chin. His eyes lock onto mine, "Do tell, why do you have the right to pass judgments as to what a drink can do to a person? Is there anything more you would like to tell me?"

"Belt-up, you bloody arse!" Olivia shouts in a rebuking tone towards Callum. "You know nothing, you bloody wanker."

"I know more than you think. And…"

"Babe, don't worry about it," Emily states, as she gently strokes Callum's shoulder. "Don't let Breanna upset you. She's nothing but a daft girl. Maybe you and I should leave and have dinner, just the two of us. "

"Hey, come on everyone, we were just having fun talking about the Hellfire Caves. No one is passing judgments here," Gavin interrupts, trying to calm the situation.

Anger begins to pulsate through me as I watch Emily throw herself at Callum while he does nothing to stop her. I am grateful I didn't let things go any further with him today because I would feel like trash right now. He had stated that he is going to make me forget 'the wanker,' but all he has done is make me miss Andrew even more. A searing wave of a foreign feeling washes over me. I have never felt like this before; if this is jealousy then I fully welcome it. My mind embraces a sudden wave of revenge, like a volcano claiming its victims.

I have survived on my own for years. I am fully aware of how to play the game. I have watched my mom manipulate the men around her to get what she wanted. If she can do it so can I. Sensually I lean close to Gavin as I place my hand on his shoulder, "You had mentioned that you have always wanted to see the Hellfire Caves, and I too have never been there. We should go there tomorrow, just the two of us." A sick wave rolls through my body as I give in to my resentful desires. Though I know how to play this game, I have never done it until now.

He glances over every detail of my revealing dress, stopping at my chest. His eyes fixate on my slightly exposed breasts, making me feel sick to my stomach.

"I think that is a bloody brilliant idea." He looks up at me with a hunger smoldering within his eyes.

"I don't bloody think so!" Callum shouts.

"What is your problem, man?" Gavin snaps back. "You've got Emily to have fun with."

I look over at Olivia's disgusted face as she shakes her head in complete frustration. "Callum and Breanna, you are the most daft and stubborn people I have ever bloody met. I am done witnessing this rubbish."

Jumping up from the table she slams her napkin down and hastily walks out of the room. A wave of repulsion washes through me, causing me to run after her. Hastily I run down the hall, shedding my vulgar actions off of me like a snake peeling its dead skin from its body.

Suddenly I catch sight of Olivia, "Olivia, wait, please." She turns to face me, revealing her sickened expression. "I am so sorry. It is just that Callum was making me so mad. I just thought I would make him jealous, that's all," I state breathlessly, from running after her.

"Do you really think you were doing it just to make him jealous, or were you just acting on your own jealousy?" Her eyes bore deep into mine, questioning my true intentions.

"Okay, yes I was jealous, but what was I supposed to do, just sit there and let him hurt me like that?"

"Yes, because he wasn't hurting *you*. He is just hurting. And until you both drop your bloody pride, you will both just keep on hurting," Her soft eyes pour over me like warm water over ice, melting the rough edges. "But you do what you feel is right. You are the one who has to live with your choices." She walks away, leaving me standing here all alone.

My heart falls to pieces as I realize I am the one who needs to change. I have been keeping secrets, trying to save my heart when all I am doing is tearing my own heart up, lie upon lie. I should have told Callum about Andrew from the very beginning instead of leading him along. A part of me has always wanted to tell him everything, but my heart wouldn't let me. Though Andrew is gone and will never return, my heart won't let me move on, as if I am cheating on his ghost. Though part of my heart misses Andrew, another part beats fervently for Callum and I cannot deny it. Tomorrow I will sit down with Callum and tell him everything.

Hellfire Cave

I woke up later than I wanted to because Noah had a rough night. I finally got some sleep around five in the morning, causing me to have to rush now. Grabbing a pair of jeans, I look out the window trying to see what I should wear. The sky is grey with a heavy fog swirling all over the landscape, giving everything a lonely feeling. The darkened sky drowns out any light trying to flood into my room. The muted light is allowing Noah to sleep longer than usual. Tucking his warm blanket around him, I throw on a plush sweater and call for Miss McNally. I feel like a horrible mother leaving Noah with Miss McNally again, but I need to talk to

Callum, alone. Quickly I head out, hoping to catch Callum.

The manor's halls are quiet this morning after the eventful night last night. I did not return to the dining room after my conversation with Olivia. I could not go back and face everyone, least of all Callum. All I wanted to do was go back to my room, take my dress off, and throw on some comfortable clothes. Though Olivia and I did not return, it sounded like the fun continued until the wee hours of the morning. I am sure the drinks were freely flowing, causing everyone's inhibitions to let down. I know Olivia told me Callum is hurting, but I wish he would choose a better way to drown his sorrows. Anger rips through me as I witness someone I care about lose themselves in the intoxicating power of alcohol. Just the bitter rotten smell of it makes me sick. The smell reminds me of what our trailer reeked of after one of my mom's binges. Sometimes I wouldn't even have to walk through the door. I could smell the fumes even from the outside. I always knew when my mom was heading into a binge. She would tell me that she either wanted to celebrate something, or she was upset and wanted to drown her sorrows. Anything simple could set her off, like missing my parent teacher conferences. Instead of just moving on she would tell me she needed just one drink to help her calm down. But my mom did not know how to do just one drink.

I began to keep all the bad things from my mom, so she would not have another excuse to pour herself 'just one drink.' Because of my adapting habit I learned how to hide things from people so they would not have to feel the stresses of the world. I know Callum is not my mother or even an alcoholic for that fact, but the fear of witnessing him running for another glass of liquor caused me to stay in my room.

As I rush down the hall I nearly slam into Gavin. "Whoa. You're in a hurry. What's the rush?" Gavin utters, as he stops me from nearly falling.

"I am sorry, Gavin. I just woke up late and… I am hungry, that's all." I stutter out, trying to hide the real reasons behind my rushing.

"I hope there is some breakfast left. Everyone has already eaten," Gavin looks as if he has been awake for hours. His warm wool sweater matches perfectly with a pair of loose fit blue jeans. He looks as if he is preparing for a cool outing today.

"I better go and grab something then," I begin to walk past him, when suddenly he grabs onto my arm, stopping me from walking away.

"Are we still going to the Hellfire Cave today?" Gavin asks point blank.

A nervous twinge vibrates within me, causing my stomach to drop. I can't tell him I was just using him to make Callum jealous, "Well, um, what is everyone else doing today?"

"Callum and Emily have left already," his normal low, powerful voice is stifled by a high, weak pitch, as if he is hiding something from me.

"What, Callum and Emily are gone?" My heart drops as I realize I missed my opportunity to talk to Callum. "Where did they go?"

"They went to the Hellfire Caves," his voice trembles slightly.

"Really? Why?" I question, as my mind recalls Callum's description of the sordid tale behind the Hellfire Club. I didn't think Callum had any desire to go there. He and Olivia seemed emphatic about their thoughts on the cave.

"Callum wasn't going to let you go with me until Emily said she wanted to go, too. So they decided to go this morning since you were still asleep. We are supposed to meet them there."

"Okay, I guess." Something about all of this doesn't seem right, but I am the last one up, while everyone else is out having fun.

"We should get going then, so we can meet up with them," Gavin grabs his things and proceeds to head out the large front doors.

"Wait, we're leaving now? I can't go yet. I have to make sure Miss McNally is okay with watching Noah for that long." A surge of anxiety rushes through me as I contemplate having to leave

Noah again for an unknown situation with Gavin. I hate leaving Noah, especially for this type of reason, but it looks like I have to if I want to see Callum. I have no desire to go with Gavin. I was just using him in a torrid game. My only hope is that when we meet up with Callum and Emily I will be able to snag some alone time with Callum. There is so much I need to tell him.

"Chivvy along then. Go and arrange things for your baby," Gavin's eyes begin to scan my wardrobe with some content. "You may want to clean yourself up, too. You look like you had a rough night."

Though he is absolutely right about my disheveled appearance, I am still perturbed by his lack of couth. I barely know him, and the fact that he has no problem telling me I basically look like crap is rude. Gathering up my deflated pride I proceed to arrange things for Noah and also freshen myself up, not for Gavin, but for Callum. I hope Callum will be happy to see me and not angry I am there with Gavin.

Gavin and I walk up to the strange entrance of the Hellfire Cave. From the outside its appearance is like a front facade of a dilapidated cathedral. Ivy grows all over the stone walls, giving it an ancient impression. The mist rolls down the hill behind the entrance, spilling over the high center wall like a scene out of a scary movie. The stones used in the construction of the outside grand entrance are blackening and turning green from years of exposure to the harsh English weather. An iron fence wraps partially around the front forming a quaint, yet odd seating area where people can sit at tables under protective umbrellas. The outer entrance has a dark, cold feeling that seeps right through me, possessing my core. It doesn't help that it is a cold and foggy day, adding to the lonely, bleak mood.

We walk through the long, white cave entrance, which is surprisingly bright for being the start of a cave. The walls of the cave almost appear to have white plaster painted over them. The sides of the entrance have plaques and pictures lining the illuminated walls. At this point I am not very impressed though. The modern appearance to the cave does not give the ancient atmosphere I was looking forward to. I hope the clean, pristine nature to the cave is just in the informational section and not throughout the entire cavity. As I look all around, I notice it is just Gavin and I here. There are no other tourists within this narrow section. Either this is a slow day or no one else wants to brave this typical English weather. I begin reading some of the plaques, trying to hide my trepidation in continuing and my slight disappointment with the cave.

Gavin looks at me questionably then utters, "This is just the entrance, the cave is through this walkway." Gavin pulls out a brochure which has a map of the entire cave on the back of it. He begins walking towards the actual cave's entrance, "Don't worry, I brought a torch with me." He pulls a small flashlight out of the pocket of his jacket, preparing for the darkness up ahead.

A deep nervous sensation pours down on me, like someone breathing on the back of my neck, causing internal chills to vibrate through me, "Where are we supposed to meet Callum and Emily? I don't see anyone else here."

"Don't worry," he says, as he intently studies the map. "We are meeting in the inner temple, which is at the very end of the cave. We will find them. There is only one way in and one way out," a sharp, deceitful tone is hiding within his voice, which causes a wind of doubt to blow over my shoulders.

As I stare into the long, narrow, and dark cavern before me, a sudden feeling comes over me, like the eerie stillness before a wild tornado. I stand here frozen as I begin mentally debating whether to go in or not. The only thing stopping me from leaving is the fact we will be meeting Callum here, "Gavin, maybe we should just wait here for them."

Gavin turns towards me with a slight irritated expression on his face, "Breanna, we are supposed to meet them inside. They are already here."

Walking over to me he hastily grabs my hand and vigorously pulls me into the cave.

The walls to the long, narrow cave have a rough hand-carved appearance to it. There are a few lights within the cave giving some kind of illumination, though they are sporadically placed. Though there are a few lights, the deep darkness within the cave mutes them out, leaving the blackness in between to send chills up my spine. The loose gravel on the ground rustles beneath our feet, causing the sound to echo within the cave. Instinctively I cling onto Gavin's arm for support as we head down the long hall-like cave.

The layers of hand-dug arches are accentuated by the periodic lights down the cave, giving the illusion of a medieval dungeon with flickering torches along the path. A dark history reverberates off of the walls, with stories of sordid and immoral actions. Just to imprint the actual history of the cave and Hellfire Club on one's mind, there are several sections decorated with wax mannequins. Several curves and turns take you on a roundabout maze. Within the nooks of the cave they have gated off wax figures of the historic people reenacting different events and situations. The wax figures add to the creepy atmosphere residing within the cave. It feels as if I am descending further into the belly of a beast. The further down we go, the eerier I am feeling, as if the air is getting colder and thicker, pressing its way into my core. The path takes a slight detour, passing by an underground river and causing a light mist to bubble around us. My nervous energy increases as we move closer to the belly of the dragon.

Gripping onto Gavin's arm for steadiness, I whisper, "How much further until we meet up with Callum?

"Why do you care so much?" his question vibrates with a thick layer of disdain.

"I just am wondering, because it seems like we are the only ones here in this eerie cave." The cold air around me sends a chill up my spine, causing me to shiver violently.

"If we weren't supposed to be meeting Callum here, would you have come with me like you had mentioned last night?" his voice is dark, causing his accent to thicken, making it hard to understand him clearly. His pace increases as he grips tightly onto my arm.

My feet are now stumbling on the barely lit ground as he drags me further down into the unknown. "What are you talking about, Gavin?" My sides are beginning to hurt from trying to keep up with him. "Can you please slow down?"

"I think you know what I am talking about," his dark voice takes on an angry, yet passionate tone. He growls out the question like a ravenous beast needing to feed.

The narrow walkway opens up into a large, expansive room. The high ceiling and vast space causes the air in here to feel even colder, making the exhalation of our breaths appear as if it is smoke coming out of our mouths. I notice a sign near the entrance of the room revealing that we are now in the – completely empty – inner temple. Hastily I catch my breath as my warm, foggy breath fills up the space between us, "No, I don't," I utter firmly.

He forcefully spins me around so that my face is now just inches away from his, "What kind of bloody game are you playing with me? You practically threw your breasts in my face last night, while begging me to take you here. And now today you would only come once you thought Callum was going to be here."

He grabs my upper arms, aggressively holding me near him.

"Gavin, let go of me!" I demand forcefully. "I am sorry if I lead you on, but there is nothing between us." I begin vigorously trying to pull my arms free.

His dark eyes pierce right through me as he examines every detail of my body. My hands are beginning to go numb from the tight tourniquet his hands are placing on me. His fingers dig into the backs of my arms as he pulls me forcefully against him, "You are obviously not a virgin, so this should be no big deal." He presses his mouth firmly against mine.

Abruptly I pull my mouth away from his as I yell, "Stop it, Gavin!"

His hands constrict around me like a vice holding its prisoner immobile. Pressing me even tighter against his aroused body he mumbles breathlessly onto my face. His thick, cold breath rolls over my skin like the searing snort of a bull before he attacks. A slight bitter aroma of alcohol swirls within his breath. I hadn't noticed the stench before, but it wasn't like I was this close to him. His mouth is now just inches away from mine.

He growls over me as his flaming eyes pierce into me, "I know what girls like you need." He aggressively presses his mouth against mine again, holding me there like a mouse trapped in his snare.

His hand begins yanking at the sleeve of my shirt. Disgust and anger take over me as a fire rages within my core. The street smarts I have been able to obtain, thanks to my alcoholic mother, reverberate within my mind like a trained lion recalling its natural instincts. Instantly I bite down on his lip as hard as I can, causing me to taste the heavy iron substance now pouring from his lip. A loud growl rips through him as his hands instantly let go of my arms. Pulling myself free from his overpowering control, I back away from him and shout, "No!"

Placing his hand up to his mouth he tries to catch the free-flowing blood streaming from his lip. "You bloody bitch!" he snaps. "This is far from over."

Quickly I turn to run out when he once again grabs hold of my arm, aggressively pulling me towards him. I begin thrashing about as he tries to pin my arms down. I was always taught to fight with all my might, taking fragments of their body parts with me, if need be.

"Breanna, stop! If you quit fighting me you will enjoy it better."

"I don't think so!" My anger takes on a new height as I shove my knee up in between his straddled legs. A loud cough rips through him as he doubles over in pain. A constant gurgling cough takes over him while he still is forcefully holding onto my arm. Just when I am beginning to run out of ideas, I hear a loud yell coming from the front portion of the cave.

"Breanna, where are you!" Callum yells anxiously from the throat of the cave.

"Callum! In here!" I scream at the top of my lungs.

Callum comes rushing into the inner temple only to discover the disgusting sight. His gorgeous soft face is now wearing a brutal mask of hate and wrath. His caramel eyes burn with rage as he witnesses his now bleeding, so-called friend, overpowering me in a repulsive way. A transforming fury rips through Callum, causing every muscle within his body to enlarge. Vicious rage exudes from him like a soldier getting ready for battle. His voice growls in a crisp rebuking tone, "Gavin, get your bloody hands off of her, now!"

Gavin stands up as straight as his now throbbing parts will allow him. "What do you bloody think, that you get to have them both? She is mine." His hand grips even tighter on me, causing sharp pain to tear through my arm. Bending my head down I latch onto his finger with my teeth, biting him again. Next thing I know his hand firmly smacks me across my face, causing a severe stinging sensation to explode on the surface of my skin. My eyes began watering heavily as I try to fight back the pain.

A loud shout echoes in my head as I notice Callum rushing towards us, "You bloody Arse!" Callum thumps his fist violently against Gavin's jaw, causing me to be thrown to the hard ground. Gavin stumbles senselessly around as Callum lands another fierce blow to the side of his head, knocking Gavin down this time. Callum stands over Gavin in a dominating stance. "If you ever touch her again I will kill you. You are no longer welcome at my house. If you even step a foot on my property I will have you arrested."

Callum immediately walks over to me, tenderly helping me up. The side of my face is on fire from the slap Gavin gave me. The furrow between Callum's eyes deepens as he looks upon my now red face with complete regret and disgust. He gently strokes the side of my face where Gavin hit me, "Are you okay?"

His cool fingertips feel like an ice pack against my throbbing skin, causing the pain to slightly decrease. Instinctively I lean against his cool touch, causing him to cup my cheek tenderly within his hand. A sudden wave of his protection falls over me, breaking down my tough façade and causing an explosion of tears to stream down my face. The raging fight or flight reaction which had been vibrating within me breaks apart, allowing my fears to creep to the surface.

"Did he…" his voice is dark and low as he struggles to force the words out.

"No. I think I was doing a good job of stopping him," I look over at Gavin still lying on the ground, afraid that Callum may actually kill him if he moves. Turning my attention back to Callum I look directly into his eyes, uttering, "But if you wouldn't have finally shown up here I know things would have gotten a lot worse. I was not about to let him destroy me. I would have done everything within my power to stop him…or kill him."

"I am having a bloody hard time fighting back my desire to kill him, also." He looks down at Gavin, who is now staring up at us with a searing expression of hate. A repulsive surge visibly vibrates throughout Callum's body, causing him to quiver in disgust.

Looking all around me I notice a small table off to the side with a group of laughing wax mannequins. Their piercing eyes have witnessed many dark situations that not only have happened in the past, but what could have happened today. The dark aura of this room mirrors the feelings vibrating within me. The deep cold from the belly of the cave presses down on me, causing me to shiver uncontrollably.

Gently I turn Callum's head back towards me, uttering, "Can we please leave this place?"

He presses his hand tenderly against my cheek then gently wraps his arm around me. Pulling me against his warm body he begins to walk out of the inner temple of the cave. Turning back towards the opening of the room he states, "Damn my great grandfather and damn all those who participated in the Hellfire Club. This is a place to which I will never return." Turning back around, he proceeds to lead me out of the beast, protecting me the whole way.

Secrets Exposed

I lay in my bed, holding onto Noah, afraid to fall asleep. The full moon is playing tricks on my eyes, making it appear as if I am still in the mouth of the cave. Everything around me has a grey, washed-out color to it, as if the darkness within the Hellfire Cave is flooding my room. Curling up within my huge, plush bed I begin replaying the events from today. Though I know Gavin is not coming back here, the fear of his aggressive touch on my body guides my night. When Callum brought me back all I wanted to do is lock myself in my room and hold onto Noah. He is the only stake in the ground I have left. I am a loose tent flapping around in the wind of reality. The only thing keeping me from blowing away is Noah.

I never left my room the rest of the day. I know that Callum had to have said something to Olivia, because she keeps coming to my door asking me if I want or need anything. I haven't been able to answer her. I just watched the door obsessively, making sure that no one is going to burst in. She keeps coming back, checking in on me. I know that she cares. I can hear it in her voice. Her typical spitfire attitude is muted, revealing a tender and truly sympathetic tone. Her soft voice pierces the door, surfing on the ripples of the warm air of my room, enveloping me with a true love of a friend. I want to let her in, but I am not ready to talk yet. My fear is still fresh and oozing.

The twilight hour has long past, leaving me laying here in the stillness of the night. All of a sudden there is a loud thump against my door. Immediately I jump out of my bed, grabbing the first heavy item I can find. Quietly I tiptoe towards my door as I listen for any possible intruder. Grasping the silver candlestick in my hand I raise it in preparation for an impending blow. Swinging my door open I jump back with fear when someone instantly falls against my legs.

"What the hell!" I scream, as I prepare to hit this person with the candlestick.

"No! Breanna, it's just me," he raises his hands up, bracing for a possible blow to his head. Callum's voice is low and gruff, as if he has not had any sleep in days.

I gaze down at his disheveled appearance as he lay crumpled up on the floor beneath my feet. "Callum, what are you doing sneaking around outside of my room?"

He sits up and begins dusting himself off, "I was not bloody sneaking around. I have been guarding your room, when I accidentally fell asleep. My head slammed against your bloody door when I nodded off, that's all."

A slight smile creeps into the corners of my mouth as I look down at his disheveled appearance. His hair looks as if someone has been rubbing a balloon over the top of his head, causing the strands of his hair to point in several different directions. His normal perfected stubble is longer than usual; while his crumpled clothes look as if they have been put through the ringer.

"You have been guarding my door for how long?"

His eyes peer square into mine as he stops straightening himself up from his tumble into my room, "I haven't left since I brought you back here and you locked yourself in your room."

"You have been on the outside of my door this whole time. Why didn't you tell me?" He is now standing right across from me, allowing his masculine features to form a protective shield for me. Though my room is dark his eyes sparkle in the moonlight as he stands here gazing at me.

"It's something I have just gotten used to doing these past few nights," his face is flat, like a soldier calling out his orders.

"What do you mean the past few nights?" I state in shock by the sudden revelation. "You weren't outside of my door the night of the dinner party. You were too busy carousing and drinking with your friends."

He walks away from me, heading towards my bed where Noah is sleeping, "Well, bloody thank you for lumping me into the same category as Gavin," his voice is flat as he gently brushes the top of Noah's head.

Shame and embarrassment flushes into my face as I stammer out, "I didn't mean…"

"No, I didn't stay with them. As soon as you ran after Olivia, I also ran after you," his fingers gently trace the edges of Noah's dark hair. Tucking the cover against Noah's body, Callum turns towards me, "I stopped as soon as I heard you and Olivia talking." The moon glistens off of him, revealing a slight smile spreading across his face, "You know… it worked."

My eyes narrow in confusion, "What worked?"

He gradually makes his way towards me, gently removing the candlestick from my hand, "The flirting you did with Gavin definitely made me jealous, along with the stunning dress you wore." He pauses slightly as he looks down like he is trying to recall a memory. As he looks up into my eyes again, his caramel eyes seem to liquefy, "You looked abso-bloody-lutely stunning."

Relinquishing my grip on the weapon of my choice I utter softly as I look down at the floor, "Look at what it almost cost me. I should have never worn that dress or flirted with him." Brutal anger rises to the surface of my skin as I am reminded of the horrific experience.

Callum lovingly places his hand just under my chin, lifting my face slightly so that our eyes now meet, "You are not to blame. You could have walked into the room naked, thrown yourself on him and he still would not have had the right to do that to you. He is a daft prick. That is why I stayed outside your door that night. I didn't trust him."

"You slept outside of my door that night to keep me safe?" I look deep into Callum's eyes with a surging wave of gratitude. All the lies and misunderstandings we have been reveling in break apart, leaving us raw and vulnerable.

His full lips part as a wide smile spreads across his face, revealing his perfect white teeth. "Blimey, I didn't sleep though. Noah was up all night crying.

At one point I almost came in to help you, but I decided to keep my post. Finally around six in the morning everything seemed quiet, so I decided to go to my room and sleep. I didn't wake up until after you and Gavin had already left. I knew I shouldn't have…"

"Wait, Gavin told me that you and Emily were already at the Hellfire Cave and we were to meet you there. That is the only reason I went with him." Confusion rips through me as I stare at Callum in disbelief. A sick, bubbling sensation rises up, causing my mouth to fill with burning acid. Callum's body tightens up as his eyes burn with a deep rage. The fear and disgust explodes from me, causing the room to electrify, "If you weren't already there then how did you know where to find me?"

"Olivia told me she saw Gavin leave with someone who looked a lot like you. I thought Olivia and you were just trying to make me jealous again. I didn't trust Gavin to be a participant in the game," rage ignites within his eyes. "I didn't think I was going to find you in that kind of situation, though. The bloody bastard must have been waiting for me to go back to my room."

Fear pushes through me as I realize how bad it could have gotten if it wasn't for Olivia saying something to Callum. Cold chills roll up my spine as everything around me slowly starts to spin, causing my knees to buckle slightly. Callum instantly grabs hold of me, picking me up and carrying me to my bed.

"How could I have been so stupid? I couldn't even listen to my mother's only advice and not trust anyone." Tears begin to pour from my eyes as I bury my head in my pillow.

Callum tenderly strokes my head as he utters, "You can trust me."

Turning sharply towards him I peer up into his face, "Really? If I can trust you then why won't you let me know how you really feel about me? I am sure you have no problem letting Emily know how you feel," my eyes blaze with jealous rage, as I attempt to sit up in my bed.

His hand remains firmly on my shoulder, keeping me in the reclined position, "You are right, I have no problem letting Emily know how I feel. I have tried keeping my distance from her since you showed up here because I bloody feel nothing for her. But you, on the other hand, I feel everything for but I am obviously having a hard time showing you," his eyes blaze with an impulsive urge that fills my body and soul. The electricity pulsating between us suddenly ignites, causing the fear within me to evaporate. The urge flowing through him transforms into a velvety expression of love as he slowly leans down just inches away from my face. He hovers above me waiting for my permission for him to continue. Grabbing hold of his head I pull him down towards me, pressing his supple mouth fervently against mine. His mouth gently moves against mine, trying to reenact what his heart desires. Life presses back into me as our mouths become one in harmony.

His hands are positioned perfectly on both sides of me as they press firmly onto the bed, allowing his body to hover delicately over me. The muscles in his arms vibrate from the strain of his weight. Gently he lowers his torso on top of me, melting our bodies into one. Slowly, my hands slide up his back, feeling his hard, lean muscles beneath his shirt. His hands grip tightly onto the blanket beneath us, while his kiss intensifies. His tongue probes my mouth searching for the same response, gladly I oblige his request. The warm, sweet taste of his mouth rolls through me. Butterflies, trapped in my stomach, instantly soar, causing a flood of passion to vibrate throughout my quivering body. Gripping onto his shirt I aggressively pull it up, allowing me to freely feel his soft, supple skin beneath my fingertips. Wrapping my hands tightly around him I pull myself closer to his mouth. His lips gently brush against mine as a pleasurable exhale washes over my face.

Opening my eyes I discover him looking at me with a sense of urgency. Instantly he wraps his arms around me, lifting me off of the bed and to my feet.

Holding me tightly against his body, his eyes bear down on me. Silence rolls through us while he takes in every detail of my face. My heart thumps rapidly against my chest, causing a sensation of yearning to consume me. Reacting to my need, Callum's mouth presses powerfully against mine. His hands grip onto the bottom edge of my shirt with a craving pulsating through them. His hands roam upwards, taking my shirt with them. The tips of his fingers gently trace my spine, causing my body to explode with goose-bumps.

"My God, your skin does feel like cream," he breathlessly utters in a low, gruff tone.

His trembling fingers reach the protective clasp of my bra, sending a nervous energy to surge within me, "Wait."

Stopping immediately, a soft laugh exhales from his mouth, "Okay. Am I moving too fast?" His breathless voice shows signs of strain.

"Can I ask you a question?" I stutter out, trying to catch my breath.

He raises a quizzical eyebrow, "Strange timing, but yes, you can ask me anything," he says, now rubbing the back of his neck in a nervous reaction.

Loosening his tight grip on me, I rest my chin in the valley of his chest, feeling his heart beat rapidly beneath me.

"Where did you run off to the other day?" I utter, while my hands remain tightly wrapped around him. The muscles in his back stiffen suddenly. The tender, slow circles he is tracing on my back stop, his hand twitches a tad.

Dropping his head down until it rests softly on the top of mine, a heavy exhale flows out of his mouth, "My father's grave."

Wrapping my arms even tighter around him, a sense of relief washes over me as I hear him finally tell me what I already know. Resting my cheek against his firm chest, I can feel his muscles quiver and tighten. His usual relaxed demeanor transforms into a stiff rod.

"You don't seem surprised by my statement," he utters in a questioning manner.

"No, I'm not surprised," I state, motionlessly.

"Bloody hell!" His arms drop away from me, attempting to back away. I hold onto him tighter, locking him in my grasp. "My arse of a sister, she can't keep her bloody mouth shut," he utters in a thick roar.

"Don't be mad at her, she was just trying to help." His muscles are still tight under my grasp though he has resigned himself to the fact that I am not about to let go.

A sharp, sarcastic laugh rips through him, "Help? How was she helping you by telling you that?" A slight pause rolls through him. "What did she tell you?" he asks with a thick realization spinning on each word. He presses me slightly away from him, so that I can look straight into his caramel eyes.

Lifting my head I meet his gaze head on, "She told me that your father died when your mother was pregnant with you. Soon after you were born your mom married your now stepfather, Olivia's dad. Olivia only told me because she knew I needed to know." Letting go of him I place my hands on either side of his scruffy face, forcing him to look down at me, "Why didn't you tell me?"

His eyes soften, breaking some of his arrogant shell away. He grasps my hands off his face, tenderly kisses them, and then sits down on the edge of my bed, "Why didn't you tell me about your late husband, before I felt like a daft prick trying to steal someone's wife or lover away?"

An expression of dubious shock streams across my face, "What do you mean?"

"Breanna, I felt like a bloody home wrecker every time I looked at you. I wanted you and Noah, and damn the man who wasn't there for you. I tried everything to push my feelings for you out of my mind. I even agreed to something I should have never agreed to," he suddenly shakes his head aggressively, as if he is pushing a horrific memory out of his mind. His firm face slowly takes on a softer shadow, "When you finally told me that your husband had died before you even knew you were pregnant, everything I thought I knew came crashing down. I wanted to hate your husband for leaving you and Noah as much as I hated my father for leaving my mum and me. I needed to confront my anger, so I went to my father's grave."

Glancing over at Noah sleeping restfully in my bed, I utter softly, "No wonder you have a strong bond with Noah. You can relate to what he has already experienced."

"That isn't the only reason I have a bond with him. The moment I saw him come into this crazy world and our eyes met, something within me turned on, like a light in a dark room. For the first time I saw what I wanted… clearly."

Walking over to the bed I sit next to him, lovingly stroking the side of his face with the tips of my fingers, "I am sorry, Callum. I had no idea you liked me, let alone wanted me. I should have told you, but the truth is I didn't want to accept it. After Andrew died I couldn't… no, I didn't want to face reality. If I had told you everything in the beginning then I would have had to confront the reality of my life. I wasn't willing to let go…until I thought I might lose you."

Callum turns towards me, grabs my hand and gently kisses the back of it. His warm, soft lips linger on the back of my hand while his thumb amorously strokes my fingers. He slowly gazes up at me while his mouth remains on my hand. His eyes bore deep into mine, like a torch melting into my core, "I wanted you the first time I saw you. But the night you challenged me, in the pub, something ignited within me. My heart seemed to awaken from a long, emotionless sleep – feeling something real for the first time."

Pulling me into him he lies down on the bed, next to Noah. Pressing my back firmly against him, he wraps his arm around me, enveloping me with his body. He holds me tightly, kissing the top of my head as he utters softly against my hair, "I am knackered. May I sleep with you tonight instead of sleeping in the hall?"

Grabbing onto his hand I pull it into me, holding him tightly against me. "Don't leave," I utter softly.

A warm, calming heat radiates off of him, soothing us into a slow lull. "Breanna, you are not going to lose me," he weakly whispers, causing his words to roll down my skin as it prickles it with an unexplained doubt. We slowly fall asleep, melting into each other, free of our own pride and assumptions.

Tell Me

The early morning sunlight streams through the large windows, setting the room ablaze. A heavy weight of relaxation swirls through me. I haven't slept this soundly in a long time. Soft, dusty sun rays cascade into the room like spotlights illuminating different areas of the room. A ray dances delicately on the bed, causing my skin to glisten. Looking at the shimmering light bouncing across my hand I catch sight of another strong hand wrapped around me. My heart skips slightly as I look down at this strong, yet gentle hand enveloping me. Instantly my mind is brought back to Andrew. This is how he would always sleep, as if he were afraid I was going to suddenly disappear in the night. Closing my eyes tightly I can almost feel Andrew's heat radiating through me. If I am having a dream right now, please don't let me ever wake up. The warmth and solidity pressing around me almost feels real. Closing my eyes I begin to tenderly stroke the hand of my illusion. His skin feels so real against my touch. Perhaps I had dreamt the whole thing and Andrew never left. A sudden ping rips through my heart with a troubling thought, as if there is now something just as important to me as Andrew. And if Andrew were still alive this person could never be in my life. My heart now seems to call out to the one person who appears to fit perfectly within the void Andrew left, Callum. Instantly a realization comes over me. It is okay for me to love again. I could not love them both if Andrew was still alive, but I can love them both now. Callum doesn't take Andrew's love away, he reminds me of what I had and what I have the right to still embrace. Andrew will always be with me in the tender eyes of his child and in the loving memories I have and will also still go through. Just like a mother fears when she is pregnant with her second child if she will be able to love it as much as her first. But as soon as her baby is born the same love is there. Her heart just grows and embraces them both the same. I can love them the same without hurting the memory of one or the future of the other.

Realization comes tearing through my dream state, as I now see that it is Callum who is in fact embracing me. Grabbing on to his hand I pull it against my chest, holding him as close to my heart as I can.

Callum's enveloping hand squeezes me gently as he kisses the back of my head, "Morning."

Callum must have never let go of me the whole night. We lay perfectly positioned, neither one of us willing to move. I now hold onto him for the same reason Andrew would hold onto me, for fear that he will vanish. Andrew left, unwillingly, and I don't want Callum to leave now. Turning towards Callum I look into his soft eyes, "Morning."

His eyes wash over my tattered body, cleansing me to the very core. We just look at each other for what feels like hours. He lovingly strokes the back of my hair, grabbing a small strand and gently twirling it around his finger. A heavy sigh pushes through him as the heat of his body increases. Looking deep into my eyes he asks suddenly, "Will you tell me about Andrew?"

Completely taken off guard by his question, I gulp audibly. I had been just thinking about Andrew and now Callum asks me this question, "Why?"

"Breanna, he is a part of you and the father of Noah. His memory should never vanish just because

I am here." My eyes widen in true amazement as a rush of emotions pour through me, slowly flooding my core. A slight smile spreads across Callum as he adds, "I just figured this is possibly the first time you have woken up with a man in your bed since your husband passed away."

Giving a slight sarcastic smile I utter, "No, there is a boy in my bed almost every night." He is slightly taken aback by my response. My smile widens in satisfaction as I tilt my head towards Noah, lying next to me.

Squeezing me tightly against him, he begins tickling me, "That doesn't count. Noah is not a man yet. And, he better not be still sleeping in your bed when he is a man." I begin screaming slightly as he continues to tickle me.

His fingertips dig softly into the sides of my stomach as I attempt to pull his hands off of me. Trying to wiggle myself free I begin twisting and turning while my laughter makes it hard to breathe. Immediately he rolls on top of me, pinning my hands above me. His weight presses down on me, allowing me to feel the quick rise and fall of his abdomen while he breathes heavily. His eyes gaze into mine with a searing fire. Slowly my laughter subsides as I return his passionate gaze. His mouth suddenly is on mine with a sense of need and want vibrating within his lips. His hands grip tightly onto mine, pressing them firmly into the pillow. I respond to his need with a want of my own. Tenderly biting his lower lip I wiggle my legs free, causing his hips to fall between mine. A sense of urgency rips through us as he releases my hands and begins pulling my shirt up. I react in the same intensity lifting his up, revealing his smooth, firm skin. As the hunger tears through us, a sudden scream belts out of Noah, shattering the heated moment.

A discontented sigh exhales out of us as Callum's head falls to the side of me. An unsatisfied laugh rolls through his mouth, "Blimey, if this keeps up I am going to explode." Kissing my overheated forehead, he dejectedly rolls off of me.

Picking Noah up I tenderly hold him in my arms, "I can't believe he lasted this long. He usually is wide awake and has eaten by now. This is the longest he has slept." Turning towards Callum I add, "Perhaps he likes you being here also."

He leans over and tenderly kisses the top of Noah's head, "Got a bung for you, Noah. Give me some needed alone time with your mum so we won't burst, and I will keep sleeping by you."

I look over at Callum with a questionable gaze, "Don't you think I have a say in this bribery you are placing on a baby?" I state sarcastically.

"No. This is between Noah and me." He kisses me ardently. "Maybe you can now tell me about Andrew while Noah eats." Staring into Callum's eyes, my heart melts with gratitude for wanting to know about Andrew and not wanting him to stay buried in my mind.

Slowly I lift my shirt, exposing one of my breasts for Noah, "Bloody hell! Maybe I should turn around while you feed him," his voice seems strained.

"Why? You know this is how Noah eats. You've seen him eat before… haven't you?" Slightly covering my chest, as Noah latches on to eat.

"No, and after having to stop myself so many times, I am liable to get a stonker just watching this."

A hearty laugh rolls out of my mouth uncontrollably, slightly interrupting Noah's feeding. The laughter is beginning to hurt my stomach as I try to contain myself.

"It is not funny. You have no idea how hard this is for me right now. I am so close to just taking you right here and now," he states in a flat, buttery tone.

I continue laughing as I add, "Well, if you thought he screamed before, that is nothing compared to what will happen if you take him away from his food." The pain from my laughter is now moving into my side.

"Well, I guess that is another thing we have in common, because I am screaming inside right now too," his frustration turns to laughter now, causing Noah to pull away and give me an almost stern expression of aggravation.

Grabbing hold of the blanket I throw it over my shoulder, giving a protective visual barrier for Callum. "Is that better?" I smile at him ruefully.

"I suppose. Why don't you just tell me about Andrew and perhaps that will take this pressure away."

My laughter immediately stops. Just the thought of retelling mine and Andrew's story sobers the room. I take in a deep breath as I gaze intently down at the tweed blanket. Grasping for strength, I realize I need to just tell him everything. Exhaling sharply I begin, "I met Andrew when I was just thirteen years old. He lived next door to me. I did not have a Norman Rockwell picture perfect life; in fact, I couldn't have been further away from that kind of life. My mom could never stay in the same place for too long. She usually irritated the landlords, neighbors, and just about anyone who knew her; except for the bar owners, they loved her. When my mom would go on one of her drunken binges I would hide out at Andrew's house. He was an only child and I think his mother always wanted a girl, so she would let me stay as long as I would like. I know on several occasions his mom wanted to call child protective services when my mom was passed out in the front yard, but she didn't want me in the foster-care system at my age. As long as I was at their home I was safe. Andrew and I became best friends, always hanging around each other, even pretending, on occasion, that we were married. We even had the names of our children picked out."

"Let me guess, the boy's name was Noah," Callum interrupts.

I smile briefly, "Yes, a new beginning, he would always say. I had to keep that name." Looking down at Noah I continue, adding, "For months I never left their home. My mom was too busy drinking to realize I wasn't there, until one day she was once again evicted. She came over to Andrew's family's house and dragged me out, kicking and screaming. Andrew's mom tried to convince her to let me stay, but my mom wouldn't even listen. Alcohol ruled her decisions. Occasionally my mom would use me to get free drinks because they thought I was a pretty girl. She would attempt to trade favors from me for a stiff drink. I had to learn to defend myself from unsolicited male advances at a very young age."

Callum's eyes shutter with pain as he pulls me against his chest in a protective manner, "Bloody blow me over, no wonder you have a severe hatred towards alcohol. I am sorry for my actions the other night. I had no right to drink in front of you, bringing back your bad memories. I was just confused and turned to something I shouldn't have."

Resting my head against his chest I continue, "It turns people into something they are not. When my mom was sober, she was a different person. As a child I would just hold onto the hope that she would stay sober, but those days were few and far between. Though we moved away from Andrew I knew where he lived. So when my mom would disappear, I would too. I would run to Andrew's house and stay with them until my mom would come and forcefully take me again. As I got older I left home and stayed with his family for good. Basically I was a runaway whose mother couldn't remember her last drink, let alone that she had a daughter. Her memory is so screwed up from the poison she is constantly consuming that she only can remember me on occasions of slight sobriety. I mourned the loss of my mother the day I left home.

"Andrew was my savior, rescuing me from a fate worse than death. He was the stability I knew. He wanted me to continue my education. I was accepted to Cambridge University the middle of my senior year and we had a plan to go as soon as we graduated. But his world soon turned tragic when his mother died of a heart attack. His father was so devastated that he turned to alcohol to numb his pain. We couldn't be there anymore. We both had just turned eighteen so decided to make it official and legal. The next day I went to the court house and married the boy I loved since I was thirteen." A thick pause pushes down on me as my tone of voice changes, "A few months later I received a call no wife ever wants to receive. Andrew and his father were killed in a single automobile crash. Their car took a turn going too fast, losing control and flipping over several times. His father was thrown from the car, but Andrew had been pinned inside. I rushed to the hospital where I got to see his battered body and hold his hand, but he never gained consciousness. I had to silently say good-bye. He died that night in the hospital."

"I'm so sorry," Callum's voice is so quiet it is almost a whisper.

A burning pain dances on the edges of my voice, "The worst part is that Andrew's father was the driver. The police performed a toxicology test and when it came in it showed that his father was more than double the legal alcohol level – Andrew had zero alcohol in his system." Anger and confusion washes over me as I utter heatedly, "Why would he have allowed his father to drive? That is a question I will keep asking myself and will never receive an answer to."

Heavy tears well up within my eyes as Callum just silently holds onto me. I look down at Noah as my tears now stream down my cheeks, along my breast, resting peacefully on Noah's face. I haven't talked about it in detail or even recalled the specifics of my memory, until now. My heart stings with a deep, surging pain. The night of his death was the worst night of my life. For the first time I was truly alone. My world had been turned upside down by alcohol. It robbed me of a mother, a family, friends, and now my husband and the father of my child. I press Noah against my chest, noticing every resemblance to Andrew, his dark hair, narrow close-set eyes, and his long, thin fingers. He is all I have left of my best friend and savior.

Callum lays his cheek on the top of my head as his arms hold onto me tightly. A warm, wet sensation soaks my head, sending gentle streams rolling down me and piercing my mind. My heart swells as I realize that Callum is also crying for me. A thick silence rolls around us, making the air feel almost pliable. This is the closest to Andrew I have felt in a long time. Mending the bridge between want and reality is a difficult thing, but when it is finally achieved one can ultimately meet reality head on.

"Thank you Andrew, for rescuing her and being the man I hope to one day be. God be with you," Callum's voice cracks slightly with emotion as he holds onto both Noah and me. "I promise you, Breanna, I will not drink again."

"Don't make promises you can't keep. I'm not expecting you to change, I just expect you to be smart and wise in your choices. Neither my mom nor Andrew's father were wise in their choices."

"Is your Mum still alive?" His usual confidence is stifled by his question, probably fearing my answer.

"Amazingly – yes. In fact, I called her from the hospital after Noah was born," I pause slightly to remember my conversation. "She barely remembered me. I could hear her heavy slur through the phone. She sold my childhood for a pint of whiskey and a life of hell. I can't wait any longer for her to change. I have a child now and I will not let her decisions affect Noah like they affected me. I am done with her."

Silence looms between us for a long time as our emotional rollercoaster slowly comes to an end. I can feel Callum's heart pounding against my back as a nervous twinge tickles the edges of his skin, "Breanna, I need to tell you something and I hope you won't hate me for it."

Confusion rushes through my mind, "Why would I ever hate you? Callum I…" Suddenly the peace and stillness looming in the room is interrupted by a loud knock at the door. Our bodies immediately stiffen at the realization that someone is about to come in, witnessing us both in my bed. Pulling Noah free I hastily cover myself up.

Turning towards Callum I utter softly, "Maybe you should hide. I don't want to get you in trouble."

A low rolling laugh reverberates out of him, "Breanna, I am twenty. I think I am beyond the age of getting in trouble for being in a bedroom with a beautiful girl. I am not moving."

Pulsating heat flushes through my face with his sudden statement, "You think I am beautiful?"

His eyes widen in exasperation, "Bloody hell, I must be doing a terrible job proving it to you. Yes I, and a lot of other people for that fact, know you are beautiful," he pauses slightly, peering deep into my eyes, "Both inside and out."

He bends down and kisses me emphatically. His warm, soft kiss causes my stomach to flip in excitement. His lips tenderly merge with mine, as we get lost in each other's touch.

Suddenly, bringing us back to reality, we hear, "It's about bloody time I catch you both in bed together."

Callum's mouth forms a wide smile across mine as his thick laugh rolls over my lips, "Olivia, you are such a child." Turning towards Olivia he continues, "Trust me, nothing happened." Olivia cocks her head in disbelief as she observes the situation. "Alright some things did happen, but not what you think. It is a little hard to do it with Noah sleeping right next to us."

"Blimey, he is staying with me tonight then," she utters with a sharp laugh.

Complete embarrassment pulsates through me, causing my face to turn multiple shades of red. Slamming my face into the palms of my hands, I muffle awkwardly, "I am in the room, too. Can we not talk about this?"

Olivia hastily rushes over to the bed, bounding up onto it, landing right next to me. "I forgot you bloody Americans get embarrassed by things like this," she utters with a thick, teasing laugh rolling from her.

"We don't get embarrassed. We just think it is a private matter, that's all."

Turning towards Callum, she utters with a mischievous smile, "What are we going to do about it?" A huge comprehending smile spreads across his face. Instantly they both leap on top of me, tickling me relentlessly.

I begin carefully thrashing about, trying not to disturb Noah as I breathlessly scream through my laughter, "Stop! What is it with you guys and tickling?"

They stop, causing laughter to roll through all of us now. I stare up at their stunning faces with a complete foreign feeling flooding through me. This is the closest to a real family I have had in a long time. I have always wanted a sister and Olivia fills that space with piss and grin perfectly. Her blatant words, sarcasm, and love have been what I needed and I will always be indebted to her.

A child-like grin streams across her face as she begins bouncing emphatically on my bed. "Callum, can we take Breanna and Noah to Carters Steam Fair at the park?"

Callum questionably gazes at Olivia, "Will you ever grow up Sis?"

"No." Turning back towards me, she stares at me with puppy dog eyes, "What do you think Breanna, do you want to go?"

Looking into her sweet face, how can I resist, "Sure, it sounds like a great way to spend my birthday."

They both gaze at me with a shocked, yet excited expression on their faces. "What?" they both utter simultaneously.

"Why didn't you tell me that it is your birthday today?" Callum states in disbelief.

Smiling ruefully I utter, "I just did."

"That doesn't count."

"Yes it does, besides it is no big deal," I utter flatly, trying to buffer their shocked expressions.

"It is a big deal." Kissing the top of my head tenderly, he adds, "Happy birthday, Breanna."

"Then it is settled, we are going to the fair," Olivia adds emphatically.

Free

It is the most beautiful day. The sun is streaming through the sporadic puffy clouds dancing in the sky. The trees and green grass shine bright from the recent washing caused by the night rain. The rolling green grass flows into a small but magnificent man-made lake. Reflections of the surrounding hills and trees dance delicately on the surface of the water. I gaze out of the car window taking in the splendid scenery while Callum drives us to this mysterious fair. Callum's hand tenderly reaches over, grasping mine within his. His strong fingers grip tightly onto mine while his thumb gently strokes the top of my hand.

We round a bend and suddenly the bright red and yellow colors of the fair shine brilliantly against the green backdrop. Olivia leans over Noah's car seat shrilling, "There it is, Noah!"

"Olivia, have you gone barmy? Do you really think Noah understands you?" Callum chimes in as he looks at her through the mirror.

"No, but he *adores* my tone of voice," she utters dramatically at Noah. He instantly smiles, sending a high pitch screech to roll out of him. "See, he loves it!"

We pull into a gravel makeshift parking lot where a multitude of cars have formed some sort of organization to the normally vacant field. Positioned seamlessly next to the edge of the River Wye is the picture perfect Carters Steam Fair. Bright red and orange colors cover the spinning rides, causing a kaleidoscope of lighted colors to fill the area. A myriad of refurbished antique rides spread across a pristine section of the park, making me feel as if I have stepped back in time.

This is not the type of fair I am used to. The clean, well-kept environment is a sharp contrast to the carnivals I grew up with. My mom would frequent our local carnivals in hopes of me being entertained while she would drink with the carnies. The traveling carnival was usually held in the parking lot of a local shopping center. The rides were ancient and poorly kept up, causing me to be terrified to go on any of them. The carnies were a scary group of misfits, usually dirty, unkempt and toothless souls. The local kids would laugh and taunt me because my mom would be hanging all over the carnies like she was their groupie. I shiver at the mere memory of my mother doing God knows what with them. I would usually go and hang out in the local grocery store trying to hide from both my mother and all the sneering kids.

This is nothing like those carnivals. Beautiful Grade 11 structures dot the surrounding areas while the Wye River weaves throughout the large property and park. Small islands are formed in the center, housing a picturesque ancient structure dedicated to music. Gently rolling hills are enveloped by trees and surrounding pasture land. The fair is placed perfectly within one of the grassy areas, giving a clean feeling to it. Several families and young adults scurry hastily from ride to ride, anxiously awaiting their next thrill.

"So Breanna, what do you think?" Olivia asks.

"This is amazing! It is not at all what I was expecting," my voice is full of youthful excitement.

"What were you expecting?" Callum utters questioningly as he takes Noah out of his car seat.

"Something a little scarier and a hell of a lot more dirty," I utter flatly, as I stare at Callum passionately. Callum's sex appeal is at an all-time high today. His brown hair is styled flawlessly, with a messy appearance matching his scruffy stubble. His slim-fitting wool sweater allows the bulges of his muscles to protrude nicely. His dark, form-fitting jeans show off his tall, slim, yet muscular physique, not to mention enhancing his firm, round bum.

"See Olivia, she was expecting bigger and scarier rides, not this," Callum utters, completely unaware of my gawking stares.

Snapping back to reality I state, "No, this is a perfect postcard fair. When I said scarier, I did not mean I want bigger rides. I meant a disgusting and dangerous environment. This is absolutely amazing." Turning to Olivia I utter in gratitude, "Thank you. This is a perfect place to spend my birthday."

Olivia turns to Callum, giving him a snarky smile, "Ha-ha, you can kiss my feet now."

"Are you sure it is your feet you want me to kiss?" Callum threatens with a hearty laugh.

Placing Noah in the baby carrier we hastily walk towards the entrance. The cheering sounds of all the fairgoers are intertwined with sounds of music, a pipe organ on the carousel, and an occasional goose honking in the background. The rides are meticulously painted with the colors of the British flag. Reds, blues, and whites flow perfectly over the surrounding temporary fairground. Two large early century replicas of a swinging boat are positioned near the front entrance. The bottoms of the two boats are painted like a large British flag. On the end of each boat are the names Britannia and Columbia. This ride and the Chair-O-Plane – the swings- are the rides that everyone seems to be gravitating towards.

Olivia nearly skips through the entrance, spying one of her favorite rides, "I love coming here. It reminds me of being a kid again."

"What do you bloody mean, *again*?" Callum teases.

"Sod off. You are just jealous because I remember how to have fun."

"I know how to have fun," Callum responds. His stunning, intense caramel eyes brighten with the obvious challenge. Gazing over at me a mischievous smile spreads across his face. He draws his eyebrows up repeatedly in a playful manner towards me.

"What?" I question apprehensively.

"We are going on a ride… my way," his voice is full of spirit, not giving me a choice in this matter.

"I can't, I have Noah," trepidation rolls through me with fear as to what he is up to.

Olivia walks over to me, unsnapping the back of the baby carrier. "Nice try, Breanna. You can't use Noah as an excuse to get out of Callum's challenge. Go and have fun, I will take care of Noah."

Placing the baby carrier on herself, she pushes me towards Callum. Anxious waves of fear rush through me. I have no idea what Callum means by *his way*. I look up into Callum's bright face. He reaches for my hand, uttering, "Are you ready?"

"I don't know. What am I ready for? Your mischievous look is scaring me."

A hearty laugh explodes from his full, soft mouth, "Come on."

He grabs my hand and we walk towards the flying swings – or Chair-O-Plane as they call it. I watch the tiny chairs spin people rapidly, flinging out in an almost horizontal position. The chains by which the chairs are attached stretch out to their full capacity. All the riders soar above all of the other rides as they hold tightly onto the chains.

This ride I am familiar with. Although this one goes much faster than the ones I am used to. Walking up to the front of the line I utter softly, "This is no big deal."

A low laugh pushes through his nose, smiling at my innocent statement. He ignores me as we walk up to the ticket taker. A well-dressed, middle-aged man stands at the gate. His professional attire is such a sharp contrast to the carnies I've met. This man has all his teeth and his hygiene is impeccable.

Smiling as Callum approaches him, he utters in a thick British accent, "'Ello Callum. All right?"

"I'm good. It has been a long time, Harry. It seems like the business is still doing well."

Harry pulls a lever, causing the swing to slow down, "I can't complain. 'Aven't seen you in a while."

Callum gives Harry a gentle slap on his shoulder, "I've been at school."

"Good, I was starting to think your father had put a dam around you, blooming stopping you from doing anything of your choice," Harry slaps Callum's shoulder in return. Callum's face stares straight ahead. Harry adds, "You got one ticket."

Shaking his head slightly, Callum corrects, "I have two."

"Oh blimey, I am sorry, two then." He looks at me, giving me a quick wink.

Harry reaches over for the two tickets, when Callum grabs hold of his hand, uttering softly, "We will be doing it my way."

A shocked smile spreads across Harry's face. As we step onto the ride Harry utters, "The best of British to you, young miss. You're goin' to be needing it."

Turning towards Callum I question, "Why is he wishing me good luck? This is just a simple ride."

Callum just smiles in response as we find our chairs. I sit in the yellow metal chair and fasten the seatbelt tightly. The top of the chair hits my lower back, making me feel insecure. My feet barely hit the ground, causing my chair to gently swing around. Grasping onto the chains of the chair I begin looking around. The center area of the ride is divided into sections, one of which is for Harry to sit and observe all the passengers. The top of the ride is ornately painted with fleur-de-lis and what appear to be different family crests. The whole ride is riddled with brilliant white lights, illuminating the spinning effect.

Looking over at Callum in the chair next to me, I notice him slouching low in his seat, leaning as far back as he can. Placing his back firmly against the now reclined chair he gazes up at the sky as his arms dangle freely beneath his nearly horizontal body.

"What are you doing?"

"Okay Breanna, it is time to bloody let go and be free," his body hangs limp in an almost relaxed backbend position. Lifting his head slightly he looks at me, "Let go."

"No! Have you lost your mind?" I grip even tighter onto the chains, holding myself safely in place.

He peers deep into my eyes uttering, "Trust me. Let go."

His gaze fills my mind and body with a sense of security. My breathing increases as I slouch in my chair. Slowly I recline my body back into a horizontal position, though still holding tightly onto the chains for security. Panic washes over me as the chair drops back, forcing me to look up at the sky above me. My knuckles are white from the tight grip I have on the chains.

"You are doing great. Now let go of the chains," Callum's soft voice echoes with an edge of relaxation dancing off of each word.

"I can't. I am too afraid," my voice quivers in terror.

"Then stop being afraid," he extends his hand across the small gap between the chairs, reaching for my hand. "Give me your hand."

Exhaling audibly I let go, quickly reaching for Callum's hand. While I grip tightly onto his hand, he begins tenderly caressing the top of mine, sending a wave of comfort to wash over me. My other arm drops to the side of the swing, dangling effortlessly. My head lies back, looking at the world from a very different vantage point.

Relaxation takes over me until the swing begins to move. My body instantly tightens up, causing a jolt of panic to shoot through me. My natural reaction takes over as I attempt to sit back up. Callum grips securely onto my hand, "Relax Breanna, you will be fine."

Closing my eyes tightly I decide to listen to Callum. Lying back down, I allow the centrifugal force to push down on me, pressing me firmly to the chair. The speed of the swing increases, pushing the chair out to the sides of the ride. Slowly I open my eyes, watching the world spin. Callum's hand still grips onto mine, as we seem to be soaring. My horizontal body is now slightly positioned on my side from the force being placed on the chairs. A sense of freedom mixed with fear flows over me with the rushing wind. Letting go of all my fear and stress, I give in to the sensation. Releasing Callum's hand, I stretch my arms out, embracing the freedom. The echoes of screams and laughter slowly dissipate like a whistling train disappearing down a long tunnel. Peace washes over me like I am soaring in the heavens all alone. The cool wind rushes over my body from my toes up over my face, like silky sheets rustling above me. The fear that was once in me shatters, leaving me no longer feeling helpless and weak. Courage takes over as I melt into the chair, releasing my inhibitions.

A strange erotic sensation charges through me, like a skydiver getting a sudden rush of dopamine after a successful jump. An explosion of exhilaration takes over my body, replacing the fear that once existed. Heat pulsates through me, causing my toes to curl under. My heart pounds against my chest while my breathing intensifies. Stretching my arms out over my head I take in the highly erotic feeling. Slowly the ride relinquishes its force as we come to a gradual halt. My deep relaxation leaves me unable to pull myself back up. Callum walks over to me, unfastens my belt and lifts me to an upright position. My eyes bore deep into his with a surging wave of passion. Wrapping my hands tightly around his neck, I bury my hands into his hair. Pulling his mouth down onto mine I kiss him passionately. Over-excited heat explodes out of my mouth feeling his with my torturous desire.

"Whoa, let's take this down a notch. You just experienced an intense chemical release. Why don't you save it for later?" he laughs heartily.

Looking into his eyes I ask, "How do you know about this sexual release? Have you experienced it before?"

A playful smile spreads across his face, "Of course, it's a pretty powerful sensation."

Gaining some of my strength back, I stand firmly in front of him, "So how many girls have you done this ride with, then?"

"One," He states blatantly.

My jealousy slowly creeps up, lodging itself in the middle of my throat, "Who was she?"

Picking up my hand he gently kisses the back of it, uttering softly, "A stubborn American named Breanna." A quick, low laugh rips through him.

Ardently I slap the side of his arm, "That is not funny."

"I thought so," he continues laughing, but also adds, "But I do have to admit that on several occasions I would come off of the ride with a high, grab the nearest fit girl and do exactly what you just did, if you know what I mean."

"On several occasions, huh," I state disgustedly. "I bet all the girls loved that."

"I never got any complaints, and I was never slapped for it, either," he looks at me with narrow, ornery eyes.

A low growl of frustration pushes out of my mouth as I turn to walk away. Gently he tugs on my arm, stopping me, "Breanna, that was actually a huge turn on for me. No one has ever said no to me kissing them, let alone slapped me for it." Pulling me into him, he wraps his arms tightly around my waist. "I wanted you that night." His eyes bore deep into mine as his voice lowers to a deep growl, "And I want you now. If we weren't in a public place…"

We stand here gazing into each other's eyes as our hearts beat rapidly. The heated adrenaline pulsates between us. Grabbing onto the back of his sweater I pull him firmly against my body. His intense sensual gaze pierces through me, causing my stomach to flip in excitement.

Suddenly a throat clears from behind us, "Callum, you need to take that someplace else," Harry utters, as he gestures towards the line of people waiting to get on the ride.

Excessive embarrassment flushes over me, stinging my ears. Callum wraps his arm tightly around me. Burying my head into his chest we proceed to walk off the ride. Walking past Harry, Callum utters, "Thanks Harry."

"Blimey, one of these days you are goin' to get me canned," Harry states sarcastically.

"If you haven't been canned yet I don't think it will ever happen," Callum turns towards Harry, giving him a friendly slap on the back. "Take care."

"You too. And tell your mum I said 'ello."

Looking up at Callum's striking face I see a new side of him, "How do you know him?"

"Harry?" Callum turns back and looks in Harry's direction. "His parents used to work at the Manor, for my grandparents. They would always bring Harry with them when he was younger. My mum and Harry would run around the grounds playing together. So I guess you would say they were childhood friends." Leaning down he whispers into my ear, "I actually think they were more than friends, but my grandparents would have never allowed it. High class never mixes with the lower class."

"That is sad. Why couldn't they date anyway?" I ask.

"Breanna, things are different here. It is not just about money, it is about position in history and society. My mum comes from a long line of noble privilege, but with that responsibility comes an apparent bloody prison. When I was little, my mum would bring Olivia and me here every time the fair was in town. Secretly I think she would come just to see Harry."

"If Harry cares about your mum, then why on God's green earth would he let you do something so dangerous and stupid?" I ask as we walk through the brightly colored rides. The warm setting sun washes over our bodies as we head closer to the water's edge of the Wye River.

"The first time it happened was by accident. I was young and having a particularly rough day with my father. He has always been tough on me. I don't know if it is because I am not his blood child, or if he just expects more of me because I am the only boy. After a while that kind of pressure starts to wear on you. I was just a boy when he laid into me, I couldn't take it so I ran to the fair all by myself. Harry saw how upset I was and allowed me to go on the Chair-O-Plane for free. I was up there crying when I accidentally fell back. As I hung there a feeling of freedom came over me, a place where no one, especially my father, could hurt me." He lets go of me as he stares out into the river, as if there is something out there. "Harry had to stop the ride; rushing over to me, asking if I was okay. Looking up at him I told him that I was never better, pleading with him to let me do it again. Ever since that day when things get too difficult I come here, letting go and feeling free. "

Compassion washes through me as I wrap my arms around him, trying to comfort him the best way I know. Tenderly he embraces me, laying his cheek on top of my head. We stand here silently holding on to each other, watching the geese land gently on the water, causing a rippling effect to break the stillness of the water. A beautiful Greek revival building is positioned exquisitely across the wide river. The soft yellow color melts perfectly with the sharp green backdrop. The building is set on a slight hill, lifting it protectively above the water's edge. The silence flowing around us is only seldom interrupted by an occasional squeal of a goose taking flight. Tenderly I look up at him. Peering down at me he places his hands on either side of my face. A sympathetic wave rolls over us as he passionately kisses me. The world spins around us while time seems to stands still, leaving us to feel the sensation of freedom again. Lost in each other, we allow the tragedies and heartbreak to fully relinquish their control on us.

Pulling his mouth away he whispers softly, "I have never told anybody about that day. Why is it that I can tell you anything?"

"Maybe there was more to me coming here than just following through on my promise. Maybe we were supposed to find each other."

He bends down and lovingly kisses the top of my head. His voice is low and muffled as he speaks softly, "Breanna, I love you."

Heat forming in my chest pushes out, causing my skin to tingle and my body to tremble. My heart embraces his words like a lost soul finally finding its way home. My heart was a delicate mess. Now his love is the super glue that is putting me back together with a new strength I never knew existed. Standing up on my tippy-toes I look deep into his eyes, "What did you say?"

A soft smile creeps into the corners of his mouth, "You really are a stubborn American."

A smile now tickles the corners of my mouth, matching his expression, "And you love that about me."

His smile dissipates, revealing a soft, sincere expression. Gazing straight into my eyes with his rippling carnal stare, he speaks with a firm conviction, "I do love you, every part of you. I love your past, your heart-ache, your trials, your stubbornness, and most importantly your son. He fills that space within us perfectly. I have never felt this way before." Gripping his arms tightly around my waist, he lifts me up slightly so that I am fully in his power. "And if you need me to say it again, I will. I will keep telling you until you believe it."

"I believe you," placing my hands tenderly on the sides of his face I look into his eyes as tears begin to stream down mine. "I wish you could look into my heart to see just how much I love you."

Our lips merge into one expression of love as we communicate our desires. Lifting me higher up, I proceed to wrap my legs around his waist as his arms fully support my weight. Taking my entire pent up passion out on his mouth, I kiss him with a new intensity. Growling feverishly, I add, "When are we going back to your home?"

Gripping my butt firmly in his hands he breathlessly responds, "Now."

Obligation

Heavy amounts of people now flow throughout the fair as we hastily search for Olivia and Noah. The sun has almost set, making it difficult to make out faces. It is taking everything within me to try and fight the surging passion flowing through me while we try to gather Olivia and Noah so that we can leave. Callum rushes through the sea of people, gripping onto my hand, nearly dragging me behind him.

"Can this possibly take any bloody longer? Where can she be?" his voice is riddled with frustration. A sense of urgency laced with an aching need guides his every move. As he turns towards me his eyes reveal the same chemical rush I had experienced earlier, "Maybe we should split up, that way we might be able to find her faster."

Gripping his hand tightly, reassuring him I utter, "We have all night. We don't need to panic."

Holding me tightly against him, I can feel his lean muscles tighten. His abdomen rises and falls quickly against me, causing an anxious sensation to roll through me, "We have had the worst luck. I am not about to let anything stop us this time."

Looking into his hungry eyes sends chills down my spine, "Okay, we can split up, but it is not like I know where I am going."

"The fair is not that big. If you find her, go straight to the car. If you haven't found her within ten minutes, head to the car anyways." Leaning down he kisses me fervently, "Hurry!"

A slight laugh rolls through me. I have never seen him like this. He is usually cool and confident in his actions, but he is guided by a male pressure I will never understand. Slowly I begin to look around, trying to get my bearings. A sea of young adults now floods the area. Groups of girls, dressed impeccably, attempt to catch the roaming eyes of all the young men. A few of the men's eyes gaze in my direction with a flirtatious call. Rolling my eyes in response I proceed to walk towards some of the smaller rides, hoping that Olivia is there with Noah. Several comments and cat calls are hollered in my direction as I push my way through the apparent meat market. It is good to know that the same ridiculous and ritualistic mating practices that exist in America are also alive and well here in England. For a brief moment I feel like I am walking on my downtown street during peak construction hours. Lifting my hand I give them the same finger I would give all the construction workers. Just one simple finger can say so much, shutting them up instantly. At what point do boys think a girl will respond to that kind of flirtation and come running to their stupid shouts?

I head straight back to the small teacup ride tucked in the back corner of the fair. This section has mostly young families with small children anxiously awaiting their tiny thrills. Slowly I walk through the crowds, trying to find a spunky blonde wearing a baby carrier. Suddenly from behind me I hear, "Breanna, what are you doing here?"

Turning around I see Olivia's beaming face. Noah is no longer in the carrier, but is now enveloped securely within her arms, "There you are. Callum and I have been looking for you."

A questioning gaze streams across her face, "Why? Shouldn't you two be having fun together?"

An instant jolt of embarrassment washes over me, "Well… um…We kind of want to head back to the house," I stumble out.

A flash streams across her face, leaving a wide smile in its wake, "Oh, I see. You two do want to have a little fun together, just not here," a mischievous grin taints her face.

Rolling my eyes I release an audible, disconsolate sigh, "Can we just leave?"

A thick laugh explodes from her mouth. She walks over to me, placing Noah tenderly in my hands, "You might want to feed him first. You don't want me walking in on you again." She walks away completely laughing, leaving me standing here mortified. Her laughter intensifies her normal bouncy walk, causing the same gawking boys to whistle and shout in her direction. Completely feeding them with empty hopes, she turns in their direction, blowing them a suggestive kiss. A scuffle ensues over who is going to catch her imaginary kiss. Her vivacious personality handles life's situations so differently than me, making me almost jealous of her innocence.

Walking down the same path, I pass the identical group of boys. Several of them start whistling. When they notice I am the same one who earlier showed them just what I thought of them, immediately they turn a different direction. A surging wave of fearlessness rushes through me. Slowly I walk over to the young men, still holding Noah tightly under one arm. They are a group of about eight, eighteen to twenty year olds, leaning casually up against a red and blue railing. Instantly several of them stand erect, preparing for a verbal attack. Walking up to the lighter haired boy in the center of the group, I stand just inches away from his face. Gradually I lift my hand, tenderly stroking his bottom lip with the tip of my thumb. His friends remain frozen like statues as he quivers against my touch. Pulling away I give him a quick, playful wink, as I turn around, walking away joyfully. The sighs, growls, and gasps happening behind me send a surge of fulfillment rushing through me, "Hopefully that just made their night," I utter to Olivia, who is now completely rolling with laughter.

Giving me a slight hug, she states through her laughter, "Now that is using your bloody feminine power. I think that boy is in shock. You did it even holding a baby. You have more sexual power than you realize."

Walking confidently towards the car I notice that Callum is in the same type of predicament that Olivia and I were in. A swarm of girls are crowding all around him as if he were a movie star. His height towers over all the girls, allowing him to look over at me. His eyes lock onto mine in a disapproving fashion, shaking his head, while his tongue makes a snapping sound. He obviously just saw my playful banter I gave to the frisky bunch of boys. Smiling back at him, I gesture with one of my hands towards his obvious similar situation.

Olivia walks over to the group of girls, completely aware of who they are. She begins hugging several of them as if they are long lost friends. Standing back I watch this exchange of shrieking, excited shrills. Several of the girls position themselves as close to Callum as possible. These are obviously some of Olivia's school friends. I am sure they must have loved sleeping over as long as Callum was there. Several girls place their hands on Callum's shoulder, while they exaggeratingly enjoy every word he utters. Enjoying this display I step back to take in more, when suddenly I bump against someone's firm build. Immediately I turn around to say sorry, when I recoil in fear. Standing right in front of me is Gavin. His large, bulky stature seems to tower over me. A large purple and blue bruise still streams across his face from Callum's attack. Carefully I back up, holding tightly onto Noah. Swallowing my fear, I grip onto my inner strength, uttering forcefully, "Gavin, what in the hell are you doing here?"

His voice is low like a tiger's guttural growl, "I saw you with the guys over there and just wanted to say hi, and that I am sorry."

"Okay, so you said sorry. I think it is best if you leave now," a firm, flat tone resonates off of my every word as I look back at Callum. He is still surrounded by all the flirting girls pining for his attention. Trying to get him to notice me I peer firmly in his direction. His eyes suddenly catch sight of mine and his relaxed face instantly transforms, noticing who is standing behind me.

Gavin continues talking, adding, "Are you and Callum together now, or is he still planning on keeping his wedding engagement to Emily, like his parents want?" His voice is firm and flat, like he is just conveying the local daily weather report.

Rapidly I snap my head back around, staring bitterly into Gavin's eyes, "What! What are you talking about?" Rage pours through me, filling my core to the very brim. He has got to be lying. There is no way that Callum is engaged to Emily. He loves me. My ears begin ringing while my body quivers in disbelief. "You are lying! They are not engaged. You are just mad about what happened in the cave."

"No, I am not. I am not the one lying…Callum is," his voice is now firm, defending his statement. "Why don't you ask him?"

Suddenly there is a low growl echoing from behind me, "What in the bloody hell are you doing here? I thought I gave you a warning, Gavin!" Callum's eyes burn with a heated rage, snapping out his warning. He rushes to my side, poised next to me like a knight ready to defend his heroine.

Callum's body takes on a defensive stance, trying to protect me.

Gavin turns towards Callum, "I am obeying you. I am nowhere near your house."

My hand trembles violently as I cover my mouth, trying to fight back the nausea. My body begins convulsing from the anger flowing through me. Callum tenderly touches my shoulder, "Are you alright?"

His touch sends a wave of electricity to shoot through me, piercing my heart. A sick upsurge explodes out of me, making me feel like the 'other woman' in a sordid love triangle. Swinging my body violently away from his touch I shout, "Is what Gavin is telling me, true?"

The furrow between Callum's eyes deepens as he stares at me in surprise towards my sudden anger and disgust with him. "I don't know what you are talking about."

"Stop lying! Are you and Emily engaged or not?" My voice is strained with emotion. Holding my position I stare deep into Callum's eyes, searching for the truth.

His eyes widen in fear, while a bolt of shame rushes through him. His body deflates as if all life has been ripped out of him. A heavy sigh rolls from his mouth, taking with it all hope. Looking deep into my eyes he utters softly, "Yes, but I tried to tell you…"

"Shut up! You are a liar." My tears that I have been keeping at bay begin to freely fall as I stare at him. He has taken everything from me. I allowed my heart to feel again only to have him step on it. The sickness swarming in my head rushes down to my body, causing my legs to go weak. I start to stumble, when suddenly Callum reaches out to help me. Slapping his hands away, I regain my own strength. Noah suddenly starts crying. Gripping tightly onto Noah I attempt to soothe him, while I am barely able to soothe myself. The world around me spins out of control like it is being flushed down a toilet. Rage now resides where there was once love.

Suddenly Olivia is at our side, trying to calm our overheated situation down, "What is going on here?"

Embracing my anger I turn towards Olivia snapping, "Are you involved in this deceit, also? Here I thought you were my friend, but you were just pimping me out to your ass of a brother."

"What are you bloody talking about?" Olivia's voice is thick with disbelief as she steps back in shock.

"Why don't you ask your brother, the liar, how he can say that he loves me, while at the same time is engaged to Emily?"

Olivia's expression drops in disbelief. Turning towards Callum she notices his deflated appearance,

"What is she talking about? Are you engaged to Emily?" Her eyes plead with him for some kind of explanation.

Callum closes his eyes tightly, trying to fight away some kind of emotion as his shoulders drop in disbelief, "You don't understand, Olivia. You don't have the same obligations put on…"

"Stop it Callum! How could you bloody do this to her?" Olivia's voice cuts through him like a knife slicing into the core. "You love Breanna, not Emily. Why would you do this?"

Ignoring his sister, Callum turns towards me, gently grasping hold of my arm, pleading with his eyes. Callum's eyes now mirror mine as tears of emotion rip through him, "Breanna, this is between you and me, please can we go somewhere private so I can explain? I really tried to tell you, but…"

A heated jolt of anger surges through my arm where his hand is touching mine. Instantly I jerk my arm away, snapping towards him, "Don't touch me anymore! I won't be going anywhere with you." Tears fill my eyes, making it hard for me to see. Drawing on the same strength I needed to raise myself and to bury my husband with, I gaze up into Callum's eyes, "I let you in and allowed you to fill a void within me. I trusted you. I loved you, but you have destroyed that. No, I will not let you explain, because I am done." As I turn to walk away Gavin stands in front of me, stopping me from continuing.

"Breanna, I was completely wrong in what I did to you in the cave. Emily asked me to take you there because Callum is her fiancé. She was afraid that Callum was going to use you. I handled things very po…"

"Stop, Gavin! You are still handling things horribly! Whether you did this by your own choice or under Emily's command it doesn't matter, you both have succeeded. You have destroyed me!" Though my voice is tattered I utter my words with conviction. I am an innocent pawn being used and manipulated by Emily and Gavin. His apology is as flat and blank as a piece of white paper.

Gavin looks at me with a slight sneer, "We didn't destroy you, Callum did. He never loved you. You are just a plaything for him."

Callum's defeated posture instantly inflates as his eyes turn to stone. Leaping onto Gavin, he grabs hold of his shirt firmly within his hands. "You bloody lying bastard! You know nothing about me! I love her. And no matter what happens I will always love her. My life is a prison and there is no escape for me, but there is one thing that is true and that is that I love her." Callum's voice quivers as he forcefully clarifies his feelings for me to Gavin. Though it is Gavin he is talking to, his words seem to bypass him, landing instead on me. Even though I was not going to let him explain, he is taking this opportunity, forcing me to hear him.

Turning away from them both I walk towards the parking lot. A wave of panic washes through me as I realize that I have no ride back to the manor. Standing here I look at the sea of cars, but not one holds my escape. I can feel my breakdown coming to the surface. My heart contracts as it squeezes out years of pain. I was able to hide my life's disappointment within Callum's love, but now that that is gone, my pain has nowhere to hide. Standing here my tears soak my face as I stare down at the only thing that will not disappoint me, Noah. He is my only link I have left to the one man who truly loved me.

Suddenly there is a gentle hand on my arm. Turning quickly to see who it is, I notice Olivia standing right next to me. Her usual bright eyes have been dimmed by the sorrows of the night. Dangling a pair of keys in her hand she tenderly states, "Callum gave me the keys to his car, asking me to drive you home." My eyes narrow in objection, not wanting Callum to ride next to me. Obviously she reads my expression adding, "Callum said that he will walk home."

Her hand stretches out towards mine. Looking into her eyes I see the soft understanding I have grown to love. Through all the crap, Olivia has always had my back. Though I blamed her, it was just my anger speaking. I know that she is as disappointed with her brother as I am. This revelation hit us both like a ton of bricks. Tenderly I reach my hand over to hers, placing it within her petite, yet firm grip.

Affectionately she smiles uttering, "Remember, don't judge a book by its cover. Though the outside may seem impossible, there is more than meets the eye inside."

I shake my head in disagreement. I know that she is trying to smooth things over, either by the request of her brother or her own desire. No matter which one, it is not going to work. "Olivia, I will go with you on one condition, don't talk about it anymore." We head to the car in complete silence.

It seemed like a very long drive back. The silence reverberating within the car washed over me like a slow poison, gradually killing me. The quiet lull of the car put Noah to sleep, while it caused me to replay every detail of tonight. Every memory of Callum's touch or kiss causes waves of anger and betrayal to rush throughout me. All I want to do is get back to their house as soon as possible so that I can make arrangements to go back to Cambridge.

Pulling up to the entrance I notice a very nice black car parked in front of their house. Olivia's face drops as she notices the car also. The air within the car suddenly thickens as she parks Callum's car next to the black Mercedes. She begins nervously fiddling with the car key while she sits anxiously within the driver's seat. The now dark night pushes down on me, matching my inner soul. Everything within me impatiently is drawn towards the manor, all I want to do is load up my things and leave.

Grabbing hold of the door I begin opening it when suddenly Olivia grabs hold of my arm, stopping me dead in my tracks, "Wait, Breanna." Turning questioningly towards her, I peer aggravatingly into her eyes. "My parents are here."

My heart instantly stops. A wave of panic bursts within my stomach, streaming up and searing my throat. This is all I need right now. After my horrific night, Callum's parents are the last people on earth I want to meet. Gavin's words echo within my ears, saying that Callum's parents want him to be engaged to Emily. What kind of hell am I about to walk into? Emily has been left at the manor all day while her fiancé has been traipsing off with another woman. My hand trembles against the handle of the car door, unsure of what I am going to do. I am completely terrified as to what I will find inside. Will Olivia and Callum's parents be waiting for us, with questions that I am not ready to answer yet? Fear races throughout me as I debate my options. I don't want to go inside, yet I don't want to stay here in the car and chance running into Callum when he comes walking up.

Olivia suddenly cuts through the silence uttering, "Emily! That bloody arse! She must have called my parents because they are not supposed to bloody be here."

Turning sharply towards Olivia I stammer out, "What do you mean? Why would she call them?" My heart beats twice as fast as perspiration now beads up on my forehead.

Olivia's eyes soften as she gazes at me with love, "Breanna, before we go in you need to understand something first. My parents are loving people and would do anything for us, but they have been raised in a very different world. We, especially Callum, have obligations that we are forced to uphold." She stares straight into my eyes, "These obligations are more like a prison sentence being placed on us."

Instantly my mind recalls the story that Callum told me about his mother and Harry, how she couldn't be with him. My heart drops as I suddenly realize the pressure that is put on Callum.

Looking up at Olivia I utter firmly, "Then why would you encourage our relationship when you knew that we couldn't be together?"

She gazes down at her keys as she twirls them tenderly within her fingers, "I wanted my brother to have real love, he deserves it. I honestly had no idea what my parents were pressuring him to do."

"Pressure or not, he should have been honest with me. It's not just me he was lying to," turning around I look at Noah sleeping silently in his seat. "He has destroyed two innocent people."

Olivia grabs hold of my hand, squeezing it gently she utters, "Let's go inside now."

Eavesdropping

T hough the main sitting room is bright, the dark, thick feeling oozing out of it vibrates within the large entrance. Olivia and I stand silently in the foyer, fully aware of her parents' presence. Not wanting to bring any attention to myself, I delicately attempt to sneak past the room. As I quietly pass the large doorway, undetected, Noah suddenly lets out a loud, hungry cry. Closing my eyes tightly I stand frozen in my tracks, afraid to even breathe. A heavy exhale followed by a slight laugh reverberates from behind me. Slowly I turn around; noticing Olivia's slightly perturbed expression.

Suddenly a low, growling voice echoes from the sitting room, "Olivia, will you please come in here?" There is a slight pause then he continues, "And Breanna, will you please join us also?"

My heart instantly drops, hitting my stomach with a loud thud. It is frightening enough to have to confront their parents, but then to hear them utter my name sends chills up my spine. How can they possibly know my name? I don't think Olivia – and definitely not Callum – have ever told them about me. I gaze over at Olivia as she gives me a sheepish smile. Hastily she proceeds to walk through the large entryway into the enormous, yet cozy sitting room. A large, pretentious smile spreads across her face as she states cheerfully, "Mum and Dad, I am so glad you are back from your holiday. I missed you."

A low, booming voice from Olivia's father immediately chimes in, "Where is Callum?"

"He is not with us," Olivia's once gleeful voice is now flat yet filled with obedient respect.

Hearing Olivia mention the word "us" in her statement, I take that obvious cue and slowly enter the room. Positioned properly on the large down-filled couch are Callum and Olivia's parents. The resemblance between Olivia and her mother is uncanny, though her posture is more refined and there is a lack of mischievous spitfire within her, unlike Olivia. Her petite frame seems even smaller next to her husband's stocky, large build. Her elegant face is soft and friendly in appearance, while their father's looks severe. His narrow, beady eyes seem out of place on his round, flat face. His thin lips form a natural frown, causing the deep frown lines on his face to stream down until they join his jowls just below his chin. His stern expression is a sharp contrast to his impeccable style. A perfectly tailored suit is thrown over a stylish dark grey cashmere sweater, softening his bulky build. Their mother's fashion sense is equally impressive, but hers blends flawlessly with her small and gentle appearance. Her shoulder length blonde hair forms seamlessly around her oval face. Looking into her eyes I suddenly see Callum's eyes staring back at me. Her eyes are the same liquid caramel color and shape as Callum's, causing my heart to flutter slightly. Their eyes widen slightly as I gingerly walk into the room carrying Noah in my arms.

A slight groan comes from a wing chair off to the side of me. Looking over I notice Emily sitting with a satisfactory smirk sprawling across her face. Her dark hair and olive skin is such a sharp contrast to the off-white fabric of the chair. Her nearly black eyes flame with hatred as she stares me down while drumming her fingers irritably against her knees. There is no doubt in my mind now how their parents found out my name. Emily obviously has told them everything she can about me. I am sure that she did not paint a pretty picture of me. From the expression on Olivia and Callum's parents' faces though, she obviously left out the information about me having a child.

Looking into Emily's eyes I give her a tender smile, uttering softly, "Hi, Emily."

She snickers forcefully through her nose, turning towards Mr. and Mrs. Hughes. Turning my gaze in their direction also, I add respectfully, "Mr. and Mrs. Hughes, it is nice to meet you." Mrs. Hughes' eyes never leave Noah. The furrow between her eyes deepens as her mind seems to wander off to a hidden corner of her memory. Her rigid posture suddenly relaxes as her eyes rise slightly, looking at my face. Surprise shoots through her gaze as she takes in my youthful appearance and the infant stage of Noah.

Shock takes over, causing her to stammer out, "Is that child yours?"

Gazing back at her questioningly I answer, "Yes, this is my son, Noah."

A stern mask covers her once soft expression. Looking deep into my eyes she spits out, "And who is this baby's father?"

"Mother! That is bloody rude," Olivia snaps in my defense.

Mr. Hughes slams his hand forcefully down on the tea table, causing us all to jump, "Olivia, you will guard your mouth when speaking to your mother." His eyes now shift towards me. "As far as my wife's question, I believe it is a perfectly respectable one. What say you Breanna, who is his father?"

"Excuse me, Mr. and Mrs. Hughes, I don't mean to be disrespectful, but I don't think the paternal nature of my child is a relevant subject right now?" My eyes stay firmly attached to theirs. Though I am young, I am not easily intimidated by people. I have had to stand firm in my choices all of my life, not bending to the constant changes of the adults around me.

"Young lady, you are standing in my house under possible questionable circumstances. I believe I have every right to question the paternity of this child," Mrs. Hughes' voice is cold and flat while she states her demands.

The air within the room is thick with suspicion as I stand here in front of them both, and Emily, defending my virtue and the paternal nature of Noah. Bubbling rage filled with insulting abuse surges within me. Turning towards Olivia I notice her eyes are full of compassion while a fuming embarrassment pours over her. Her eyes narrow with an apologetic expression within them. Gazing back at Mrs. Hughes I suddenly see the possible fear within her eyes as she looks inquisitively at

Noah. Internal strength rushes through me like my bones have transformed into iron.

Standing here erect I face my accusers. They obviously feel it is more important for Callum to marry someone he doesn't love but is of a higher class than to be shamed by the possibility of him fathering an American trailer trash's child – but that he loves.

"I have been insulted in every way possible. You sit here in front of me, questioning my morals and also who the father of my son is. You have no right. My standards should not be judged nor put under scrutiny by someone who doesn't know me. I am worth as much, if not more, than anyone else in this room. Just because my value cannot be measured by currency doesn't make me worthless. And as far as my son is concerned, you have no right to ask his paternal nature. Whether he is Callum's or someone else's is none of your business."

The heat rises to my head, causing my face to turn a bright shade of red. Tears start to well up within my eyes. Trying to fight them from spilling over I begin biting down on the inside of my lip.

"Excuse me, but if that child is Callum's then we have every right to know, especially since he is engaged to Emily. Your virtue *is* at stake," her voice is unaffected by my emotional state.

"No mother, you don't have a bloody right to know!" a firm familiar voice echoes heavily from behind me. "If Noah is my child then that is our business, and if he is not then it is still our business. Her virtue is and will always be in impeccable condition as long as I have something to say about it," Callum now stands firmly behind me glaring furiously towards his parents. He had silently entered the room behind me. From his obvious facial expression, he has heard most of the accusations, also my subsequent response. Though he looks slightly weary from his long walk back, his voice still reverberates strength.

Callum's mother jumps to her feet, revealing her true petite stature. "Callum, do not shame this family and the Hughes name." Though she is a small woman, her strength and fiery nature cause her to appear as if she is six feet tall.

Callum's tone instantly matches hers as he growls, "Mother, it is hard to shame the Hughes name when I am not a Hughes. I am a Holden and you know it. Sam is not my biological father. No matter how much you have tried to erase my father's memory from me, I am and will always be a Holden. His face screams from my reflection in the mirror every day," his voice softens slightly as his eyes meet their twin, liquid caramel battling for understanding.

Her voice cracks slightly, "I have not hid him from you. I have always told you that Sam is not your biological father." She walks closer to Callum, gazing up into his eyes, questioning. "How do you know what your father looks like? I have never shown you a picture of him."

"Mother, I am not daft. I don't look anything like you. So that must mean I look just like my father. There have been times when you cannot even look at me." Turning towards Sam he utters respectfully, "I know that you have tried to be a good father and I love you for that, but I have felt your jealousy towards my father displaced onto me." Turning towards me, his eyes wash over my face with a pleading edge of regret. Our eyes lock, causing a throbbing sadness to rise within me. Tears flood over the protective dam, rolling down my face. Facing his parents again he continues, stating with a trembling voice, "Breanna is innocent. This is my entire fault. Don't drag her or her son's name through society's rubbish."

His mother turns towards all of us stating boldly, "I would like to converse with my son…alone."

Mr. Hughes begins corralling everyone out of the sitting room, "You heard her, everyone out." His stout arm presses against me, almost dragging me out of the room. Locking my worried eyes onto Callum, he gives me a reassuring smile, yet his eyes tell a very different story. Sadness envelopes him, like an invisible prison cell, as I am pushed out of the room.

"Sam, I would like you to leave also," her voice is soft as she gently asks him to leave.

"Charlotte, I don't think I should leave you two alone." She stares at him persuasively, giving him a firm, yet tender expression. Acknowledging her request, he hesitantly leaves the room.

A multitude of emotions fill the foyer, while everyone begins staring accusingly at each other. Emily slowly paces back and forth, wringing her hands firmly together. Her dark eyes sear into me like laser beams cutting into my core. A thick disdain oozes off of her, filling the room with palpable hatred. Walking over to me and standing just inches away from my face, she warns, "Stay away from Callum, you bloody slapper. If only Callum wouldn't have interrupted Gavin, things would be bloody different right now," her face lights up with a malicious smile.

Rage pushes its way through me as I stare at her smug, arrogant face. What type of a person wishes that kind of act on someone? If it wasn't for Callum my world right now would be very different. Only to discover that it was all her idea. The muscles within my arms coil up, preparing themselves for an attack. Rage elevates within me, when all of a sudden Olivia's fist swings violently across Emily's face, knocking her across the room.

"You bloody wanker! You set up Breanna to get attacked by Gavin," Olivia's voice reverberates off of the walls. Her hands are still tightly gripped, preparing for another blow.

"Olivia!" her father yells in reaction to the sudden attack. Rushing over to Emily's side, he begins tenderly helping her.

Instantly Callum and his mother rush towards the foyer. Callum's face matches Olivia's, completely disgusted by what he has just heard. My body is still trembling from the intense amount of anger flowing through me. Out of the corner of my eye I notice Callum giving Olivia a thumb's up in response to her brilliant blow. Callum's mother pulls him back into the room, noticing that Mr. Hughes is taking control over the situation.

"Olivia, take Breanna back to her room while I take care of Emily. We will deal with this outburst later," he proceeds to tenderly walk Emily towards the kitchen.

Olivia gives me a large satisfied smile as we walk away, "That felt abso-bloody-lutely incredible," her voice was quiet, but filled with enthusiasm.

Giving her a reassuring smile, I utter intensely, "Will you do me a favor?" She gazes at me curiously as I continue, "Will you please take Noah to my room? I need to stay here."

Olivia's excited eyes transform, resonating a serious expression, "Are you sure you want to hear it?"

"I don't want to, I need to," I correct.

Tenderly taking Noah from my enveloped arms, she gazes up at me with a loving smile. Slowly she walks down the long hallway towards my room. Quietly I head back to the foyer. Finding a hiding place that will still allow me to eavesdrop on their conversation, I tuck myself into the corner. A quiet lull vibrates out of the room, though I can hear a soft clicking sound of heels passing on the wood floor. My heart hammers in my throat as I silently wait for someone to talk.

As I raise my eyes to heaven I notice the intricate carvings and design on the ceiling. Ancient beams lay crisscross above me. The secrets that they hold within them over the past hundreds of years, is innumerable. I share their quiet eavesdropping right now as I blend into the woodwork. Suddenly a soft feminine voice breaks the silence, "Callum, you know that I loved your father."

A loud sigh vibrates out of the room, "Yes." His voice sounds strained, as if the weight he has been carrying is finally taking a toll.

"He was so striking. Every time he looked at me my heart would skip a beat. You are correct in your assumptions, you look just like him. And there are times when it hurts to look at you." There is a long pause, causing fear to consume me. Holding my breath, trying not to make a sound, I continue intently listening. I am grateful when the silence breaks, "My parents fought our engagement because his family's income did not match mine, though his ancestral line far surpassed my history. After heavy persuasion we were allowed to marry, to the shock and horror of the social aristocracy. When he died and I was left a single mother, my parents arranged a more suitable union."

"What, you didn't choose Sam?" Callum's voice was thick with shock.

"No, but I choose him now. He has been a good husband, provider, and father. His social status matched my parent's, he also loved me from the moment he saw me. He also loved you as his own. We thought it was best to have your name match ours," though her voice remained flat, as if she were relaying her grocery list, there was a slight trembling of hidden emotion within her words.

"Why didn't you tell me the truth? I had a right to know and a choice in my surname," his voice was thick and firm as he rolled out his questions.

"No, you didn't. Those were my choices, which affected you for the better. I share these things with you only to show you that our choices affect our family's respect and class. This girl, Breanna, could destroy all of that."

Instantly my ears perk up with the sudden mention of my name. I know that I come from a very different world, but to state that I could possibly destroy an entire family's reputation is a concept that is foreign to me. If the price of wealth and prestige is your happiness, I don't want it.

"No, she wouldn't. I love her. You missed out on an opportunity of love in your life because of your obligations, like Harry. I am not about to."

"Harry? You mean my childhood friend?" Her voice perked up in pure amusement.

"I know he was more than a friend, but you turned away from that. I saw the way you would look at him when we were younger," he almost seems to plead with her to recall all that she has lost over stupid obligations.

"Callum, that was just a childish crush, it wasn't real. I never wanted the life he was capable of giving me. If that is what you have with Breanna, then by all means, get it out of your system. Use her up and then move on."

Her cold reference to me swirls within my gut as I listen to her sickening advice for Callum to just use me up then throw me away like rubbish. Gripping my hands tightly together I fight back the urge to run in there, giving them both a piece of my mind. The only thing stopping me is that I need to hear what Callum's response is.

"This is not a childish crush. If anything I wish she would use me up, and never move on. Breanna and Noah are important to me. I only agreed to the engagement because I thought that Breanna could never be mine – but I was wrong." His warm, buttery voice flows through me, washing away my anger.

"Is that child yours?" she snaps out.

Silence pours out of the room, dragging with it anger and trepidation. A firm, yet dejected response follows, "No. His father is a much better man than I can ever be."

"Then let her go. From what I understand she is a poor American, most likely using you for your wealth and prestige, wanting the fairytale story. Emily is the better fit. Besides, you are already engaged to her. Her father and Sam are best mates. It was humiliating when they called us stating the betrayal you were putting their daughter through. You made a promise to her..."

"...only because you forced it on me!"

"It doesn't matter why. To break that promise will destroy this family's reputation."

My heart breaks as I suddenly realize the reality of what needs to happen. Quietly I leave my hiding place, heading back to my room, dragging my dreams behind me. The world has trampled on me my whole life. I was born into this world by a mother who cared more about her alcohol than me, and a father who was just a one night stand for her. I then marry my friend and lover only to have him ripped from me. Thus leaving me with a constant reminder, every time I look at Noah, of what I lost. The final nail this cruel world has hammered into my coffin is allowing me to love someone I can never have.

The reverberating pain pushes down on me, making it difficult to walk. Dropping down in front of the door to my room I expel all of my pain. My tears stream down my face, soaking my knees as I sit with my arms tightly wrapped around my bent legs. Even if Callum hadn't proposed to Emily, we still wouldn't be able to be together, we are from two different places. I was damned from the very beginning to live a hellish life. No matter where I run I cannot escape the world I was born into. Though I want no part of it, it still haunts me wherever I go. Who am I kidding? I am trailer trash trying to pass off as something of worth. No matter where I am placed, in an apartment or a palace, one thing stays the same, I am garbage, and now I have just been taken out.

Staring at the intricate door in front of me, I utter softly to myself, "Andrew, you may have thought that I was worth more than what life has given me, but you were wrong. I can't do this any longer." Standing up I grip tightly onto the doorknob, completely aware of what I have to do.

Let Him Go

Olivia's eyes fill with tears as she looks at me in disbelief. Externally I maintain a hard, distant shell, while internally I am falling apart. I didn't realize how hard this was going to be on her. For me though, I knew it was going to be more difficult than distancing myself from my mother. Olivia has been my only friend here. It is killing me to watch her so upset. I am used to seeing her so full of life, it is as if I have killed that part of her.

"Breanna, I don't understand, did I do something wrong?" Her eyes are blazing red while her tears freely flow.

Pushing down my natural instinct to comfort her and tell her I was just kidding, I clinch my jaw tightly, uttering, "You didn't do anything wrong. I just can't be your friend anymore. I have been fooling myself. I am not ready for a friend or…" I swallow hard trying to spit the rest out. "…anything else right now." Trying to muster up my strength I add, "I was just using you because I didn't know anyone here."

Her eyes narrow as she glares deep into mine, "I don't know why you are bloody doing this, but if this is what you want then fine, I will no longer talk to you." She storms past me, heading towards the door to exit my room. Suddenly she turns around, eyes blazing with emotion. "I am not so easily dismissed. Trust me, I will find out the truth." She slams the door behind her, taking my heart and soul with her.

Instantly I throw myself onto the bed, screaming forcefully into my pillow. Olivia was the closest thing to a sister and I just broke her heart. The only way I can successfully separate myself from Callum is to distance myself from them both. If I were to remain friends with Olivia, she would be constantly giving me unwarranted hope for Callum until the day of his marriage. I also can't be around Callum or anything that reminds me of him. The pain would be too unbearable. I can't allow my presence to ruin their family or their reputation.

Having a family that loves you is worth my sacrifice. I know what it is like to not have a family. I could never live with myself if I was the reason behind their destruction. Though I don't agree with their rigid obligations, it is their prison to bear, like loneliness is mine.

The immense pain within my chest cripples me as I expel my sadness, soaking my pillow with my tears. A thundering knock at my door interrupts my emotional breakdown. Gathering myself together, I hastily wipe away my tears. Rushing to the door I internally prepare myself for another confrontation with Olivia. I exhale a heavy sigh, opening the door, "Olivia…"

Surprise rolls over me as I notice Callum looking at me with emotional eyes, "I don't think Olivia will be knocking on your door any time soon. You have crushed her." Though he is trying to put on a strong act, his face is worn from the night's events. Everything that has transpired tonight has been a rollercoaster effect on both of our hearts. I have felt the emotional high from Callum's declaration of love to the severe low of deceit, heartbreak, and shattered dreams. As Callum stands before me, my heart jumps back onto the rollercoaster ride once more. Not wanting him to see through my façade, I gaze down at the floor, trying to avoid eye contact.

Placing his hand firmly against my partially open door, he asks, "May I please come in? We need to talk."

Positioning myself between the door jamb and the door, I hold securely onto the door, blocking him from entering. "I don't think it is a good idea. It is late. Noah is asleep and I don't want anyone to get the wrong idea."

His voice and posture stiffen up, "Bloody hell, let them get the wrong idea, we need to talk."

Still gazing down at the floor I hold fast to my position, "No. I think you need to leave."

"Damn it Breanna, look at me…Please," his voice is thick with emotion, like syrup on a cold day.

Pushing down my pain I quickly look up at his face. His gaze locks onto mine, revealing his pleading pain. My soul breaks apart as I witness his broken hearted expression. Dark circles have formed around his eyes from stress and exhaustion, while the deep furrow between his eyes deepens as he peers devastatingly into mine. Fighting back my tears I turn my heart off as I utter flatly, trying to hide my trembling body, "Callum, I am done. Noah and I are leaving first thing in the morning. Please don't talk to me again." With every word I utter it rips a piece of me out with it.

Slowly I push the door closed between us, leaving him standing out in the hallway, alone.

Walking into the center of my room I expel the pain I have had to push down. A heavy weight of regret rolls up my spine, crawling over my shoulders and pouring down my body. Uncontrolled tears rush down my face as I begin sobbing uncontrollably. A thick air within the room envelops me, making it hard to breath. I teeter on the edge of hyperventilating and passing out. Everything around me spins out of control, when suddenly there is a loud slam behind me. Fearfully I spin around, noticing Callum standing next to the pushed open door. His eyes blaze with desire as he growls, "You are not leaving. I won't let you. You may have dismissed Olivia, but I will not walk away that easy."

His highly erotic eyes rip through me, causing my heart to pound against my chest. He rushes towards me, wrapping his arms around my waist, lifting me up off of my feet. Holding me tightly within his arms he presses his lips firmly against mine. Our tears unite in sorrow as they mix delicately within our kiss. Heat pulsates through us as he takes his aggression out on me. Gripping my hair firmly within his hands he holds me against him. The salty taste of his tears mingles inside of my mouth as his tongue stimulates the cocktail. Wrapping his arm beneath my butt he holds tightly onto me as he eagerly walks us over to the bed.

"Breanna, I love you, please love me too," his voice is rough, with a pleading need. I know he is trying to rebel against his parents, showing them that this is what he wants, but I now know he can't have me.

A heavy weight pushes down on my chest. Though this is what I want with all my heart, I can't. Pressing my hands securely against his chest, I push him away from me. His eyes are red from his tears and emotional need. His face shows the heavy burden of what he wants and what is inescapable. I grasp at every ounce of strength within me, forcing myself to complete the horrible task I know I have to do.

"I did, but Callum, I don't want this. I don't love you anymore," his face drops as if I have just stabbed his heart. If his heart isn't breaking I know that mine is. Though my lies are tearing me apart, I know that I have to do this. I have to let him go.

He buries his head into the hollow spot between my neck and shoulder. Gripping me tightly against him he pleads, "Please don't do this. You are killing me." He swallows firmly, pushing down a large knot in his throat, "You still love me. I felt it. You can't turn off love that quick. You are just mad. I know I should have told you about Emily, I honestly tried, but Olivia interrupted us and then...well, I forgot about it."

Disbelief surges within me, giving me the fuel I need to continue letting him go. Pushing myself free from his grasp, I slide down out of his arms, "You didn't try that hard! Besides, how can you forget something like that? I am not an idiot. You purposefully kept it from me, lying to me. Telling me that you love me, knowing the whole time you are engaged to Emily. You made me feel cheap," acidic anger pours through every word.

Grabbing hold of my anger I use it for my benefit, allowing the rage to consume me, invading the passion that was encompassing me. Peering into his eyes with daggers, I search for some kind of answer. Though in my core I know what the real answer is, I am trash. I don't contain the same bloodline or fortune, making our relationship a shameful one.

Feeling the heat of my anger, he instinctively backs up as he utters in defense, "Breanna, I was finished with you and all the bloody unanswered questions. I thought that you and Noah's father were still together. You led me to believe it too!" Looking deep into my eyes he adds, "I thought I was done until you showed up here. When I saw you and Noah my hope was rekindled and all I wanted was you."

He remains immobile as he gazes at me with a pleading understanding. I stand here soaking in every ounce of anger and disappointment flowing within the room. My heart pounds vehemently against my chest. I stare at his face, wishing he would just be honest with me. He has no idea that I heard him and his mother talking about me tonight and how his father and mother disapprove of our relationship. Yet he stands here in front of me, lying right to my face, trying to tell me he only proposed to Emily because he thought I was still with Noah's father. The sooner he is honest with me, the sooner we will be able to move on.

Standing resolute in my position I question, "So you are telling me that as soon as you thought Noah's father was still in the picture, you rushed off and proposed to Emily. Isn't that awfully fast?"

"Well yes, but…"

"But what? Why did you really run off and propose to her?" I snapped. The acid within my tone of voice burns my tongue as I spew out my request.

"What do you bloody want from me?" his voice is thick with anger as his hand aggressively glides through his hair, gripping onto a chunk of hair on the back of his head. He begins nervously pacing back and forth, wearing a path in the floor.

"I want the truth," though my voice is firm, there is a pleading tone to it.

"I don't understand you. This is a bunch of rubbish. I have already told you the bloody truth." His pacing increases in speed as he forcefully pulls at his hair. Frustration engulfs him while he seems to be losing an internal battle.

Firing one more bullet in his already riddled body, hoping this will break him, causing him to utter the statement he is refusing to say, "No, you haven't. You have not told me why you proposed to Emily so hastily. Why Callum? Just tell me why!"

He spins around and looks me deep in my eyes, "What do you want? Do you want me to tell you how you are just poor American rubbish in my parents' eyes? While Emily was not only born with a silver spoon in her mouth, but her father is one of my father's best mates. Is that what you want to hear?" His eyes blaze with irritation.

Though I already knew the truth, hearing him finally say it feels like a nail gun firing at my heart. The pain of his words instantly brings my reality to life. I have been living a lie this whole time. I knew it the moment Olivia pulled up to their mansion. I was just kidding myself if I thought for one minute his family would just embrace me with open arms. The vision of my world flashes in front of me with vivid color. The silver spoon of prestige, wealth, and opportunity was not given to me. Mine was a plastic spoon of alcoholism, homelessness and pain, a disposable and useless upbringing.

Instantly his eyes fill with regret as he looks into my hurt eyes. Rushing over to me he attempts grabbing my hand, "Breanna, please forgive me for my cold and callous statement."

Instinctively I try to pull my hand away from his. Looking down at my hands I see the worn down un-manicured nails, crying out in simplicity. The hand that belongs in his is not mine. His requires one of feminine grace and polished perfection. Looking up into his eyes I state flatly, "No matter how you say it the words are true, I am not meant for this world."

Reacting to me trying to pull away, he tenderly releases my hand, "You are meant for me. Breanna, I don't care if you came from a hole in the ground or a castle in the sky, if you are American or English, I need you."

"Stop kidding yourself. A river can never flow upstream, I am meant to stay down here in the lowly valley. And no matter how much you want this to work, it won't. Deep down, you have always known it or else you wouldn't *have* proposed to Emily."

"You don't understand the pressure my parents are putting on me. You speak as if yours is the only tragic and tough life. Do you have any understanding for my life and what I am going through?" His voice is stiff, clicking out each word in a precise manner. His slight accent intensifies with every word he utters. His posture is now erect, taking on a more prestigious appearance.

My voice softens slightly, trying to tame the situation, "Yes, I do. That is why it is best if I leave," I state plainly, trying to bring some reason to his irrational thinking.

A heavy weighted silence presses around us, making the air feel thick. We stand here in silence for what feels like hours as the world around us spins with clarity. Callum's eyes reveal a shattering pain tearing through his face. Grasping at anything, he suggests, "I was a fool to ask Emily to marry me and I will be a fool to let you go now."

Tenderly I walk over to him, standing just inches away from his face. Looking into his eyes I lift my hand and place it on the side of his cheek. His skin feels soft and warm against the cool touch of my hand. My fingers softly stroke the stubble on his face as my hand lovingly glides across his warm cheek. He leans against my hand, closing his eyes as he takes in every bit of my touch. Tears begin to fill my eyes as I gaze at his face. My mind burns into memory every detail of him; his soft, sumptuous lips, firm jaw line framed by his perfect whiskers, his sensuous eyes that can gaze right through me. But most of all, my mind burns into memory his genuine love towards Noah.

Letting my tears wash my face, I lean in, affectionately kissing the side of his cheek. Pulling away I utter softly, "Then let me be the one to let you go. Thank you for everything. But most of all thank you for letting me feel love again, even if it was just for a brief moment in time. I didn't think I could ever love again and now I know I can," a slight pause rolls over me. Fighting back my trepidation I add, "You will be able to love again, it just won't be me."

His eyes rip open, staring at me with an incredulous expression. Pulling his face away from my hand he raises his hand, gripping onto my wrist firmly, "Bloody hell, stop! If it means that I lose everything, so be it. You are being a bloody stubborn arse right now. If you think I will be able to love anyone else you are being ridiculous!" His grip on my wrist tightens with his emotions, causing my fingers to go numb.

Looking deep into his eyes I spit out, "I am not being a stubborn *arse*! I am the only one being reasonable. I will not allow you to lose everything, least of all a family that loves you. I know what it is like to not have a family and I will not curse you with that kind of life. You are engaged to Emily, let yourself love her."

"No! I could never love someone who so maliciously sent you into the depths of hell to be attacked and even almost..." his eyes blaze in anger as I witness his need for me transform into bitter disgust.

"Lower your voice, Noah is asleep," I command.

The heat penetrating off of his hand burns my skin. As I attempt to pull my hand away he tightens his grip, "I will not let you both go." He holds onto my arm as if it is his last attempt at keeping me close to him.

"Callum, let go of me," ripping my hand free I firmly stare into his eyes. Our eyes lock in a surging battle. His usually calm nature evaporates, revealing a fiery side to him. He seems to be fighting for more than just me, but a sense of freedom in his choices. His world has been scripted his whole life and this is the first time he has been able to make a choice in his life.

Grabbing hold of my nerve, I end this battle stating in a commanding voice, "Good-bye, Callum." Turning my back on him so he won't see my tears, I add, "Leave now!"

A furious wave rolls behind me, surging up my spine as my back remains to him. I can feel Callum's eyes peering right through me, making me wish I didn't have to make that statement. Holding my breath, I maintain my firm stance.

Suddenly the door behind me slams, sending shock waves into my soul, shattering the courage I have been pretending. Dropping down to the floor I expel all my tears. Pulling a blanket off of the bed I wrap it around me, attempting to feel some kind of warmth. Gripping the blanket tightly within my hands I cry vigorously, soaking the blanket.

Looking down at the tweed cover, I instantly recall the night I first realized I was falling in love with him. Pain rips through me even more. Gazing around the room I remember all the details of this past week, like a tortuous nightmare, dangling everything I want just outside of my grasp.

Sitting in this agonizing room I instantly realize that I need to leave, tonight. I can't stay here any longer. I can't chance running into Callum, Olivia, or even Emily tomorrow. I know what I need to do and I can't allow any trepidation to invade my courage. Hastily I start throwing all my things together, trying not to wake anyone in the process. I have run away from homes before. I am very capable of sneaking out unnoticed, but I have never done it with a baby. Quietly I call for a cab, explaining to the driver not to enter the property but to pick me up at the end of their private road.

Placing Noah in his baby carrier, I gather all of my things as I quietly sneak out of my room. A wave of relief washes off of me as I walk away from the room. My hopes shed from my mind with every step I take down the long hall. Carefully I maneuver the winding hallway, making sure I don't accidentally run into Callum. Silence looms all around me, making the whistling air almost scream in my ears.

Softly I walk past the large sitting room. Gazing in at the vast emptiness, my mind replays the scene from tonight. Peering into the darkness I notice the large ceiling-to-floor windows at the end of the room. As I look out into the night I catch sight of someone leaning against the large cement railing. My heart stops as I realize who the figure is. Callum is standing dejectedly, looking out into the empty night. Gripping onto my courage I fight back my innate desire to comfort him, turning my back on him.

I cautiously head towards the front door, trying to escape unnoticed. Sliding out the front door, the cold, moist air hits my body with a stinging sensation. The moisture pierces Noah, causing him to whimper slightly. Wrapping a blanket around the carrier, I begin running towards the edge of the property.

The thick fog wraps around me, making it difficult to see anything. My feet stammer on the ground, traipsing across the road on just instinct. The fog has a silver glow to it from the moonlight trying to break through. The mist encapsulates the surrounding trees lining the entrance, appearing as if a black and white photo has been smeared with water, causing the sharp lines to blur into the surroundings. A sense of loneliness whispers on the edges of the mist, enhancing my emotional situation. Moisture seizes me to the core, soaking all my belongings. The cold, wet air dances on my face mixing with my warm, salty tears and leaving my skin soaked from this tango of moisture.

The blinding surroundings cause me to stop, trying to get my bearings, when suddenly I notice the bright lights of a car up ahead. A jolt of relief springs within me as I hastily head towards the safety of my escape. Breathlessly I reach the cab, open the door and proceed to throw everything inside. Turning back towards the manor I suddenly notice a light within the room I was staying in turn on. Panic washes over me as I realize someone is discovering my unexpected escape. The light instantly turns off, sending a surging wave of panic over me.

Jumping into the cab I utter forcefully, "Drive now." He peels out, causing a slight sputter of gravel to spew out from behind the car. Gripping tightly onto Noah my tears begin to expel down my face. Unsuccessfully I try and fight my urge not to look, turning around I notice the lights of the front porch turning on. The shimmering rays of the light bouncing off of the fog send a beam straight through my heart. My heart breaks as the glue that once held me together shatters apart, leaving me a raw, vacant shell. Things will now be very different.

Promise

The steady hum from all the returning students vibrates off of the surrounding buildings. The rough bark of this large, unique oak tree is such a sharp contrast to the soft, supple grass as I sit here watching Cambridge come back to life. All the students are the city's life blood. The city and Cambridge University are one; without all the intricate workings of the colleges which form Cambridge, this town would be an empty shell. Even above the myriad of shops and pubs are several lecture rooms. I watch as some professors scurry out of their classrooms and into the awaiting pubs for a quick pint before heading back up to get their rooms ready for the influx of students tomorrow.

Leaning back I look up at the large branches of the oak tree dancing over my head. Bright green leaves swirl over me, causing the sunlight to skip across my face. A warm breeze whirls across me with the smells of sweet flowers, wet grass and strong, dark tea. Taking in a deep breath I fill my lungs full of all the surrounding smells. A strong, retched stench suddenly overpowers everything, stinging my nose. Noah had been sleeping nicely on my lap as we both soak in the needed fresh air. Looking down at Noah I notice his once restful expression has now transformed to one of deep concentration.

Instantly I realize how unprepared I am for this situation. Since we arrived back at our flat yesterday, I couldn't stand sitting around looking at the crib set Callum had let me use anymore. The crib was just a constant reminder of another loss in my life. Deciding to wipe my slate clean, I packed up the crib set this morning. After my expressive purging I needed to get out of my flat as soon as possible. I had hastily left my flat, wanting some sort of escape. I grabbed hold of Noah and nothing else, leaving his diaper bag back at the flat.

Another strong aroma invades the sweet smells around me. Bending down, I utter softly, "Well, Noah, I guess you have decided that our time out here is done." A full smile spreads across my face as I gaze down into his brilliant eyes.

Getting up from my restful spot I notice out of the corner of my eye a large group heading into one of the pubs. Their joyful laughter rings in my ear with a sudden sense of familiarity. A low, yet shrilling voice cuts through all the noise.

"Breanna," this strange yet familiar voice calls to me.

A sudden bolt of panic explodes throughout my body. Looking up I notice a fellow classmate from my only other class heading towards me. Because of my late acceptance to the University I was only able to get two classes, English and American History, which I thought was funny to take here. Conner Fairfield is a sweet, yet kind of irritating boy. As far as his age goes he is probably older than Callum, but socially he acts like a know-it-all young boy. He always tries to assist me with my classwork, assuming that I know nothing about my own country's history. He has strong, handsome features, but as soon as he opens his mouth his features transform from good-looking to nerdy. His sandy blonde hair is always perfectly styled with a sharp, straight part just slightly off the middle; making me want to put my hands in his hair and vigorously mess it up. He would actually be good looking if he knew how to relax the imaginary solid rod that is shoved up inside of him – even just a little bit. Everything on him is perfectly placed and polished. An air of arrogance and superiority rolls all over him as if everyone else is beneath him. His proper posture and manner gives off a slight feminine edge. As long as he keeps his mouth shut I don't mind being around him, but in this particular situation I can tell that he is definitely planning on talking to me.

His seamlessly pressed khakis and polo shirt mirror his rigid personality perfectly. Not a single item of clothing is out of place or wrinkled. A large smile spreads across his face as he rushes over to me. Suddenly he stops just inches away from me. His nose slightly wrinkles up, pulling up the top of his lip with it. An expression of horrific disgust rolls across his face, twisting his looks into a humorous expression. Gazing around curiously, he utters, "What is that most wretched smell?" The pitch to his shrilling voice increases, causing me to laugh.

Quickly I cover my mouth, trying to hide my apparent snicker. He has talked to me before but I have never heard his voice sound like this. Mixed into his squeaking tone is an occasional gag reflex ripping through him, causing his face to twist and crinkle up. His smooth skin and masculine features transform into a scary and quite wimpy expression, now complementing his piercing voice.

A wave of revulsion crawls up my spine and rolls over my head. I have never seen a man react this way to just a baby's diaper. I watch him continue sniffing, trying to figure out where the smell is coming from. I bite down hard onto my tongue, trying to fight a bubbling urge within me to tell him to just "grow a pair." Pushing down my arsenic words I simply utter, "The smell is coming from my son. I need to get him back to my flat so I can change him."

"Wow, I never knew babies could smell that atrocious," a true shocked expression mingled with revulsion consumes his face.

Instantly my eyes open wide in astonishment. A force of disbelief drops down on me, nearly pushing me to the ground. How ignorant and sheltered is this stupid prick? I can't believe he just insulted my son right in front of me, "Yeah, isn't it amazing? I am sure your shit smells like roses and honeysuckle." His face drops in astonishment towards what I just uttered.

I am not in any kind of mood to deal with him today. I just want to leave and go back to my lonely flat and change Noah's diaper. Immediately I turn my back on him and proceed to walk away. My annoyance with him instantly mixes with the anger I am feeling towards Callum, forming a dangerous cocktail. The brew flows through my veins, causing my body to bubble with a vengeful heat.

"Wait, Breanna!" Conner calls out to me. "I am sorry! I didn't mean to offend you," though the tone to his voice is still high, he has regained some control to it.

Turning around I gaze forcefully towards him, "What do you want, Conner?"

Suddenly my heart drops down to the pit of my stomach as I notice Callum and several of his mates walking up to a pub just behind Conner. My eyes narrow as I stare right through Conner. Though his mouth is moving, I can't hear anything Conner is saying, my attention is transfixed onto Callum. My heart spins around within my stomach, causing the vengeful bile ripping through me to taint my heart. Piercing rage flows through my body as I watch Callum happily mingling with his friends, while I stand here in misery. Heartbreak and hatred explode out of me, flowing across the street and hitting Callum directly in the chest, causing him to turn in my direction. Suddenly his caramel eyes meet my gaze. His expression abruptly changes, revealing a sorrowful countenance. Our eyes lock onto each other, causing my anger to break apart like shattered glass. A sensation of want mingled with heartache rips through me now as I am forced to look at him, knowing that I can never taste his lips or his love again.

His eyes quickly glance over at Conner, who is still talking to me, triggering a glimpse of jealousy to roll through his eyes. He glances back at me wearing a mask of distrust and envy. Both of us silently call to each other, but neither one is willing to move. This is the first time I have seen him since I left his house. I knew I was going to have to face him. I just thought it would be in class, not here and not now.

Our world is moving in slow motion as our eyes remain transfixed onto each other. My chest swells, causing my bra to feel tight against it. The only sounds I can hear are my slow, deep breaths and heart slamming against my ribcage. The one thing keeping me grounded to reality is the occasional whiff of Noah's dirty diaper still penetrating the air surrounding me. A pleading sensation rolls off of Callum, burning me to the very core. My heart is pulling me closer to him. He is what I want and need. I don't think I can fight it. Suddenly the bubble we are enveloped in is burst by a female's hand sliding tenderly across Callum's shoulder.

Shaking my reality back into view, I notice Emily now standing next to Callum. The anger that had been shattered instantly envelops my heart again, slamming the door to my heart once more. The vengeful bile once again creeps through my veins like black blood feeding my damaged heart. Turning towards Conner I notice that he is still talking to me, completely unaware of the hypnotic state I have been in.

"Well Breanna, would you like to?"

Looking at him questioningly I utter, "Would I like to what?"

His pompous expression drops, revealing for the first time a sense of vulnerability, "Would you like to accompany me on a date this weekend?"

I had been zoning out the whole time he had been apparently asking me out on a date. I have been too busy locked in my heart's true desire, that I didn't hear one thing Conner had said. Didn't he even realize that I was not listening to him, let alone even looking at him? Quickly I glance up at Emily, whose hand is still placed on Callum's shoulder lovingly, causing my anger to intensify. Callum's eyes are still locked onto me, completely disregarding Emily's touch. His eyes, though, are now bouncing back and forth between me and Conner, completely aware that Conner is asking me out.

Reality washes over me. Callum is moving on and so should I. Why fight my world anymore? It nips at my heels like an unruly dog. I am not allowed to have what I want. I was born into hell and no matter how hard I try to escape it or change my situation it will always suck me back in.

Turning back towards Conner I utter reluctantly, "Yeah, I will go out with you."

A pretentious smile creeps across his face, "You mean, yes, I will go on a date with you," he corrects my grammar.

Irritation rips up my spine, tearing at my flesh. I silently stare at him, trying not to disclose my anger I am feeling for him. It is bad enough that he insulted my son, but then to go and correct my response is unfathomable. His blind arrogance and complete stupidity is amazing. I wonder if he has ever gone on a second date, let alone a first. If he thinks that I am blessed to be able to go out with him, he is living a lie. I only accepted his date because of my present mind set and discouraged situation. My hands begin quivering as I try to fight away the urge to just tell him off. Turning my back on him I begin walking away before I regret my decision.

Yelling back at me, he utters, "Fantastic. I will communicate with you in class about it, then."

My walk home was spent shaking my head rapidly back and forth, recalling the events of today. Walking into my flat, lying in the middle of the floor is the dismantled crib set. Irritation wraps around me like an old familiar friend. I have spent my whole life being mad and irritated at the world and those who are supposed to love me. The only one who exacted any love for me was repossessed from life, like he was never supposed to be for me in the first place.

Walking over to the changing table I quickly remove the cause of Noah's smell and discomfort. A sense of relief shines within his eyes as he begins kicking and cooing joyfully. Lying him down inside of his portable crib, I allow him to play. Walking over to my dresser I grab an envelope from my top drawer. Tracing the wrinkled envelope with my fingers I sit dejectedly down on my bed. I begin gazing at the dirty fold line cutting right through the middle of my name like a symbolic sword splitting me in two.

Andrew's handwriting was always better than mine. He would take time printing each one of the letters in my name with precise placement and technique. I used to have him write my school papers for me because the teachers could read his writing better than mine, which was unique for a boy. Usually it is the girl who has better handwriting. Slowly I take out the long lined paper containing a letter that Andrew had written to me before he died. The pain of that day is so real that it still glides across the surface of my skin like a razor scraping off the epidermis layer, exposing the soft, unprotected dermis layer.

I can remember lying in a fetal position on the floor of our apartment, looking around at all Andrew's things like he was going to walk through the door at any moment. His change of clothing was still strewn across the floor from the day before. I used to get so mad at him for not putting his clothes away, but on that day I was grateful he didn't. I remember walking over to his shirt and gently grabbing hold of it, sniffing it tenderly. His shirt smelled of a strong, clean, musky odor intertwined with the aroma of soap and a fading hint of cologne. He always used to wear cologne that enhanced his natural luscious smell. I used to place my nose on the nape of his neck, inhaling him softly while kissing him.

Tenderly I began folding his shirt for him, gently caressing the soft flannel fabric. Walking over to his drawer, I went to place his shirt inside when I discovered an envelope with my name lovingly printed across the front of it. This same letter now rests carefully across my lap. I have only read it one time, and that was the day I decided to accept my endorsement into Cambridge University. I have held his letter many times within my hands when I needed to feel him near me, but have never opened it again. This time though, I need to hear his voice in my head and feel his words touch my soul. Holding his letter in my trembling hands I begin to read his words, allowing myself to hear his voice ringing in my ears.

Breanna,

I have to first start by saying that I am so sorry. I wanted to keep you away from the pain and sorrow caused by the stupid effects of alcohol. I never thought that my father would start drinking because of my mother's death. He loved my mother more than anything and for the first time I can understand his pain. Breanna, if you were to leave me my heart would be ruined. I would hope that I wouldn't fall into the depths of alcohol's arms, but I am lucky I still have you, whereas my father no longer has my mother. Sometimes the haunting call of what we know is wrong is too strong. I hope that you will someday forgive him for turning to drinking. He is a good man, stupid but good. I knew we had to leave his house, because I was not about to have you live through my father's actions. I love you too much to allow my father to stifle your happiness.

This leads me to my main concern. I saw you hide your acceptance letter to Cambridge University after my mother died. No matter what, you are going to school there even if I have to sell everything I own, promise me. You are my wife, not my maid. You are not here to take care of me. We are to take care of each other and this is my time to take care of you. You deserve this. Though you were dragged through a crappy life by your mother, you have been able to maintain all A's. You are an incredible student. Me, on the other hand, I suck at school work. You have no idea how wonderful you are. If you could only see what I see on a daily basis, your ego would be huge.

A huge smile spreads across my face, allowing the tears I am shedding to stream into my mouth. The salty stings of my tears roll within me, bringing with it memories of Andrew. I can remember on several occasions I would catch him just staring at me. I would always ask him what he was staring at and he would just simply reply, "Someone who has no idea how wonderful she is."

My heart is dancing with pain and joy right now, pain being the dominating lead. Turning my gaze back to his letter, I continue reading through tear filled eyes.

You are the smartest, kindest, and most loving girl I have ever met. I knew that the day this obnoxious girl came knocking on my door, interrupting my video games, asking if I wanted to play. You weren't afraid of anything, least of all a gangly thirteen year old boy. The moment I looked into your hazel green eyes I knew you had me. I never wanted to be separated from you. And still to this day your eyes and all of you have me. I will go with you wherever you go. We may not have much, but at least we have each other. You deserve the chance to find out how special you are. You have always felt some kind of pull to England. I have no idea why! It is a God awful cold country, but I am willing to freeze my ass off for you. I love you, don't you ever forget it. I want you to be happy.

He had scribbled through a sentence, trying to block it out. For the first time I try and decipher what he had written then promptly scratched out. Gazing deeply at the long black mark, I try to unearth some magical x-ray powers hidden deep within me. My eyes are beginning to feel the strain when suddenly I figure out the sentence, causing my heart to stop.

If anything should ever happen to me, please go on with your life and find someone who makes you happy. You deserve it.

My heart drops to my toes, leaving my soul feeling empty inside. Andrew's deep voice rings within my ears and echoes in my chest. A warm sensation wraps around me, enveloping me in an invisible mist. The warm sensation explodes over me as it crawls on my skin, up my spine, taking residence within my mind. On occasion I have heard of loved ones finding letters or pictures after someone's death explaining their desires if anything were to happen to them. I have heard people call these things tender mercies. Perhaps the person is given a glimpse, allowing them to give these gifts before they can't. A sense of immeasurable love consumes me as I once again read his words, as if he is giving me permission from the grave, permitting me to fall in love again and be happy.

My hand tenderly strokes the paper, gliding across each word with great care. I read his final sentence carefully.

I hope that you will listen to me this way. You are sooo stubborn (and I love you for that), but don't let your stubbornness stop you from getting what you deserve.
I love you,
Andrew

Gently folding the letter I place it tenderly back in the envelope. Holding his letter close to my heart I begin to expel the sadness pressing down on me. The silence in my flat is deafening. I gaze around at all the tiny furnishings, noticing that nothing in here is mine except a few pictures, some baby things, and my clothes. I had left everything behind when I decided to come here. I can remember not knowing how I was going to be able to afford the plane ticket here, let alone living in one of the most expensive places. I knew I was running to an unknown country, pregnant and poor.

I didn't know how I was going to keep my promise to Andrew and go to school in England when I couldn't even afford a city bus ticket, let alone my living expenses. Until a few days after his funeral, I received a call from a life insurance company stating that Andrew had taken out a life insurance policy declaring me as sole beneficiary. They had informed me that his parents also had a policy with them, stating Andrew as their sole beneficiary, thus transferring everything now to me. Andrew not only took care of me in life, but he made sure I would still be taken care of if he should die.

This is the only reason I have been able to go to school here. Guilt rips through me as I stare out at my furnished flat knowing that I am only able to pay for this because of Andrew's death. I would give this all up, be homeless and starving if Andrew could be next to me again. He was right, we may have been poor, but we had each other and that was enough. Money doesn't fertilize the joy deep within. It can cause pain, eating at your soul like a poisonous spider slowly devouring you. I opened up my heart to Callum, but money is what separated us and shoved the door shut, forcing the both of us to live in misery. There are so many things between us stopping us from ever coming together. The space between us is filled with pain, loss, deception, obligations, and yes, even Noah drives a gap between us. Though Callum loves Noah now, would he someday transfer resentment towards him, like Callum's stepfather resents him?

I was doomed from the very beginning. No matter how hard I try to get off my inevitable path, I am flung back on with great force. Walking over to

Noah, I gaze down at his sweet sleeping face. His resemblance to Andrew is amazing. He even sleeps like him. Both arms flung up over his head, free from any restraint binding them down. Tenderly I stroke his dark hair, causing him to grunt slightly. His full lips begin forming tightly around an imaginary nipple, making a soft sucking motion. Looking down, I utter softly, "Well, it looks like it is just you and me here."

Suddenly there is a loud knock at my door, causing a jolting vibration to run through the both of us. Noah twitches violently, but then slowly regains his sound sleep. Hastily I rush to the door so whoever this person is won't slam on it again, causing Noah to wake up. Trepidation rolls over me as I grip onto the door handle, pausing slightly. Shedding my over-excited imagination off of me like useless dead skin, I proceed to open the front door.

Shock and dismay hit me like a hurricane, nearly knocking me over. Standing in front of me is Charlotte Hughes, Callum and Olivia's mother. Her small, petite frame fills the doorway like a giant. Her slim-fitting slacks flow seamlessly with her silk button up shirt. She is wearing elegant high heels, making her appear taller than she actually is. Her shoulder length blonde hair is styled impeccably, not a single strand is out of place despite the rainy, wet weather here. Her round, pixie face mirrors

Olivia's perfectly. The strong genetics given from mother to daughter is uncanny. Mrs. Hughes hides her age flawlessly, causing her to look more like Olivia's sister than her mother. Gazing up into her eyes I am taken back by the sharp resemblance to Callum's eyes. This is their only similarity. Her liquid caramel color eyes stare right at me, almost solidifying right before me.

"Mrs. Hughes, what a surprise. What are you doing here?"

Her eyes bore deep into mine, ripping at my soul with firm, flat eyes, "Is Callum here?"

Confusion streams across my face, "No."

"Good, because my dear, we need to talk," she pushes her way past me, entering my flat with no hesitation.

Leave

Charlotte Hughes stands quietly in the middle of my flat, staring at the dismantled crib set which was Callum's ancestral crib. Her long, thin fingers delicately trace the large H carved on the headboard. Carefully she dusts off her fingertips as she gradually turns, assessing my small, yet clean flat. The furrow between her eyes deepens slightly as she takes in the size and meager furnishings. It may not be much but it is conducive to my needs. I have everything a young college student and single mother needs. There is a small bedroom, basically a bed shoved into what looks like a large closet; an adequate kitchen, married brilliantly with the living room, forming one great-room. If you were to stand in the center of what is organized as the living room you can see the entire flat just by spinning around.

The furnishings that came with the flat are plain, but comfortable. The mattress, though old, is quite comfy and clean. Growing up I used to sleep on the floor or perhaps some mattress that God knows what happened on it, so this one is perfect. There is a small couch positioned just under the only window in the flat. In front of the couch is a large glass coffee table that also doubles as a kitchen table for me. In the corner opposite the couch is where the crib that Callum let me borrow used to be, but now holds Noah's portable crib. On either side of the crib are the cherry wood dresser and the soft blue club chair. Mrs. Hughes stops in front of the club chair, eyeing it dubiously. Running her hand along the back of the chair allows me to catch sight of her large diamond ring balanced poorly against her delicate fingers.

"This is an exceptionally nice chair, made of high quality," her tone holds a hint of skepticism as she eyes me suspiciously.

"Thank you…" Standing in front of the chair she turns facing me, pulling on the upper thigh section of her slacks as she sits gracefully in the chair. "Have a seat," I add sarcastically.

"I will, considering my son most likely bought this," she utters enigmatically as her caramel eyes look upon me with a heavy air of distrust.

"Why would you think that? I can afford my own furnishings," I utter in a flaccid tone, trying to hide my insincerity.

A corner of her mouth pulls up faintly as her head tilts slightly to one side. Her eyes never waver from their intention – me, "Breanna dear, look around…" Her eyes scan my scantily decorated flat. "This is a meagerly decorated flat while this chair and bureau are of a higher quality. Besides, the crib and bureau belong to my son. Do you really expect me to believe they just magically showed up here?" an acidic edge rolls off her high pitched voice.

The duplicity undulating through me shatters instantly, causing my palms to sweat nervously. Walking over to the small couch I sit down, wiping my hands aggressively on the tops of my thighs. My heart slams against my chest as I meet Mrs. Hughes' eyes dead on. Though Callum's mom is a petite woman she is very intimidating. She is aware of every little detail and has her fingers on society's pulse, allowing her to breath in every bit of gossip.

Staring at her confidently, I utter, "In a way, yes, they did just show up magically."

"I am not easily fooled."

"Good, because I am not joking." Straightening my posture to mimic hers, I add carefully, "When I came home from the hospital they were already in here. I did not ask for them or use Callum or Olivia in any way to get what I want. I didn't want this. Callum also hired a nanny…a Miss McNally. But I am going to be paying for her myself until I can find someone else to watch Noah while I am in class. I am not an avaricious person," my voice is firm yet flat, holding a respectful tone yet defending myself vigorously.

Her face relaxes somewhat, "So you did not ask Callum to help you financially?"

"Let me reiterate one more time. No, I have not and will not ask for his financial help. I am not in love with him for his money, Mrs. Hughes."

Instantly she sits back in the chair, crossing her legs effortlessly as she stares at me with her cool, liquid eyes, "You love my son?"

"Yes," I utter softly, wishing that my heart didn't.

"Why?"

"Excuse me?" The furrow between my eyes deepens as I am taken back by her question. Adjusting in my seat I lean forward, making myself clear, "He is your son. I would hope that you know all the reasons why someone would love him…"

"Breanna, don't bloody patronize me. I know all of Callum's great qualities…"

"Do you? Because I distinctly recall you asking if he was the father of my child like he is some heartless bloke just spreading his seed everywhere. He could have run from Noah and me, but he didn't," the heat within my core pulsates out, quickening my breathing as I choke out each word.

"Why is he so drawn to you and your son, anyway?" she did not ask facetiously, putting down my appearance, but sincerely wanting to know. "He is bloody irresponsible. He cannot fanny around anymore like a rebellious child. It is time for him to grow up." Mrs. Hughes' features remain in complete control, guarding her every action as if the mere idea of losing her temper is something a lady cannot afford to do. The only indication she is getting upset is the occasional drop of a British swear word and slang.

"I am not completely sure why he is drawn to us. When I went into labor in our class he rescued me, staying with me the entire time. I knew no one here and he was willing to be there for me. He is not being irresponsible or messing around." My mind slowly gets lost remembering that day, as my voice twirls with sincere love and respect, "Perhaps we formed a bond that day, or perhaps it's because he and Noah come from a very similar situation."

A sharp, disbelieving exhale pushes out of her nose, "How is your fatherless son anything like Callum?"

My eyes narrow in response to her sudden demeaning statement. A bubbling force pushes through me, causing the bile in my stomach to increase. "He is not a fatherless child. He had a wonderful and loving father, my late husband, whom my son will never know," my voice is thick with an acidic edge as I spit the words out.

Stillness pushes through the room as if someone has hit a pause button, freezing everything and everyone. The thick air envelops the both of us as her eyes widen with a horrific parallel memory. Silence looms between us, when suddenly Mrs. Hughes walks tenderly over to Noah's crib. Her shoulders relax as she gazes down at Noah. A heavy air of reminiscence washes over her normally rigid appearance, revealing a softer side. Her eyes transform, divulging a painful memory.

She reaches into the crib, tenderly stroking Noah's head, "Callum hates me for the things that I have done. Though a mother will do anything for her child."

Regret mingled with an aching need for understanding ripples on the soft surface of her skin. A shimmering tear glistens in the corner of her firm eyes. Compassionately I add, "Callum doesn't hate you."

A tremor of irritation crawls across the floor vibrating up her legs and through her spine, causing her body to stiffen back up. Turning towards me again she utters in a controlled tone, "Breanna, you may think you know about Callum and my situation, but you don't. If I want your words of encouragement then I will ask for it, but as of now you need to mind your own bloody business."

An offensive jolt rips through me, "Mrs. Hughes, I was just trying to help because I know where you are coming from."

Her eyes instantly narrow, causing her liquid caramel eyes to solidify, "You know nothing about where I am coming from."

Placing myself on the same defensive level I stand up, meeting her gaze head on, "Callum told me about how his father passed away before he was born. I also heard you and Callum talk about it the other night." An instant regret of what I had just divulged consumes me. I had accidentally revealed my apparent eavesdropping.

Taking a few steps towards me she looks up into my face firmly. Though Mrs. Hughes is several inches shorter than me, her self-assurance and tough personality make her appear like she is overpowering me, causing a sudden surge of anxiety to roll up my spine. A gleam of vexation explodes within her eyes, revealing a frightening side to her. The furrow between her eyes narrows, causing her face to match the anger within her eyes, "You were bloody listening in on a private conversation!" The air within the room drops several degrees, causing a shiver to roll up my spine.

"I am sorry. I just needed to know the truth. Callum had already lied to me and I thought this was the best way to discover the truth," a soft strain takes over my voice, causing my breathing to increase.

Though I knew my actions were wrong that night I held firm to my decision, pleading my case. The cold that had been radiating off of her, transforming my flat into an icebox, slowly dissipates. She forcefully shuts her eyes, blocking out any visual communications. A heavy sigh rips through her, causing her chest to heave. Her soft, full lips form a gentle pucker while her breath escapes out her mouth. Composure flows down her body, allowing all of her muscles to slowly deflate.

Gradually she opens her eyes, revealing a soft liquid caramel appearance. My heart leaps slightly as I gaze into Callum's mirror image. Her expression now imitates Callum's perfectly. Her once cold demeanor has shattered, revealing a sympathetic core. A capricious tone comes over her, "Did you discover the truth?"

A heavy weight pushes down on me, deflating my puffed up appearance, dropping my shoulders in defeat, "Yes."

"And may I ask what the truth is?" Her voice is now soft, exposing a deep understanding.

Closing my eyes, I try and fight back the tears now knocking on the doors to my eyes. The once cold environment now has transformed, sending warm currents to push through me. The tension that had been surrounding us evaporates, leaving a sincere empathetic comprehension. Slowly I open my eyes, still fighting the tears attempting to invade my eyes, "The truth is I can never be with Callum. He is bound by obligations."

Another forceful sigh rushes through her, dropping her protective shield even further. Her soft face now exposes a crippling pain. She walks back over to Noah, compassionately checking on him. Her gaze stays locked onto him as her mind gets lost in thought, "Before I met Callum's father there was someone that I loved, but it would have been a public disgrace if I would have divulged my feelings for him. I had to let him go. It destroyed me. For years I wondered what would have happened if I had chosen him instead of my social responsibility." Turning back towards me, her eyes are full of emotion, yet expose a stern recognition, "If I would have acted on my impulse I would have been a fair worker's wife."

Shock explodes over my face, setting me back slightly, "You told Callum that Harry was just a childish crush."

A corner of her mouth pulls up, giving a disdainful smile, bringing recollections to her mind of my apparent eavesdropping, "Do you think I was about to give him fuel to throw on his fire…not bloody likely. Besides, the truth is, if I would have not walked away from Harry then I would have never met Callum's father. Though my family still disapproved of our union, Neil, Callum's father, came from an aristocratic history. So you see, Breanna, it may be a hard thing for you to comprehend, but leaving him is the best possible scenario."

My tears now are betraying me, falling freely down my cheeks. Understanding rips through me. Though Callum's mother has been harsh towards me, I suddenly realize her true motivation. She is just trying to protect her son from public ridicule, which will inevitably come if he were to stay with me. I have been looking at his situation through naive rose-colored glasses, refusing to see how things work here in the upper class of England.

"Mrs. Hughes, I have already told Callum we can no longer be together. I understand that I am not only from America, but I come from a very different world. The only heritage I have to offer is an alcoholic mother and a non-existent father. I have no idea what I was thinking, falling for Callum. I will never escape my destiny. The sooner I grasp it the better."

"Breanna, you are an American, where anybody can become what they want to be… in America," she states flatly, with a subtle persuasive hint, which is as subtle as a bomb going off.

"What are you saying? Are you asking me to leave and go back to America?"

Her voice lowers in respect, "Yes. As long as you are here Callum will never let you go."

My heart drops deep into the pit of my stomach. Everything I have been trying to run from suddenly catches up to me. I have no idea how I can go back and face everything. My life in America is empty. I have nothing to go back to, no house, no apartment, no belongings, no family, I have nothing. Everything I owned I have gotten rid of. I hired a realtor to sell Andrew's parents' house, and when I left to come to England I donated all mine and Andrew's belongings to the next tenant. I can't humiliate myself even further by knocking on my mother's trailer door. I will not put my son or myself through that kind of life again. I left that world. It will kill me if I am forced to go back to it.

The air within the room thickens, making it hard for me to breath. Anxiety pulsates throughout my chest as I try and grasp the reality of my life. The faster I run the harder my past pulls on me, like a mouse attempting to free an elephant from quicksand. Looking up into Charlotte Hughes' eyes I notice a glimpse of remorse streaming through them. My breathing intensifies as a chill runs up my neck, causing the hair on my neck to stand erect. Slowly I go to give her a response, when suddenly there is a loud knock at my door. My body jumps at the sudden sound, breaking the silence. Quivering jolts vibrate throughout my body, causing me to tremble slightly.

Hastily I walk over to the door, trying to avoid answering her question. Swinging the door open I am suddenly taken aback, "Breanna, we need to talk. You cannot bloody run away and then avoid me. I am going off my trolley right now."

"Callum, is that you?" Charlotte Hughes echoes from behind me.

"Mum?" he replies in complete shock.

An instant wave of irritation slams against me. Of course Callum would have to show up when his mother is here. Let's just make the prospects of my life a Hughes family decision. Looking up at Callum's face I notice his eyes narrow, causing the liquid caramel color to solidify like his mother's. A firm expression now consumes his face, holding his once soft countenance hostage. He gazes down at me, translating his apologies with his eyes.

Firmly pushing the door open he stomps aggressively into my flat. "Mother, what in bloody hell are you doing here in Breanna's flat?" his voice is firm with a thick layer of acid spewing off of each word.

Charlotte's eyes harden, mirroring Callum's, "Callum, do not talk to me like that." Her voice is firm as she spits out her demands like an angry parent correcting a willful child.

"I will bloody speak to you as I damn well please, Mother. You have no right coming here, putting your bloody demands and qualifications on Breanna!"

Suddenly Noah begins to whimper slightly as Callum and his mother continue arguing. I feel like an intruder in my own home as a sea of angry comments, laced with a now heavy British accent, rolls out of them. A continual rapid fire of incoherent slang, swear words, and rebuking flows out of their mouths. I can now see where Olivia gets her tempestuous nature from. Callum's mother had been able to control her emotions with me, but now both Callum and his mother have given in to the gutterick speech, causing their accents to thicken into a garbled mess.

Tenderly I pick up Noah, cuddling him close to my bosom. His soft, yet wiry features melt into me as a significant amount of arguing continues behind us. Holding Noah against me I attempt to soothe him when suddenly a clear statement vibrates out of Callum, "I know she is American trailer rubbish, but I don't bloody care, I still love her."

Though Callum knows where I come from, he has never made me feel like trash…until now. I have never heard him refer to me in a derogatory way, even if he is just repeating what his mother had stated. His words pierce my heart with a sting that can never be repaired. Words don't leave your body black and blue, but they bruise the soul and taint the mind. His words definitely bruised my soul. My mind spins rapidly as the atmosphere within my flat intensifies. The heated anger expelling from them matches my own heated rage, causing the tension to affect Noah's mood. He is fussing and fidgeting with aggressive jerks, as if his body is mimicking the contentious atmosphere.

Walking over to the dresser, I grab a diaper and persist in freshening him up. Neither Callum nor his mother is aware of me or Noah. They are still consumed in their heated debate. My flat has transformed into the one thing I always resented, my mother's home. Growing up our home was filled with yelling and contention. It was never a place to escape to – it was what I always tried to escape from. A resolute awkwardness presses down on me as I listen to them fighting about me and my disreputable history. This environment is becoming poison for both Noah and I. Instead of throwing them both out, I decide to flee. Remembering to grab Noah's diaper bag this time, I rush out my door.

Heading out of the building's main exit, I am hit by the cool, twilight air enveloping me as it begins extinguishing the raging fire that burns within me. A heavy mist delicately falls, tainting the surroundings with a coruscating sparkle as it sticks to everything like glitter being poured over the entire city. The roads are quiet, as usual. Most people walk or ride bikes from place to place, despite the weather. This night is no different. The roads are dotted with groups of people intermingling with each other, a perfect backdrop for me to get lost in. Wrapping a blanket tightly around Noah, I abscond through the crowds of people, hoping to intertwine with the throngs of individuals.

The twilight sky mingles with the delicate mist, covering everything, setting the city ablaze. The black shadows of buildings and trees invade my vision with their colorless images against a lit backdrop. The fading skylight washes away everyone's details of their faces, leaving only their silhouettes. The darkening street suddenly is brought to life by the illuminating power of street lamps and interior lights radiating out from all the windows. The lights heighten the crystal appearance caused by all the millions of droplets over everything. The brilliant lights delicately dance on the surface of the River Cam with a glistening kaleidoscope of bright yellow lights.

Peace begins to envelop me, shedding the tension and heartache of tonight from me. Standing on the edge of the River Cam, I watch as the light bounces off of my mirror reflection. The girl within the water echoes the call uttered by Callum's mom – leave. Staring down into the reflection I catch sight of someone approaching me. Abruptly I spin on my heels, facing the invader of my respite.

"Callum, what are you doing here?" I utter in breathless surprise.

Callum apprehensively approaches me. Though the twilight sky has dissipated into darkness, the glowing lights from all the buildings bounce off of his face, revealing his incredulous expression. Sweat glistens around the top of his forehead like he has been ardently running, trying to find me. Grabbing hold of my shoulders he utters, "Please tell me that my mum is wrong," though his voice is firm, it is laced with an almost pleading demand.

His hands grip tightly onto me, holding me firmly in front of him. His fingers dig into the soft hollow spaces on the tops of my shoulders, causing my arms to tingle in pain. The lights shimmer off of his heavily shadowed face, exposing his tortuous expression. The torrid nature of the argument he and his mother had been in shines vibrantly off of him, like red hot coals left smoldering.

"Callum, let go of me. You are hurting me," I state firmly, as I gaze at several bystanders looking in our direction.

"Tell me Breanna, are you leaving?" He continues holding onto me but loosens his grip slightly, allowing the pain in my arm to dissipate.

"Why do you care anyway? I am just American trailer rubbish, remember?" I utter vehemently.

A disconsolate exhale rushes through his full lips, causing his body to deflate. Relinquishing his grip on me, his eyes lose their luster as he looks down upon me apologetically, "Breanna, I didn't mean…"

"Stop," I interrupt, not wanting to hear a frivolous apology, "What I do is no longer your concern." A heavy sigh rolls off of me, "I come from trash. I have always known it, and now I know you believe it, too."

Turning my back on him I begin hastily walking away when suddenly I hear him softly utter my name. It rolls along the surface of the mist, slamming against my back, piercing into my core, revealing his internal pain. Ignoring his pleading call I continue to walk away from him, leaving all my hopes and dreams behind. My decision is made. I am leaving as soon as my classes are done.

Apologies

A monotonous routine has ensued this week. I attempt to avoid Callum in every situation. It has been very difficult to achieve that goal when he is in my class. He has tried to talk to me on several occasions, but has been stopped by either our professor or Emily. She has managed to weasel her way into every aspect of his life, though he tries to avoid her persistent advances. I have locked myself back into the iron-clad vault I had built around myself after Andrew's death, allowing me to focus solely on the things that can't hurt me, like Noah, school work, and packing. Gratefully I have been able to retain the services of Miss McNally at a greatly discounted price. She has agreed to sit with Noah during my class time only, thus allowing me to finish the last two weeks of schooling for this Easter term.

My dreams of getting a college degree evaporated that night with Callum and his mother. Once I leave England my fate is sealed. The future of a nineteen year old, working, single mother on welfare is bleak. I am completely aware that I am now heading down the same path as my mother, and though it should frighten me, I have dolorously come to grips with it. The road I am now on is a familiar one. There are no surprises allowing me to get hurt along the way. I just need to get through these next two weeks with very little incidence. Once I am back in America I will be able to retain my hard outer shell and just live day by day. The only obstacle standing in my way now is the pointless date with Conner I fatuously accepted.

Walking down Queens Road towards my class, I suddenly notice Olivia sitting under a large, ornate tree. Her eyes are closed as if she is meditating. Her soft blonde pixie hairstyle frames her chiseled features perfectly. Her usual feisty expression is hidden by her contemplative state she is succumbing to. Sadness radiates off her, pressing into my chest, filling my mind with regret. Tumbling waves of guilt surge within my stomach as I watch my only friend's spirited personality diminished by my traitorous behavior. I had cut her deep since I had filleted our friendship, gutting her to the core. Regret over my tumultuous behavior causes me to realize that I need to mend the bridge between us before I leave. I had only pushed her away because I was hoping to completely sever my connection to Callum. Since I will be leaving soon, I need to apologize.

Apprehension consumes me as I walk towards Olivia. My heart slams against my chest, causing my breathing to intensify, while my body reacts like I am walking towards a hangman's noose. The warm sun ripples down my exposed arms, seeping under my skin, attempting to eliminate the goose-bumps covering my apprehensive body. My anxiety slowly recedes into the far corners of my mind as I watch Olivia's face soften.

"You know, I should tell you to bugger off after the way you treated me," she utters fastidiously. Her eyes are still closed while she leans back against the tree's trunk languidly, like a sleeping sprite.

Stopping instantly in my tracks I utter in astonishment, "What…How did…"

"Breanna, you are about as sneaky as a damn elephant. I could hear your heavy breathing from far away," her body still lies dreamily against the tree, but her eyes now slowly regain their conscious awareness. Though her soft brown eyes ripple with tender emotions, her chiseled features are firm with skepticism.

A cool breeze rolls over me, instantly reigniting my goose-bumps, sending a rolling chill up my spine. I am not completely convinced the breeze is the culprit behind my sudden chill; Olivia's firm expression is most likely the cause of my sudden sensation. Wrapping my arms tightly around me I begin vigorously stroking my exposed arms, melting the dappled bumps back into my skin. This time I firmly walk towards her, taking no care in trying to be subtle about it. Standing now just inches away from her I dejectedly sit down next to her, gazing back into her eyes.

"Olivia, I am so sorry for the way I treated you. You have been an exemplary friend and you did not deserve that."

A long silence looms between us as her eyes remain locked onto mine. Nervously I begin fidgeting, attempting to detach the death stare she has on me. My foot starts bouncing rapidly beneath my pretzel-folded legs. The only thing cutting through the silence is a flock of small birds swirling above us in the tree. Breaking free from her gaze I look up at the acrobatic birds, flipping from branch to branch like trapeze artists demonstrating their skills. Their light blue bodies and painted yellow breasts swirl through the tree with a kaleidoscope of spring colors. Chirps and vibrant songs escape their tiny beaks, giving some kind of reprieve from the ominous silent treatment Olivia is dishing out.

"Do you think that is long enough?" she asks with a hint of sarcasm twirling within her solid tone. Her eyes remain locked onto me, as I look at her dubiously.

"Is what long enough?"

A slight smile tickles the corners of her mouth, illuminating a mischievous grin, "The silent treatment and death stare."

Pulling my eyes tightly together, deepening the furrow between them, I gaze at her incredulously, "Were you just messing with me?"

A full smile creeps across her face, causing her eyes to twinkle with roguish delight, "I wanted you to squirm in your seat a little bit. Did it work?"

"What the hell? Of course it worked! Your eyes can burn a hole through steel!" A loud belly laugh rolls through her, causing her to double over in abdominal pain. "That is not funny! You had me sweating in my boots. I almost got up and left!"

Her laugh is consuming her, making it difficult to talk, "You are not wearing boots," she stammers out, hissing through her teeth.

"I know, it is just an expression." Her laughter is getting contagious. I try and fight the vibrating sensation rolling in my stomach, but the urge is too strong. The deep belly laugh explodes out of me, sending me into an uncontrolled fit of laughter. The pendulum of emotions undulates through me, causing my mind to spin, not quite sure of what we are laughing about.

Breaking free from our facetious laughter I gain some control asking, "Does this mean you forgive me?"

Slowly her laughter dissipates, leaving her slightly panting, "Breanna, I forgave you that night. I knew why you were pushing me away." Her breathing slowly resumes its normal pace. A sympathetic expression comes over her, causing her eyes to glisten with respect, "You love my brother. And for some bloody reason you feel you don't…no, you *can't* have him."

A flood of tears threatens to spill over the protective dam holding them at bay. I have never cried this much. I was always the tough one, constantly holding myself together. Now it seems like all my pent up emotions have been set free. Her hand tenderly envelops mine, squeezing it with a reassuring grasp. "There is a reason. When I left you to listen in on Callum and your mother, I heard the truth. My world can never mix with yours." Swallowing firmly, I push the thick lump in my throat back down, forcing my tears to stand down. Continuing I add, "Your mother also paid me a visit this past weekend, reiterating what I already knew."

"What in bloody hell was she thinking? My mother never raised us to treat people like that."

Anger now takes ownership within her body, causing her voice to quiver.

"She was thinking like a mother, wanting the best for her son and the best is not me." Closing my eyes I exhale forcefully, pushing out the trepidation surging within my chest, "I am leaving, going back to America, as soon as this Easter term is over…"

"Like bloody hell you are," she interrupts, tossing my hand away as her body erupts to an erect position, gazing at me with a firm look of dissidence.

Her rigid voice causes me to recoil, startling me slightly, "Olivia, it is for the best. As long as I am here Callum will not be able to move forward, neither will I. Besides, my life is an alcoholic mother and a trailer trash future," my voice vibrates with self-loathing.

"Bloody hell Breanna, that is not your life, it is your *excuse*," her teeth bite off the last word, cutting through it like a crisp apple.

"It is not my excuse! I have tried everything to break free from its tenacious pull. But no matter how hard I try to escape, my reality slaps me in the face." A surge of anger bubbles inside of me, "Besides, you don't understand, you live in a picture perfect world…"

"Blimey, you're right," she utters facetiously. Her voice is thick with disdain as she mocks my comparison, "We just had a bloody photographer out at our house, taking pictures of our *perfect* family," her tongue snaps on the word perfect. "There is my overbearing mother who only married my father for his social stability. Next is my emotionally distant father, who cares more about his public career than his own family. My half-brother, who is being forced to take a path that will unavoidably ruin his life. And then there is me, the daughter who screams to be heard over all the chaos. So, yes, I guess you are right, we do have a picture perfect family. Or shall I say, a normal family. Though our residences are different, we are still the same. I am also trailer rubbish, just shut behind a posh door. Everyone has trials, no one is immune to them, but you don't see me running away from them."

"Exactly, I ran away from them when I came here. Perhaps I need to face my world head on, and the only way I can do that is to go back." Shaking my head dejectedly, I utter softly, "Why did I come here? I should have never kept my promise to Andrew, he would have never known anyways."

I hunch over, burying my face in my hands, attempting to hide my emotions. A sudden quiet stillness rolls over me. Even the chirping birds have ceased in their joyful singing. The echoing hum of all the students heading to their classes rings in the far corners of my ears, making it sound like they are walking through a long tunnel. My body slowly quivers as I try to push my emotions back down into the pit of my stomach.

"Breanna, you were supposed to come here, not because your late husband told you to. Blimey, can't you see why?" Olivia's voice drops to a near whisper, enhancing her sharp British accent, "You leave now, you *will* be running away from your future and into the arms of your torrid past."

"At least it will be into the arms of something willing to hold me," I chime in. "I am sorry Olivia, but there is nothing you can do or say to change my mind, so you might as well give up." I stand up quickly, causing my weak legs to quiver under my weight. I have been sitting pretzel style for so long my feet and legs have gone numb. Fighting through the prickling sensation, I stand erect, gazing down into Olivia's firm yet tender eyes.

"Well, Breanna, I guess I misjudged you. I thought you were a bloody fighter, but I was wrong. You just submit to whatever is thrown at you."

"That is not true. I have had to fight for everything in my life."

Olivia stands up, attempting to meet my gaze head on, but her petite frame causes her to stand several inches below me, "If you leave then it is true, and my brother deserves someone who will fight for him as hard as he is willing to fight for her."

"I am exhausted. I can't fight any more."

"Then good-bye Breanna, I hope you will be happy in the life you have chosen," she walks tenaciously past me, sending tingling vibrations rushing through me. Her firm, distant face reflects her vexation towards me.

A cold chill brushes over the epidermis layer of my skin causing my body to prickle with goose-bumps. A sick feeling deep in my gut pushes up as I watch Olivia walk away. Though Olivia believes it is my choice to leave, she is wrong. Choice is a luxury saved for those with hope, and hope disintegrated the moment I overheard Callum and his mother's conversation. Resolve now spins rapidly in my head, grasping the unyielding truth of who I am and what I will become. Firmly gripping hold of my emotions, clenching down on my jaw, I hastily head to class.

Awkward

A lingering wave of negative tenacity brushes over the surface of my mind, expelling a pessimistic attitude. The dark aura seeping out of me like deadly gas from a toxic waste facility fills the classroom with a thick layer of tension. The herd of fellow classmates pours through the entrance to the room, adding a layer of their exuberant attitudes into the mix, diluting my nay-saying attitude. Slowly I encompass the dark, street-smart temperament I was raised with yet fought so hard to deny, causing everyone to avoid me like the black plague; which is what I am right now, a plague infecting those around me.

The door to the classroom is left ajar, allowing all the students to freely flow into the room. Turning towards the entrance I instantly notice Callum and Olivia standing out in the hall talking. Olivia's petite frame is dwarfed next to Callum's tall, lean physique. His frame instantly increases in girth and height as he reacts to something she has just divulged, causing him to look like a medieval warrior. The muscles in his jaw quiver in revolt from the strain he is inflicting on them. Gripping his fists tightly together triggers the lean muscles in his arms to amplify, putting excessive pressure against his sleeves. An awkward silence looms between them as Olivia continues divulging – I can only assume – my surreptitious decision to leave. His eyes narrow with rage as his gaze deliberately turns in my direction. His normal soft caramel eyes blaze with disappointment while he stares deep into my eyes. A piercing sting sears through my soul with regret, yet a subtle glimmer of satisfaction ripples on the surface of my mind. Though I did not want Olivia to divulge my plan to Callum, the subconscious part of my mind clearly knows what is taking place. As if my mind is attempting to take revenge on him for the deceitful lies and pain he inflicted on me.

Reacting to his ominous stare I twist the corner of my mouth up revealing a treacherous smile. His head shakes slightly back and forth as he utters something to Olivia. She too turns in my direction, giving me a matching smile, though hers is filled with satisfaction over her obvious choice to tell Callum. Deep down I know she is hoping that her apparent tattle tailing may perhaps hinder my decision to leave. But there is nothing she or Callum can do to change my mind. Olivia stretches up on her tiptoes, giving Callum a strong hug as she whispers something in his ear. The subtle words obviously have something to do with me, because he turns once again in my direction with a look of complete understanding searing within his face.

Mr. Bramble walks past Callum, tenderly giving him a double 'man slap' on his back, bringing his attention to the forefront that it is time to start class. Callum proudly walks into the room. Walking past me he lightly taps the top of my table, getting my attention. He softly utters, "We need to talk."

Shaking my head in refusal, I whisper firmly, "No, we don't."

A determined smile spreads across his face as he adds threateningly, "You are not physically strong enough to stop me. If I have to throw you over my shoulder and carry you someplace – I will." He arrogantly strolls off to his table, wearing a triumphant smile.

I am left sitting, unable to move at my table, feeling the reverberating, alarming and yet slightly lascivious remark spin within my mind. The thought of Callum forcefully overpowering me leaves my body burning in want. My skin becomes highly sensitive, feeling the air dance across the surface. My mind instantly recalls all the times Callum claimed his power over me. Though I try hard to push the mental image down, my mind is not cooperating. Olivia is right, I love Callum, and as long as I am around him I will be in his power. This is a perfect example. Though I know it is best to stay away from him, just the thought of having him grab hold of me, refusing to let me go, sets my skin on fire. Heat pulsates through me, causing my skin to ignite as I stare down at my table, trying to gain control. Vibrating from the far corner of my mind I hear my last name echo in the distance.

"Miss Hayes!" the booming voice explodes through my torrid thoughts.

A rumbling roar of laughter bursts all around me, instantly bringing my mind back to reality. Looking around the room I am completely taken back by the sudden change of seating arrangements. There are several groups consisting of two or three people sporadically placed throughout the room. Complete dismay washes over me as to how I could have missed the obvious shuffling of students all around me. My mind spins in confusion as the students continue their laughter. Echoing from the front corner of the room a female voice reverberates above all the laughter stating, "Bloody barmy wanker."

"Emily, belt up!" a smooth, low voice coming from the back of the room cuts through the noise.

"Miss Hayes, are you alright?" Mr. Bramble states questioningly.

"Yes, I am fine. I am sorry, I was just lost in thought, that's all."

"You are lost al 'right," Gavin chimes in. Suddenly a deep and forceful throat clearing echoes from the back, causing Gavin to utter a quick apology.

"Miss Hayes, we are separating into groups to prepare for the final exam."

"Okay, what group am I in?" I state hesitantly, not wanting to necessarily be paired up with anyone right now.

"You are back with your same partner…Mr. Hughes. He is waiting for you in the back of the room."

My heart instantly drops into the pit of my stomach, causing me to feel slightly sick. Callum had just stated his intentions on talking with me, but I am not ready to talk, let alone sit so close to him right now. My mind is still vibrating with all the lewd thoughts spinning around in my head. I am not trustworthy right now. No matter how hard I try to lock my heart into the ironclad safe, Callum's sedulous eyes hold a mysterious key, emancipating my heart.

Laboriously I get up, walking towards the back of the room where Callum sits languidly wearing a large mischievous smile. His well-built body is heightened by his aged blue jeans and a soft, athletic cut V-neck shirt silhouetting his substantial pecks and smooth valley between them. His velvety skin rolls up his neck and marries beautifully into his clean-shaven square jaw. The soft skin of his neck vibrates slightly just under the sharp corner of his mandible. His buttery smooth caramel eyes scan mine for any emotion he can use against me. Fighting back all my anxiety, I hastily transform my lascivious emotions into hate, knowing that where love lives hate resides there also. The opposite of love is not hate, but indifference, and until I don't care about Callum I am in danger of still loving him.

Placing my chair gingerly in front of him, I gaze angrily into his eyes. A conflicting sensation encapsulates me, wanting to both slap him and kiss him at the same time. Masking my capricious desires with a firm poker face I am able to retain the searing stare he has on me.

"What are we supposed to go over?" I ask firmly, trying to hide my quivering voice.

His eyes suddenly lose their arrogant luster, revealing a soft, yet serious expression, "Olivia tells me you are leaving as soon as your classes are done." His eyes scan my motionless body, waiting for me to unearth my plans.

Our eyes begin a dueling match over control. Holding onto his gaze I utter flatly, "Yes."

"She says that you are running from what you want, back to the life you think you should have."

A heavy sigh rolls out of my mouth, "I don't care what Olivia told you. Callum, you no longer have a decision in what I do or say."

"I don't believe you. I think you are being a bloody stubborn girl. You are so afraid of getting the life you not only want, but deserve…"

"I'm not afraid. You are what I want, but I can't have you. You know that I'm right. Your mother laid it all out for me. I am trying to save you from public humiliation and disgrace."

He sits straight up, erect, as his body pulses with an irritating substance, causing his muscles to quiver, "Screw the bloody society! It is my life."

"And your family's life."

"Then to hell with my family, too," he spits out.

"Callum stop, I am done. I have moved on and so should you," I stutter, pushing the lump in my throat down. The palms of my hands are beginning to sweat as my lies start to reveal their ugly head.

"You haven't moved on any more than I have, I can tell." Leaning in he begins examining my body with a voracious look consuming his face, "Your pupils dilate slightly whenever I am close to you."

"Stop, Callum," I breathlessly add in an unconvincing tone.

His fingertips lightly trace my thighs, causing my heart to palpitate, "Your heart rate still increases when I tenderly touch you…" He slides his chair closer to mine, allowing him to now fully overpower me. Both of his hands firmly grasp onto my upper thighs, digging his thumbs into my sensitive inner thighs. His need pulsates within his trembling hands. Deliberately his hands begin gradually sweeping into the inner portion of my thighs, causing my breathing to increase into a nearly hyperventilating state. Resting his warm, smooth cheek against mine he causes his hot, sweet breath to pour down my neck, "Your breathing quickens to an almost dangerous level…" I can feel the corner of his mouth pull up slightly, forming a luscious smile against my cheek. "The best part is how my breath…" he exhales softly onto my skin, "…causes your skin to break out into goose flesh." A hypnotic state washes down my body as a joyous tingling sensation ripples throughout my body. Melting into my chair, I am slowly becoming a puddle of boiling flesh within his grasp.

He is winning this battle as I close my eyes in pure joy, forgetting where I am until a booming voice knocks me out of my trance, "Mr. Hughes, I am assuming that your close proximity to Miss Hayes is to do with the assignment, correct?"

My eyes instantly snap open like a stretched coil ricocheting back to its primary position, immediately recalling my original will.

Callum slightly turns towards Mr. Bramble, keeping his hands firmly gripped onto my thighs. "Yes, in fact it does have to do with the lesson. Thank you, Mr. Bramble."

Pulling my cheek free from his allows the cold air to invade the section of my face where our cheeks seemed to be melting together. The cool air quickly extinguishes my smoldering skin as it screams in a tingling sensation, wanting his warmth to once again reside there. Reluctantly leaning back in my chair I peer into his face, grabbing hold of my internal strength I state flatly, "I have moved on. I have a date this Friday." Placing my hands firmly on top of his, I begin prying his hands off of my thighs.

His hands aggressively spin around, capturing my wrist within his iron clasp. His long fingers easily envelop my wrists within a heated prison. Surging warmth pulses against my wrists as if his hands have their own heartbeat. Firmly pressing my hands on top of my thighs, he hunches his torso over my lap, resting his head just inches away from my face. I can feel his quick breath rushing out of him, sending a warm sensation to roll over my hands, flowing gently onto my thighs. His breath slowly comes to a steady rhythm, causing the heat radiating out of his hands to subside.

Looking up into my face, his eyes lock onto mine, "You have a date?"

His caramel eyes sear deep into my soul, causing a rippling current to flow throughout my body. A sick sensation spins in my stomach, pushing up the thick bile, lodging itself firmly in my throat. Fighting back my instinct to kiss him, I utter hoarsely, "Yes."

"Is it by chance that bloody wanker Conner Fairfield you were talking to?" his voice is thick with an incredulous tone.

"It is none of your business who it is. You have Emily now," my razor tongue slices through him.

Squeezing my wrists even tighter he snaps, "I am not, nor will I ever be with Emily, you bloody, stubborn, daft girl."

"I am not daft. I saw Emily put her arm around you the other day, besides you have every right to be with her. She is your future wife and we are not together."

"You are bloody driving me barmy. How many times do I have to tell you? I am not with Emily. And she is not, nor will she ever be my future wife. Of course she put her arm around me, she saw me looking at you. She will do anything to keep you away from me. Look at the bloody situation she put you in with Gavin."

A shiver runs up my spine as I recall my terrifying experience in the Hellfire Cave with Gavin. If it wasn't for Callum things would have turned out much worse. I am amazed I can still sit in the same classroom with Gavin after what he attempted to do to me. But because of Callum's threat he has tried to avoid me, fearing Callum's retribution.

"Okay fine, you are not with Emily, but it still doesn't change the fact that you cannot be with me." Trying to pull my wrists free, he clenches tighter onto them, still holding me prisoner. Relinquishing my attempts to break free, I add dolorously, "I am still going on my date and I am still leaving."

Leaning further away from me but still gripping onto my wrists he utters with fastidious care, "I don't trust Conner. You don't know him like I do."

"How do *you* know him?" I question disbelievingly.

"He's a ponce. He likes to find out who the minted students are then try to weasel his way into their wallets. He is a greedy, conniving bastard and you are not going out with him."

"Yes, I am. You are not my father. I can take care of myself. Besides, I don't have any money he can weasel out of me," I firmly state.

Peering deep into my eyes he adds cautiously, "What about the inheritance you were left after Andrew died?"

My eyes widen, completely taken back, "How do you know about that?" My voice is quiet as I stammer out the question.

"My mum, you told her how you are able to pay for Miss McNally. Besides, I knew you had to have some money in order to go to school here and not have to work. I don't want Conner getting hold of any of it. It is Andrew's final gift to you and Noah."

I exhale sharply, shaking my head in frustration. The class, which was previously buzzing with scholastic discussions, is now beginning to dissipate, revealing it is the end of our class. Several students turn in our direction, attempting to eavesdrop on our conversation. Callum's eyes remain fixed on me, undeterred by their prying ears.

"Callum, will you please let go of me. My wrists are beginning to hurt."

He stares at me suspiciously but gradually obliges with my request. His hands peel from my wrists like an orange rind freely pulling away from the soft fleshy center. My wrists are slightly red and moist from the heat of his hands causing warm sweat to develop between our skins. Slowly I begin rubbing my wrists with my hands, wiping away the perspiration and reinvigorating my skin.

"Thank you for your concern, but I am going on the date." Gathering my things I proceed to get up and leave.

This time he softly grabs hold of my hand, tenderly stopping me from leaving. "Breanna, will you at least tell me where he is taking you?" his voice pleads with an underlying concern. His eyes remain fixed straight ahead, not meeting my gaze.

Letting out a sigh of defeat as my body deflates to his will, I utter reluctantly, "Fine, I am meeting him at a place called 'The Black Boar.' I hope you are happy now."

Gradually I walk away from him when suddenly I hear him respond. "I am," his voice is bright, full of resolution. A hidden plan vibrates off of each word, leaving me with a surprising sense of relief in telling him where I am meeting Conner.

You Don't Drink

The cab stops outside of a wide, brick lined, pedestrians only alley, with several different entrances leading into small pubs and inns lining the inside of the alleyway. I stare skeptically down the long, thin alley, not quite sure as to where the pub is. The cab driver points down the center of the backstreet, stating in a thick gutter accent, "Oi' the Black Boar down th' road o'bit."

Staring down the dark alley causes my stomach to twist and turn viciously. The only lights down the road are dimly lit electric lanterns positioned next to the main entrances of the establishments. One lone, large gas lantern hangs above the entrance to the alleyway with a rustic worn-down sign reading 'Historic Pubs' placed just below the lantern. A few groups of young adults stammer out in a state of disequilibrium, laughing and carrying on in a robust manner. Rolling the cab's window down, a strong aroma of bitter, dark ale laced with an unnatural earthy scent pulsates through the window, stinging my nose. Though I am vastly familiar with the strong stench of alcohol, this smell has a heavy, darker, almost rancid meat smell mingled with malt to it. The strong aroma turns my stomach slightly, heightening my already queasy state.

Handing the cabbie his fair, I gingerly proceed down the dimly lit passage. The narrow brick road has hundreds of years' worth of heavy use put on it, tainting the color from a deep brick red to an almost dirty grey. There are several pubs flanking the sides of the road such as: The Rabbit, The Blue Ox, and a tiny one tucked in the corner called The Lion's Mane. It seems that each pub invokes the name of a wild or type of hunted animal. Decent-sized painted wood signs hang crosswise out from the brick walls near the pubs' entrances.

Though the night is cool with a slight mist rolling over the buildings like water-falling down into the alley, the air oozing out from the pubs is thick with a dank, hot smell to it. Occasional belts of laughter intermingled with songs ring out of the different pubs. Tinkling noises of several pint glasses clanging into each other pierces out into the now narrow alley. The road narrows slightly the further in I go. I haven't seen a sign for The Black Boar yet, causing a nervous shiver to roll up my spine.

This area of town is lit with a lower, more serious partying type of clientele than what I am used to here. These were my mom's type of people when she was young and attractive. She would use her good looks and sex appeal to lure young men into offering her an assortment of alcoholic beverages. On some occasions, she would agree to let one of the men satisfy his needs on her. She has told me on more than one occasion that this is how I was conceived, not quite sure who my father was exactly. Knowing my whole life that I was a product of one of my mother's many manipulative one night stands caused me to grow up with a feeling of disgust towards myself. I can't help but look down this alley and feel like my mother, out on the prowl for alcohol and sex. Several guys standing outside of one of the pubs take in my tantalizing appearance. My form fitting jeans enhance my long, slim legs, balancing nicely with the curvy portion of my rear. The slim, cut button down, white shirt frames my trim yet hourglass figure perfectly. I let the top three buttons of my shirt hang open freely, exposing my heightened cleavage. My appearance seems to be luring several male gazes in my direction. An instant wave of anger mingled with satisfaction slowly consumes me, allowing me to embrace a dark side I always tried to run from. Relinquishing my internal fight to become something I know I can never achieve, I slowly concede to the inevitable. I never wanted to be my mother. But no matter how hard I have tried to push her life away I have naturally succumbed to it. I am a young, single mother, homeless, no family, and now walking into the gut of the beast – a bar. I am on a runaway train holding on for my dear life. A dark cloud envelops my heart as the sign for The Black Boar finally comes into view.

Inside the pub I am hit by a wall of thick, stale air mixed with smoke, and a concoction of fried food laced with the strong aroma of dark, heavy alcohol. Swarms of young people fill the small yet surprisingly cozy environment. Loud music pulses through the pub, vibrating within me, causing my heart to beat to the same rhythmic, yet energetic rhythm. A wave of contagious excitement presses through me, allowing my surrendering attitude to embrace this situation. The call towards the dark side is paved with cheers, fun, social acceptance and escape. But what will I have to give up in answering the dark side's request?

Though the smell takes some getting used to, the surrounding environment is quite pleasant. The large, ancient, wood planked floor looks as if people have been enjoying this establishment for the past hundreds of years. The dark mustard colored walls add to the warmth. There is a large trophy plaque of a black boar's head hanging on the wall above a roaring fireplace. A large fire burns within the mouth of the fireplace, heating up the already warm atmosphere. Crowds of people are standing around the open bar while others are positioned nicely in small alcoves. Burgundy velvet loveseats and brown leather club chairs are placed in groups around small tea tables, allowing people to visit while they eat and drink. As I look around the crowded room for Conner, I am sucked into a group of pissed young men. The alcoholic state they are in has completely melted away their inhibitions. One young man says some incoherent vulgar remark to me, while at the same time offering to buy me a drink. The smell of alcohol pours out of his mouth as if something has died in his stomach, forcing the rotting smell to push its way up out of his mouth. Reacting to the foul smell I lean away from him, trying to locate Conner. Suddenly I see him sitting on one of the burgundy velvet loveseats placed in front of the fireplace.

Pushing my way out of the over-aggressive group of young men, I briskly head over to Conner, noticing that he has already taken the liberties of ordering the both of us a dark pint of beer. Walking up to him I utter loudly, trying to talk over all the noise, "Hi Conner, how did you hear about this place?"

A quirky and slightly nerdy smile spreads across his flawlessly manicured face, "This is a perfect place to drink." Gracefully he gestures down at the two large pints of dark beer placed on the small table in front of him. One of the stouts of beer, which I am assuming is his, is nearly gone already, leaving the sides of his glass covered in thick, frothy foam.

I gaze down at Conner with a slight perplexed expression radiating from me. Pulling my eyes firmly together, twisting my face in disbelief, I watch Conner with a puzzled countenance on my face. He is a conundrum. He is wearing perfectly polished attire with everything precisely placed, as if an overbearing mother has laid out his coordinating outfit. His hair is neatly plastered with a heavy amount of styling gel, giving it an almost helmet appearance. Though his natural looks are quite handsome, his style is attempting to allude towards English uptight aristocracy. His neurotic and almost nerdy appearance is such a sharp paradox to this beer drinking, party going guy in front of me.

Silently I sit next to him on the small sofa, pressing myself into the arm of the couch, trying not to sit close to him. I begin fidgeting in my seat, attempting to decide if I am going to fully give in to the darkness gnawing at my ankles. The condensation forming on the glass from the cool drink meeting with the warm, almost hot air from the crowd and fire, sends rivulets of water droplets down the glass, making my mouth water. I stare at the thick, dark brew glistening in front of me, as dangerous thirst consumes my battling mind.

Conner picks up the large, moist glass, handing it to me, "I took the liberty of ordering you a strong stout..." passing it to me he forcefully adds, "Now drink it so my money doesn't go to waste. You are the lucky girl here who gets a drink from me."

His pompous attitude sends nails ripping up my spine, tearing away at my nerve. If I am going to have to sit here with him I am going to have to do it under the influence. Wrapping my hand around the tapered portion of the moist glass causes the water droplets to collect on the top part of my hand, between my thumb and index finger. Closing my eyes and fully deciding to drink it, I bring the glass to my mouth, smelling the vile stench oozing out of the glass. Holding my breath I slam a large amount down my throat. Pulling my mouth free I aggressively wipe the dense, thick foam from my upper lip. The burn of alcohol stings my throat as it pours down my esophagus, landing firmly in my empty stomach, filling it with warmth. The taste is not as bad as I was expecting. Though there is now a heavy, lingering bitter taste rolling around in my mouth, mingled with a slight roasted flavor, and a surprisingly dry sensation coating my tongue.

"That is better," Conner adds. "Now you can relax. Shall we converse?"

"Um, what do you want to talk about?" I state suspiciously.

"Well, for starters, what brought you here from America, with a child nonetheless? And how can you afford to be here?" his high pitched voice squeaks out.

My mind instantly recalls Callum's warning about Conner and his desire for money. Trying to avoid his questions, I hastily guzzle another large amount, firmly pushing the thick substance down my throat. Shock and dismay roll over me as I look down into the hollow opening of my glass, realizing I have downed an entire glass in just a few moments. Looking over at Conner his eyes widen in amazement, "Since your drink is gone, why don't you answer my questions now."

A nervous wave rolls through me, mixing with the nasty bitter brew, slopping around in my hollow belly. I hadn't eaten anything, thinking that Conner was going to at least offer to buy me dinner. Realization rolls through my mind, if I am going to survive this I need to drink a hell of a lot more, "I need another drink."

His eyes widen in dismay, "Umm, brilliant, I was hoping you liked to drink," he states in a lascivious tone.

"I am hungry, too."

"You can go order yourself something to eat. I will wait here while you pay for it," he states plainly, making sure I understand he is only purchasing the alcoholic beverages.

Shock rolls over me. What kind of guy asks a girl out, and then doesn't buy her dinner, only offering to pay for the drinks…a cheap one, "Well Conner, if you want me to stay, you better keep those drinks coming or I am leaving." An instant thought shoots through my mind – *leave*. But I just go on ignoring it.

"Fine, but you need to make it worth my money." Raising his hand he motions to the waitress, "Two more strong Stouts, now please."

"Make it three." If I am going to succumb to my new life then I am going to jump in with both feet.

The more I drink the more Conner's voice gets on my nerves, forcing me to drink even more, attempting to block out his high pitched shrill. Conner, surprisingly, is freely offering me Stout after Stout, perhaps it is because of my now close proximity to him. My head starts spinning out of control as I gaze around the room, listening to Conner's shrilling voice constantly echoing in my ears. I am in a state of disequilibrium, watching the room and all the occupants move back and forth like we are trapped on a violently rolling ship. Though my belly is empty, I am beginning to feel sick to my stomach. Looking up, trying to find a bathroom, I suddenly catch sight of Callum walking into the pub, hastily scanning the entire room. His eyes instantly find mine, staring at me in a disapproving way. For a brief moment it feels like I am hallucinating until a deep, smooth and sexual voice loudly cuts through the noise.

"What are you doing, Breanna? You don't drink," his voice is firm with an acidic edge, berating my obvious condition.

Looking up at him through my beer goggle eyes, I stutter joyfully, "Oh…hi Callum. This is my date." Turning towards the person sitting on the couch next to me, I take in his face trying to recall his name again.

Callum chimes in, interrupting my thought process, "Conner, what in the bloody hell did you do to her?" His voice is thick with disdain as he bends down, tenderly examining me, "How many has she had?"

Conner's erect body and blazing eyes reveal his disgust with Callum's apparent arrival, "I have only given her what she's asked for."

"– Except food," I slurred out.

"She has had all this alcohol…" he points to the multitude of empty glasses lining the table in front of us, "…on an empty stomach? You bloody wanker! She doesn't drink! And you gave her all those Stouts on an empty stomach. Do you realize what you could have done to her?"

"She wasn't acting like someone who doesn't drink. Besides, she was drinking them faster than I could give them to her," he adds gratuitously, in a pompous tone. His shrilling voice rings in my ears, sending sharp needles piercing into my brain.

"Ouch!" Grabbing firmly onto my head, I close my eyes adding, "Conner, your voice is killing my head, do shut up."

I hear a small snicker push out of Callum in a satisfying manner. Putting his arm around me he tenderly lifts me to my feet, causing the room to move even more with vertigo, "Come on Breanna, I am taking you home to bed."

Looking up at his striking face I take in his strong, chiseled features, blazing caramel eyes, and a soft, sumptuous mouth, "You are so good-looking. It is about time you take me to bed," I mumble.

Shaking his head in dismay he hunches down, kissing me tenderly on the top of my head, adding softly into my hair, "I wish."

Conner explodes off the couch, staring at Callum with blazing eyes, standing in front of him and preventing us from leaving, "You aren't taking her anywhere! She is my date and…"

Instantly Callum slugs Conner square in his face, knocking him over a club chair and flinging his flailing body down to the ground. Conner's hands instantly ricochet up to his face, covering his now bleeding nose. A slight whimper rolls out of him, sending blood splatters all over his hands. "Blimey! You broke my nose!" a suppressed cry tickles the edges of his voice, causing his words to quiver slightly.

"Good! You bloody arsehole! And if you know what is best for you, you will stay down there on the ground where you belong, you slimy snake, or I'll pummel you again." Wrapping both his arms around me, he nearly carries me out of the pub.

As soon as the crisp, cool air hits my face, life jolts back in me like being thrown into a cold shower, causing me to suddenly become aware of my nauseous state, "Callum, stop. I think I am going to throw-up. Quick, take me to a bathroom!"

Walking me over to a dark corner of the alley lined with bushes and low shrubbery, he demands, "Go here, because I am not about to let you walk into a bathroom alone. You are staying by my side."

"Callum, I am not going to throw-up right h…" my words are cut off by a thick, vile substance choking its way up.

He grabs hold of my hair, pulling it back away from my face as he places his cool hand on the back of my neck. A tingling sensation ripples on the soft surface of my overheated skin, causing a light shimmering of sweat to wash over my body. His cool hand placed on the back of my neck slowly begins lowering the temperature of my boiling blood. Though I was able to expel some of the poison from my body, I am still feeling nauseous and weak. Slowly I stand back up, wiping my watering eyes and mouth with the edge of my sleeve.

"Here," Callum hands over a white linen napkin with an embroidered boar down in one corner of it.

"Where did you get this?" I weakly ask.

"I nicked it on our way out of The Black Boar. I figured you were going to be leaving a pavement pizza and would really appreciate having something to wipe your face off with," a dense layer of satisfaction and anger ping-pongs out of his voice, like he is unsure whether to yell at me or laugh at me.

Slowly standing up I gaze into his tormented eyes as I hold tightly onto the napkin, covering my rancid breath. "Thank you," I whisper against the cloth.

Silence looms between us as his eyes pour down upon me with an expression of discontent, "I am so bloody angry and disappointed right now. I don't know whether to verbally flog you or go back in there and beat Conner back to hell!" A firm tone of seriousness cuts through each word as if it isn't a threat, but simply stating what he is about to do. He begins pacing back and forth within the narrow alleyway, slightly kicking the bottom of each wall as he alternates between them. His hands are aggressively clinched together, fighting back the urge to verbally assault me and then beat Conner.

Pulling the linen napkin away from my mouth I firmly add, "Why in the hell are you mad at me? I just did what you and every other stupid British person do here…drink."

Hastily he stomps over to me, standing just inches away from my face, causing me to instantly cover my mouth again. Peering down right into my eyes with his now solid caramel color eyes, he clarifies resolutely, "You don't drink! And now, neither do I!" His eyes hold mine prisoner as he berates me with his searing look, "What would Andrew think about your actions?"

Fury explodes within the pit of my gut, expelling out a toxic surge, causing a subterranean quake to roll just under the surface of my skin. Gripping my hand into a tight fist I vigorously take a swing at him. My hand instantly stops against his. Clutching onto my hand with both of his, he steadies my wobbly, drunken state as I nearly fall to the ground. Attempting to pry my hand from his I tearfully utter, "How dare you…" My tears now freely flow as I drop down to the ground, realizing the price I just paid for my choice. I have betrayed Andrew, but most of all I have betrayed myself. I gave into the vile medicine which rips your heart out, destroys your dreams, but most of all takes your choices from you, leaving you a slave to its call. I have seen the ugly side of alcohol and yet I still chose to embrace its seductive call.

Callum bends down next to me, enveloping me within his warm grasp. Several bystanders outside of the pubs are watching my emotional breakdown, which I am sure is being heightened by the alcohol pulsating through me. Callum relinquishes his grasp on me as he stands up, pulling me with him, "Come on. I will take you home."

We walk into my flat. Callum's arms are still around me for support as the vertigo, caused by the alcohol, still has a firm grip on my mind and body. Suddenly a high pitch shrill comes from the far corner of my flat.

"Ah! Miss Hayes, are you alright?" Miss McNally anxiously belts out, observing my…questionable state.

"She will be fine. She is just going to have a bloody headache tomorrow," Callum utters as a slight laugh ripples within his voice.

"Oh my dear, next time you need to slowly sip your drinks, not devour them," she states in a crisp, clear accent, demonstrating her poise and sophistication.

"Thank you, Miss McNally, but trust me, there will not be a next time. I am done with alcohol. You can sip that shit as much as you like, as for me – keep it far away from me." Miss McNally's eyes bulge in complete shock with my sudden use of foul language. A sharp laugh explodes out of Callum's mouth. Instantly he tries to stop his laugh with his hand. Feeling another wave of nausea come over me, I utter quickly, "I've got to go to the bathroom."

As I rush over to my tiny bathroom I hear Miss McNally ask Callum, "Should I stay here tonight, in case Noah wakes up?"

"No, I will stay and take care of them both. You can be dismissed now. Thank you, Miss McNally."

Closing the door to the bathroom I proceed to splash my face with cold water, trying to soothe the revulsion spinning in my stomach. Needing to get the nasty taste out of my mouth I begin vigorously brushing my teeth, scraping the scummy taste off of my tongue. Looking in the mirror at my disheveled reflection, I see the horrific effects alcohol has had on me tonight. Stripping down to my birthday suit I jump into the shower, washing off the night's rancid smell and smoke coating my body and hair. The water and soap strips my skin of the events from tonight, washing them down the drain. Drying my body off, I now smell clean and fresh, my mind is still a foggy mess though as if my thoughts and actions are being decided for me by some foreign being residing within me. I have very little control over what I am doing, let alone saying. I am so grateful that Callum is staying to help with Noah tonight. There is no way I can be a good mother right now. I have no idea how I survived with my alcoholic mother without getting seriously injured or even dying in the process.

Wrapping my hand around the doorknob to walk out, I suddenly freeze realizing I only have the clothes from tonight in here, and I am not about to put them back on. Enveloping my towel tightly around me, covering up all the important parts, I gingerly open the door, trying to sneak into my closet size room. As I walk out I notice Callum sitting in the blue checkered chair he had bought for me. His eyes are firmly locked onto me, taking in every nearly exposed detail. An uncomfortable wave of insecurity mingles with my relaxed inhibitions, causing a conundrum of emotions to twist around within me.

My mouth blurts out, "I guess it is only fair you see me out of the shower, since I saw you." Immediately I want to slap myself for blurting out the one event that still rings vividly within my mind. Incessant images of his naked body pop in my mind like an instant replay button constantly being hit, burning his image into my mind.

A smile tickles the corners of his mouth, giving me a tantalizing grin. His eyes give a slight mischievous wink, as he scans down my body, then back up, peering into my eyes with a surreptitious look, "If I remember correctly, this is not even close to being fair…you have a towel."

"I can always make it fair," I quickly stammer out. My inhibitions and usual self-control have fully been possessed by the lingering effects of the alcohol.

His eyes narrow in a disdainful look, bringing his thick brows nearly together, shielding his true emotions. Standing up he walks dolefully towards me, causing my heart to pound nearly visibly against my slightly exposed chest. He stands just inches away from me, causing my hands to tremble against my towel and then suddenly he snaps, "Is this some kind of joke to you?"

"What do you mean?"

"Is this you speaking or the bloody alcohol? You cannot play with my emotions like this," his eyes pierce deep into me with more than just rage.

"I wouldn't be so quick to judge. You have had no problem playing with my emotions. Yes *I* want you, but you know we can never be together. You don't think it is tearing me apart? When I leave next week, I will be going home to nothing. You, on the other hand, will have your family's support and someday a wife you will love more than me."

"Bloody bullshit, if you think I will love anyone more than you and Noah," his voice, though quiet, pulsates with rage and frustration.

"You may not love her more than Noah, but you will love her more than me. You may have a bond with him, but I am just another girl to you."

"Just another girl, my bloody arse. I love you. Do you hear me? I love-*you*!"

He pulls me aggressively against him, enveloping me in his firm, muscular arms, imprisoning me within his control. He leans down just inches away from my mouth, causing his sweet breath to wash over my damp skin, exploding my body with goose-bumps. A smile spreads across his face, "I love when your skin reacts like this, when my breath hits you," his breathing transforms to hot waves quickly pouring down on me. Matching his grip I embrace him fully, giving in to the possessive desires ringing in my head. Gripping my wet hair in his hands he pulls my head back, tenderly stroking the soft surface of my neck with just the supple tips of his lips. Pausing just under my chin, he begins to slowly drag his full bottom lip up my neck, stopping on the point of my chin. I hold my breath while quivering waves of pleasure cascade down my legs, sending out an explosion of butterflies to inhabit my core.

My breathing quickens to a ragged beat, with a slight shudder pulsating through me, causing my legs to weaken slightly. Gripping onto me tightly, he supports my weight as he bends me back into a near backbend while his mouth still strokes my neck. His tongue now takes over where his bottom lip left off. His tongue traces up my chin, stopping just at the base of my full lower lip. Our breath now intermingles as he slowly pulls me back up to a standing position. Our bottom lips scantily touch, causing a need to pulsate through me like wild horses thundering throughout my chest. My heavy breathing expands my tingling chest firmly against the binding towel, which is now in the way. Reacting on my need, my tongue slowly strokes his soft, supple lip, causing an exquisite moan to roll from him, merging our exhalations into one breath of pleasure.

Opening my eyes I notice his soft caramel eyes gazing upon me with a flaming intense love surging within him. He holds me locked into his loving gaze as our hearts beat as one. Leaning in he presses his mouth against mine, releasing our carnal desires. An aggressive need rips through us, as we begin thrashing at each other wildly. My breathing increases to a dangerous level as I lift myself up into his awaiting arms. My mouth is biting at his bottom lip, holding it captive within my nibbling teeth. He presses me against the wall near my room as his hand tenderly slides up my thigh.

My rough, panting voice pleads to him, "Please take me to bed before I leave. Give me something to remember you by."

He suddenly stops kissing me. A wave of frustration vibrates through him, causing his body to tremble. Slamming his fist firmly yet quietly against the wall next to my head, he roars, "No!" A quick breath rushes out of his mouth, continuing with his rant, "Damn it Breanna, are you still planning on leaving?" His hot air rolls against my neck.

A heavy sigh pushes out of me as I hang against the wall, still supported by the weight of his body pressing against mine. Hesitantly I answer, "Yes, I will not ruin your life or your family's life. I have to leave – your mother wants me to leave."

Dropping me down to the ground he walks away, trying to regain some kind of control. Turning towards me he states flatly, "To hell with my mother. Don't you care about what I want? When I take you to bed it will be for love, not need, and definitely not an alcohol-induced need, either. Until then I will not bed you."

Disappointment swirling with anger pushes out of me, "You will have sex with some random slut, but you won't have sex with me!" I shout.

"That is correct." He now stands inches away from me, making sure I clearly understand his demands, "I don't want to have sex with you. I want to make love to you."

"But I do love you and you love me, too. So what is the problem?"

"You are choosing to leave. And as long as that choice resides within you it is not the kind of love I want from you."

Paroxysms of fury expel out of me, "Then leave. If you are so stubborn that you refuse to see where I am coming from, then I don't want you." My anger is holding my tears at bay as I berate him.

"I am not the one being stubborn here, you are. Besides I don't want to leave you and Noah alone while you are still under the influence…"

"I am fine! Besides Noah and I are no longer your concern. Leave!" I aggressively push him towards my door.

Opening the door he turns to face me, "Good-bye, Breanna. I hope you find happiness in the life you have chosen."

I watch him walk out the door, causing my heart to drop to the pit of my stomach with regret. An empty feeling envelops me as the word stubbornness reverberates, rolling around within my mind. "*Who is the one really being stubborn here?*" echoes in the far corners of my mind.

An Act of True Love

It is the last day of my class, my final exam and the day before I leave. These past few days have been the most emotionally draining on me. My capricious emotions have teetered on the edge of insanity at times. My heart screams at me to stay while my mind points out the logical reasons behind my escape. My mind took a turn for the worse when mine and Noah's airline tickets showed up at my nearly empty flat.

The day after Charlotte Hughes' surprise visit she sent for the removal of Callum's baby crib and dresser, leaving me only the beautiful club chair to deal with. Luckily my flat came completely furnished, giving me very little to have to ship back to America. Sitting in the club chair waiting for Miss McNally to show up, I hold Noah tightly within my enveloping arms. His soft, ivory features melt effortlessly into my forearm as his eyes gaze up at me with an expression far beyond his understanding. Gnawing pain pricks at my heart, as I look down into Noah's innocent face. I have tried to protect him from the life I was exposed to at such a young age, but I can't stop it. He is so young yet he has lost his father, his next closest thing to a father, he is homeless, and has a mother who has given up on life. No matter how hard I have tried to give him a better life, his destination is paved by my stubbornness and cynicism. Bending down slightly I kiss the top of his forehead, uttering softly, "I am sorry."

A deathly lull in my flat melts down on me as I look out at the stark walls surrounding me. The flat has been robbed of life and vivaciousness with every little item I have placed in a box. I look out at the two suitcases and one box that contain my entire existence. I can sum up my life in these few things in front of me. When I first got here these walls held an optimistic future, with hope of a new start waiting to be filled. Now these walls hold disappointment, loneliness and regret. Though who am I disappointed with? Who has been the one placing stubbornness at the helm of choices?

My eyes grow heavy as I watch Noah now sleeping in my arms. The heat radiating off of him like an electric blanket warming me to the core, causes my languid body to seep into a deep, soporific state of relaxation. A heavy weight pushes down on me when suddenly a vibrating knock rolls through the room. Placing Noah in his port-a-crib, I walk over to let Miss McNally in.

Opening the door I am taken back, "Olivia, what are you doing here?"

"Though I want to bloody flog you for leaving, what kind of friend would I be if I didn't say good-bye?" Her excessive chipper attitude is masking some kind of scheme crawling up her sleeve. Her eyes narrow in with duplicity as she takes in my suspicious gaze. "Besides, you left this," she hands over the thin wardrobe box containing the stunning black tee-dress she purchased for me while at her parent's house.

My hand tenderly strokes the top of the box, recalling the night I wore it and how Callum's jaw nearly dropped to the floor. It was Olivia's plan that night to make me completely irresistible to her brother, but it made me irresistible to not only Callum, but Gavin as well, opening the door to a terrible situation. Still holding the box firmly in my hands I ask, "Are you giving me this dress?"

A swirling mixture of offence and amazement pour through her eyes, "Breanna, I gave it to you that night. This is your dress."

"Thank you Olivia, but where will I ever wear it?" Realizing that I am just going back to a life of poverty, I hand over the box containing the dress. "You should have it. You would look absolutely stunning in it."

She pushes the box back into my hands, "I am not about to take this back. We did not go back to my parent's house so I could bloody come back here and give it to you, only so you could tell me to keep it. You are bloody taking the damn box," her voice holds an unusual sternness to it, as her eyes plead for me to take the box.

"Alright, I will keep the dress." Her face instantly beams with satisfaction. "Do you want to come in?" I ask tenderly, opening the door a little wider.

"No, I think seeing your flat empty and your bags packed will make it all too real," her face pushes back her emotions as she swallows firmly. "Besides, I have a final test in thirty minutes, and then I am going home to meet my br…to meet up with some friends." She leans in giving me a firm hug, pulling me strongly against her body, holding me here for what feels like eternity. A soft sniffle echoes from her as she fights back her emotions. Pushing me gently away from her she adds, "You might want to take the dress out of the box before you leave. The airport won't let you carry it on the plane like that."

Confused by her statement I stammer, "O-kay?"

"Good-bye, Breanna." She slowly walks away, stops, and then turns back towards me. "Remember, choices are made by those who have the strength to fight for their outcome. Fight for the outcome you want, Breanna," She gives me a disconsolate smile. As she walks away I can hear a soft cry echo down the narrow hallway, causing my heart to break.

Rivulets of tears stream down my face as I press the box firmly against my chest. Standing here I hold onto the gift as if it has arms embracing me with peaceful memories. A great void is left in my heart where it once tickled the edges of a real family. I not only lost Callum, but I lost the closest thing to a sister I have ever experienced. Releasing my embrace with the box I stare down at the physical reminder of what I had. Remembering Olivia's instructions, I pry the lid off of the box. There on top of the black tee-dress is a single, yet slightly wilted red rose. My heart nearly stops when I notice below the rose is a newly developed photograph. Tenderly I pull the picture free from the slightly wilted rose, as tears begin to pour freely down my face. There in the picture is Andrew's headstone, with the same bouquet of red roses placed respectfully in front of it. Collapsing to the floor, I hold the picture affectionately within my trembling hands. My mind encapsulates this amazing act of love, causing my stubbornness to shatter, revealing the real reason why I am leaving. The fear of betraying Andrew has always rippled on the edges of my love for Callum. I love Callum, there is no doubt in that, but I am afraid to be in love with him. I have only had one other love in my life and he was taken from me. I could not handle it if Callum, too, is taken from me. So subconsciously I decided to be the one to leave.

I know that Callum's mom doesn't support our relationship, but if I truly love Callum like he loves me, then I should be willing to fight for it. Olivia is right, choices are made by those who are willing to fight for their outcome, and I have made my choice. Pulling the airline tickets out of my purse, I look down at the one-way flight information. Holding the tickets firmly in my hand I begin to rip them up, making my decision final.

Walking into my class I am mentally prepared to confront Callum. A thick layer of anxiety mingled with excitement fills the room, as all the class-mates buzz about the room trying to get any last bit of information before the exam. I sit at my table eagerly watching the quiet door, waiting for Callum to enter, but stillness remains. Everyone but Callum is in the classroom. My stomach drops to the pit of my abdomen as I realize that Callum is not going to show up. The classmates begin to move at a slow pace, as my mind spins with regret. Fear pricks my soul as I wonder where Callum can be.

"Everyone take their seats please," Mr. Bramble begins handing out the tests as he continues, "When you are done, you may leave. It has been a fascinating term – to say the least. I have experienced more…interesting situations this term than any other. You can take that statement as you may. Good luck everyone."

He walks over to me, placing the exam on my table. "Mr. Bramble, is Callum going to be taking the test today?" I whisper softly.

"I should hope not. He asked if he could take it earlier this week because he was leaving."

My heart nearly stops as panic takes over my body, "Did he say where he is going or when he will be back?"

"No," he taps at my awaiting test, "Good luck, Miss Hayes."

"Thank you."

Facing my test, I have no desire to take it. I can barely see the words through the tears filling my eyes. The dam hasn't broken yet, keeping the salty stings at bay. My mind begins replaying everything Olivia told me this morning, trying to find a clue as to where Callum may be. Pounding my head slightly, I instantly recall a flub she said as she was forcing me to take the dress. She had mentioned that "we" went to get the dress, along with saying that she was going home to meet up with someone. But she was very vague about who it was. Facing my test I begin quickly answering the questions, not caring if I get them right. The faster I answer them the sooner I can get the hell out of here.

Finishing my last question, I rush it up to my professor, slamming it on his desk as I run out of the room. My mind becomes a jumbled mess as I try to figure out how Noah and I are going to get out to West Wycombe without having to have to take an expensive cab ride. Everything around me spins in fast motion, from the anxiety flooding my mind with 'what if…' scenarios. I can't give into that kind of thought process right now. I have to find Callum and I need to tell him that I choose him.

Suddenly my mind catches sight of a petite, spirited sprite rushing across the street. Joy rips through my heart as I yell at the top of my lungs, "OLIVIA!"

Instantly she turns towards me. A huge, radiant smile spreads across her congenial face, as a sigh of relief drops down upon her. As I rush over to her she yells loudly, "It's about bloody time you decide to fight!"

Running up to her I slam myself into her, causing her to nearly fall over as I give her a voracious hug. A warm sensation pulses through my heart as the tears I have been able to keep down now freely flow, knowing that as long as Olivia is still here I will be able to find Callum. She wraps her arms tightly around me while she whispers threatening actions mingled with loving responses towards me in a thick British brogue and quirky slangs. I can only understand a few things, about me being stubborn and wanting to hit me at the same time as kiss me. Olivia possesses the same fiery, yet loving, temper as Callum, a capricious tongue when they are frustrated, wishing to hurt and love you at the same time. They must get it from their mother, considering they have different fathers. I just hope that someday their mother can love me at the same time as hating me.

"Olivia, are you done berating me in some incoherent language?"

"It is not incoherent, it is English. The language you bloody Americans got from us," she states with a thick, taunting accent, "And yes, I am done."

"Good, because I need to find Callum, and I know you know where he is." A large villainous smile spreads across her face, showing her perfectly white teeth.

We pull into the gravel parking lot, causing the tires of her car to spittle out rocks from under them. The bright colors of the Carter's Steam Fair are such a sharp contrast to the thick green foliage surrounding it. The divergence of the fair against the ancient landscaping and buildings give a modern feel to the surrounding area. The fair is beginning to wind down. Some of the rides have been broken down, getting them ready for the travel to a new city. There are herds of workers surrounding the dismantled rides as they begin covering them with colorful tenting, loading them into large trucks.

"Olivia, why are we here? They are closing down the rides," I utter inquisitively while I look out her passenger window at the dismantling of the rides taking place.

"Like I told you, Callum has a way of getting whatever he wants," she states, gesturing with her head towards the Chair-O-Plane.

The ride is in full swing, with one person hanging in a limp reclined position, freely flying. Turning to Olivia I state, "He needed to escape and feel free."

"Yes. He couldn't be around and watch you leave. I was to give you the box, then come here, letting him know when you left." A silence looms between us as we watch Callum soar. "Breanna, I love you like a sister, but if you ever break my brother's heart again – I will hurt you," though her voice holds a mocking tone to it, sincerity encapsulates every word.

I give her a reassuring smile, and then spring out of the passenger's door. Turning back towards her to ask a favor, she suddenly replies before I am able to fully ask it, "Don't worry, I will watch Noah." Turning around, she gazes into his vibrant face, watching him kick joyfully, "Besides, he loves me anyway."

I rush through the swarms of on-looking workers as their eyes gaze towards me questioningly. Deep imprints in the plush grass are left by the vacating rides, leaving only the memories of their existence. The Chair-O-Plane is the only ride left in complete functioning order. Weaving my way to the far corner of the grounds where the ride is still positioned, I notice it is beginning to slow down. Hastily I push my way past the ticket box when suddenly a loud voice shouts towards me, "Stop, you can't bloody go 'n there. W'er closed."

Turning around I notice Harry standing next to the control box. "Please let me go in there, Harry. I need to talk to Callum."

His head tilts curiously, as he cocks his eyebrow in a revealing manner, "Blimey, you're the reason why that barmy bloke is up there."

Pain rips through my heart as he brings to the forefront of my mind the reality of what I have put Callum through. Gazing up at the swing now slowly stopping, I notice Callum's languid face. Though his eyes are tightly closed, a searing ripple of anguish pulsates through his face and down his body, leaving a relinquishing appearance to flow over him.

A warm hand tenderly pushes on the mid-section of my back, "He's a great bloke, go get 'im."

Turning towards Harry I give him an understanding smile. He at one time walked in the very same shoes as me but his outcome held a different scenario, one that I almost had. His eyes beamed with satisfaction as if I am completing the choice he always wished he had the strength to make. Giving him a slight wink I walk over to the now lowered and motionless ride. Walking up to the only inhabited swing – his, I stand firmly above his relaxed, dreamlike body. His eyes are still tightly closed as if he is refusing to face the world. A sharp ping pierces my heart as I stare down at the man who has loved me through all my stubbornness; the man who I am not only willing to give my heart to, but also my trust, my future, and my soul. I would have never thought that I was actually running towards something instead of running away when I came to England.

Leaning over his face I utter lovingly, "Hey stranger, what are you doing here?"

His eyes instantly snap open, revealing a wave of shock rolling within his stunning eyes. His thick eyebrows flow perfectly over his eyelids, causing his soft caramel color to explode vehemently from his face, giving him a seductive appearance. A large smile spreads across my face as I gaze down at him. My heart rolls open in a sense of relief as I realize that I am not too late.

"What are you bloody doing here? How did you find me? I thought you were leaving," he breathlessly stumbles out the questions as his body starts to catch up with his mind. Quickly jumping to his feet, he begins surveying me skeptically, as if he doubting his own eyes.

"I am not leaving, I choose you, Callum Hughes. I am so sorry for my stubbornness and fear. I love…"

Instantly he grabs hold of me, pulling my body firmly against his as his mouth presses down on mine, stopping me from finishing what I was going to say. His soft lips move with an urgency, showing me what I was about to tell him. The sweet taste of his mouth fills my mind with pleasure as I aggressively squeeze my body against his, melting our heightened forms into each other. His hands press into my back, refusing to let me go, as if I am going to truly leave this time. Our tears mix sweetly within our mouths, coating everything with untainted ecstasy.

His mouth forms a soft smile across my lips, causing me to open my eyes in response. Liquid caramel eyes blaze down on me as he peers into my face, causing my heart to melt, seeping down into the tips of my toes. I look into his gaze, owning every part of him, knowing that he wants me as much as I want him. His lips gently brush against my mouth as he pulls his mouth tenderly away.

"Are you telling me that you are staying? You are not going to run away…"

Backing slightly away from him, I reach deep into the pocket of my jeans, pulling out a wad of crinkled and torn up papers. Tenderly I reach for his hand, placing the wad symbolically within his grasp, "Yes I am staying here."

Lifting his hand up he begins unraveling the crumpled pieces of paper. A congenial smile spreads contagiously across his face as he looks down at the destroyed airline tickets. Giving a final blow to the tickets, he adds another destructive tear through them. Picking me up within his arms he spins me vivaciously around while he presses his mouth against mine, kissing me passionately. A soft laugh rolls through me as the world twirls effortlessly around us. He puts me down next to him, locking his hands tightly around mine, facing each other we gaze fervently at each other.

A villainous smile spreads across my face, "What is your mother going to say about this?"

"Nothing, she can't."

"What do you mean?" I question.

He drops one of my hands while still gripping onto the other firmly within his, he begins walking me towards the bank of the River Wye. The plush green grass feels like we are walking on a thick bed of carpet beneath our feet. Geese glide across the river, leaving slight ripples behind them. The trees dip the tips of their fingers into the river, gently stroking the surface of the shimmering water. A soft breeze blows gently across us, causing him to wrap his arm protectively around me.

Stopping at the river's edge he adds, "Olivia confronted my parents, explaining in her own way." A smile spreads across his face, alluding to the fact that Olivia's way is not always diplomatic. I have been on the opposing side of Olivia's blatant comments on several occasions. I can only imagine what her parents were thinking. "That if they were going to force me to stay away from you then she was going to disown them."

"She basically threatened them, for you."

"No, she threatened them for you."

A smile spreads across my face, feeling for the first time like I have a sister who is willing to give up everything for me. Turning back towards where the car is parked, I notice Olivia lifting Noah into the air and spinning him around as she plays with him enthusiastically. My eyes take in the vision of Noah now being surrounded by a family who will love him as if he is their own. Suddenly my mind recalls the picture of Andrew's headstone, with a fresh bouquet of red roses placed delicately in front.

Turning back towards Callum I utter respectfully, "Callum, when did you go to see Andrew's grave?"

He hunches down slightly. Kissing the top of my head, he utters against my head, "The day after you drunkenly threw me out of your flat."

"How did you know where to find it?"

"Breanna, there is only one cemetery in your town. It was not difficult to find it."

Eagerly I gaze up at his face, still bent towards mine, "Why did you go?"

"Because, I was hoping to be able to give you this," reaching into his pocket, he tenderly pulls out a small black velvet box, holding it within his trembling fingers. Dropping down to one knee, he peers into my eyes with a fervent love blazing within his face. My body quivers as my heart vibrates against my chest. Tears begin to pile within my eyes, pouring over the protective dam, causing them to now stream down my face. My hand begins trembling within his still enveloping hand, as he grips onto mine tightly.

"I couldn't ask you this without first asking for Andrew's permission, and telling him thank you. If it hadn't been for his request for you to come to England, I would have never met you. I promised Andrew that if you let me, I will always love you and Noah and I will be the kind of husband and father he would be proud of." I look down at him through tear-filled eyes as an abundant surge of warmth fills my soul, like a warm blanket is being wrapped around me. "Breanna Hayes, will you marry me?"

Dropping down to my knees, placing us on equal levels, I tenderly look into his eyes, "Yes! Yes, Callum Hughes, I will marry you."

Enveloping me within his arms, he holds onto me tightly as the rippling laps of the River Wye break effortlessly against the bank where we sit. Life has a strange way of showing us that incredible happiness can come out of the darkest nights, if we only have the strength to persevere, choosing to fight for what we deserve.

Callum's warm, soft body lies next to me in our bed as I look out the window at the crisp morning air. The cold cusp of winter is blowing out our window. The trees outside have long since lost their vibrant colored leaves, leaving their bare branches to scrape gently across the frozen glass, giving a slight screeching sound. The thick crystal fog shimmers around the grounds, coating everything with a gray frozen mist. The rising sunlight dances on the tips of the mist, illuminating the fog with a slight orange glow.

Callum's bare arms are wrapped tightly around me, melting his skin onto mine. Our legs are intertwined, making it difficult to know whose legs are whose. The warmth within the covers is heightened by our bare bodies merging perfectly into one another. His soft, sleeping breath rolls down my exposed neck, causing my skin to explode in goose-bumps.

A heavy breath flows down my spine, sending chills racing up my back. He gently kisses the base of my neck. "I love when your skin gets goose-flesh from my breath against you. Will that always happen?"

I spin around so that we are no longer spooning, but are now face to face. Responding tenderly to his question I add, "Yes, you will always give me goose-bumps."

His stunning morning face is illuminated by the filtered sun now flowing through our window. I take in every part of him as I gaze at his light caramel eyes. His arms that are still enveloping me habitually pull me against his exposed body. My hand tenderly traces the soft ridges of his chest, the deep valley between them, down his rippling stomach muscles. A soft moan escapes from his mouth, causing a slight shudder under my fingertips. "I love when you make that sound when I touch you. Will that always happen?"

A wicked smile tickles the corners of his mouth, "No."

"What!" I shout, slapping his chest teasingly.

A loud laugh rushes out of him as he grabs hold of my now thrashing body, rolling firmly on top of me. "Shhh, don't wake Noah up."

"I won't. He has been sleeping through the entire night for a long time. We are so lucky he is now sleeping a good ten hours a night, because when he is awake I do nothing but chase after him. I can actually sleep now."

"I can think of better things we can do than sleeping," he utters mischievously, as he presses his naked body down onto mine.

A soft groan escapes through my mouth as his warm, firm body merges with mine. "Will our passion for each other ever end?" I add, wrapping my arms and legs tightly around him.

"I bloody hope not," he smiles ruefully, as he begins tickling my completely exposed body. Wriggling jolts of laughter rush through me, as I thrash around, attempting to get him to stop tickling me. Trying to grab his hands, he suddenly envelops mine, aggressively pinning them above my head. His mouth drops onto my neck, softly kissing my now heightened skin. A lascivious moan escapes through my teeth as his hands press mine open, intertwining our fingers together. The new life of marriage has settled into us perfectly, like the final pieces of a difficult puzzle. His thumb begins to slowly spin the diamond on my ring finger around. Nibbling on my ear he utters breathlessly, "I love you, Mrs. Hughes. You have given me everything I have ever wanted."

"I have something more to give you," I whisper back.

His body freezes against mine. Lifting his head up his eyes pull together quizzically, deepening the furrow between them. Raising a brow in a perplexed manner, he adds, "What do you mean?"

Looking deep into his eyes I state joyfully, "I am pregnant." Excitement rolls through me as I realize that I am able to tell him. I was robbed of the excitement with Andrew, and the memory of that situation has been giving me a heavy burden of anxiety lately. Fear that something was going to happen to Callum haunted my mind these past few days. But now after telling him, I am left with a peaceful wave of warmth washing through me.

Callum's eyes widen as he gazes down at me in complete shock. His naked body lay frozen against mine, like a horizontal statue of David. Sitting up slightly I tenderly ask, "Are you alright?"

A sudden smile explodes across his face. Wrapping his arms around me he spins onto his side, exposing my torso. His hand gently glides down my breast bone, along my ribs, tenderly resting on my lower abdomen. His gentle touch sends chills throughout my body. Looking into my eyes, he responds, "I have never been better." Leaning over me he gently kisses my stomach, resting his soft lips there for a long while. "You have allowed me to be a part of Noah's life, and now you have given me a part of myself back. I love you, Breanna Hughes."

He lays his cheek against my stomach as I affectionately stroke his hair. Twirling a strand of his hair within my fingers a sudden sense of peace washes over me. I have fought my whole life to try and have some kind of solidity to it. Andrew was the only anchor I thought I had, and when he was ripped away from me it felt like everything around me was spinning out of control. Now that I am able to look back I know I wasn't spiraling out of control. There was someone at the helm guiding me to the place where Noah and I are today. Love is an amazing power. There are no borders to it. I had thought I could never love again when Andrew died, but love doesn't work that way. The more you give love, the more it allows you to receive it. I have been led to a family I always dreamed of, a spunky and vibrant sister-in-law, a devoted and passionate husband who loves Noah and me unconditionally. And yes, parents who will someday, I hope, come to fully accept me.

As I lay here with Callum I know that we were lead towards each other. I will always love Andrew, but now I know I can love Callum too. Bending down I softly kiss the top of Callum's head as I whisper earnestly, "I love you with all my heart, Callum Hughes."

Though trials may be hard, hold onto the fact that there are brighter days ahead if you are willing to fight for them. The End

ABOUT THE AUTHOR

L. R. Johnson is the founder and President of The Inspired Writers League – an active community writers group. When L. R. Johnson was a child she would live in a world of her imagination. Her teachers would have to put her in the front row of the class or she would drift off into a story she was creating. Though she studied Psychology in college she never lost her imagination, constantly creating stories in her mind. Bringing to life her characters and writing great love stories filled with adventure, dynamic characters, and brilliant surroundings is something that L.R. Johnson has a natural gift for. She lives in California with her husband and two wonderful children.

9 780692 565537